PRAISE FOR THE
STEEL BROTHERS SAGA

*"Hold onto the reins:
this red-hot Steel story is one wild ride."*
~ A Love So True

*"A spellbinding read from a
New York Times bestselling author!"*
~ BookBub

*"I'm in complete awe of this author. She has gone and
delivered an epic, all-consuming, addicting, insanely
intense story that's had me holding my breath, my
heart pounding and my mind reeling."*
~ The Sassy Nerd

"Absolutely UNPUTDOWNABLE!"
~ Bookalicious Babes

FLARE

FLARE

STEEL BROTHERS SAGA
BOOK TWENTY-THREE

HELEN HARDT

WATERHOUSE PRESS

For Marit

S.I.G.I.

PROLOGUE

Brock

I study my father's profile as I sit on the passenger seat of his pickup. The two of us are driving across the Wyoming border. Donny and Dale were both unavailable, so it's just Dad and me.

I wish my cousins were here for backup. I love my father—I do—but I feel like I don't know him anymore.

He's quiet. When my father's quiet, I begin to worry. It means his mind is working. He's thinking. He's thinking about things that I probably don't even know about. Sure, he came clean about some of the stuff, but it's clear.

There's a lot I still don't know.

Finally I speak.

"Tell me. Tell me who tried to kill Mom. And why."

He doesn't answer at first. Instead, he stares at the road in front of us. Driving to Wyoming is driving through a lot of nothing.

Finally, "Your mother had a patient. Her name was Gina. She was Aunt Ruby's cousin."

I widen my eyes.

"Your cousin Gina was named after her. Anyway, she was a patient of your mother's, and she committed suicide."

My jaw drops.

"Except she didn't actually commit suicide. That's what

we were told, at first. But the person who took her wanted your mother to believe it, so he kidnapped her and left her to die in a garage, tied up, while a car was running."

I feel sick. My stomach's about to come out of my mouth. How did she escape? I want to ask, but the words don't come.

"You know how smart your mother is. She managed to get her wrists untied, got into the car, and backed it through the garage door. She was treated for carbon monoxide poisoning."

Still, I say nothing. My beautiful mother. My brilliant mother. All this happened before I was born.

"Funny," Dad says. "I haven't thought about this in so long. But that's how your brother came to be."

"What?"

"Your mother was kept for several days, and she didn't have her birth control pills with her. So she missed a few days, and when she escaped, and she and I got back together, she got pregnant."

Pregnant.

Before they were married.

With this new knowledge, I feel a kinship with my father I never felt before. A different kind of kinship.

"So I guess you could say that if none of that had happened, we wouldn't have your brother."

Talk about a silver lining. "Look, I get that you love Brad. I do too. But for God's sake, someone tried to kill my mother."

"Yes. So much bad happened to our family during that time. So much we've all tried to bury. To keep it in the past. And when we do think of it, we try to think of something good that came out of it. The good that came out of your mother's kidnapping is your brother."

I pause for a moment. My father's philosophy is not a bad

one. Will I look back on what I'm going through someday and see only the good that came out of it?

So far, I'm not sure any good has come out of it.

The more we uncover, the more horror we seem to find.

"What you need to remember," Dad says, "is that your mother lived through it. She saved herself. Part of it was luck, of course, but part of it was her own intelligence and shrewdness. She's a clever woman. And I thank God every day that I have her and the two of you boys."

I nod.

"Brock, our family made it through the horror of those years, and we will make it through this. I promise you that."

"How can you make such a promise?"

"Because I will *will* it if I have to. That's how much I love you and your brother. That's how much I love your mother. That's how much I love this entire family. Everything we've done, we've done for family."

Then my father does something completely unexpected.

He laughs.

I turn to look at him, regard his profile once more.

"What the hell is so funny?"

"It's not funny, Brock. Just something that occurred to me, and it made me laugh. The absurdity of it all."

"Okay. You will have to clue me in here because I really don't understand what you're talking about."

"My own father," Dad says. "That was my own father's excuse for so long. For everything he did in his life. He did it for family. For my mother. For his children."

I say nothing. I don't like where this is going.

"And now here I am. Sixty-three years old, and I'm making the same excuses. We buried all of this for you—for your brother, your cousins—so you wouldn't have to live with the darkness that our family had been through. And I'm laughing because . . . in the end, it didn't work for my father. Everything he tried to protect my mother from, us from, came barreling into our lives twenty-five years later."

And then I understand.

History is repeating itself.

Now.

The horrors of the past are resurfacing.

And I vow. I vow here and now as I stare at my father, his laughter finally subsiding, that I will never, *never* bury the past again.

"Tell me, then," I say. "Tell me about your father's half brother. The descendants who have come out of the woodwork. Do they have names?"

"Only one so far. The report came in late last night."

"What's the name, then?"

"It's a grandson, or so he says."

"Okay. Has he consented to a DNA test?"

"A DNA test may not be conclusive. We're talking about a half sibling from two generations ago. Every family has second and third cousins floating around that have no claim to anything."

"It's a start, anyway."

Dad nods.

"What else do you have? Anything?" I ask.

"A last name," Dad says. "Lamone."

CHAPTER ONE

Rory

I clear my throat. "Davey, like I said, I'm flattered. You're very attractive and obviously intelligent and caring, but... Can I think about it?"

"Sure. You have my number."

"I appreciate that. Part of me wants to say yes right now, but I guess..."

"You guess you should talk to this other person? This guy?"

"Yeah, I should."

I need to do some serious thinking, and not just about what I might want with Brock.

About the fact that I may very well be carrying his child, and that changes everything.

"Not a problem," Davey says. "It was nice talking to you again."

"You as well. Bye, Davey."

I end the call and then stroke my abdomen.

Until my phone buzzes yet again.

I don't recognize the number, so I ignore it, but then I change my mind almost instantly.

"Hello?"

"You won't get away with this," says a distorted voice.

My stomach drops.

"Who's this?" I demand.

The call goes dead.

Damn. "Hello? Hello, are you there?"

But the call was dropped. No way to trace it now. But at least I have the number. I quickly call Callie.

"Hey," she says into the phone.

"I just got a phone call. A very ominous phone call that has my nerves on edge."

"Okay, Ror. Calm down. What happened?"

"It's a number I don't recognize, but it appears to be a Colorado area code."

"Okay."

"It was a distorted voice. And all he said was 'you won't get away with this.'"

Callie is silent for a moment.

"Callie? Don't leave me hanging here."

"Can you come down to the office?" she asks. "I can have Donny run the number."

"Yeah, sure. I'm still at the studio, and I'm done for this morning anyway."

I haven't heard from Brock today. And right now? I can't be distracted by my growing feelings for him. Right now I need to figure out what's going on with this phone call.

I walk the block and a half to the courthouse and enter the spacious lobby. Reception is a circular desk in the middle of the room, where, to the left, a hallway leads to courtrooms, and to the right is a waiting area for prospective jurors. It's small, as we don't have a lot of jury trials in Snow Creek. The city attorney's office and the mayor's office are upstairs.

"Hi, Rory," the receptionist says to me.

"Hi, Elaine. I'm just going up to see Callie."

"Is she expecting you?"

"Yep."

"All right. Go on up."

I ascend the staircase—it's a circular staircase, which I always thought was off for such a small town—and walk toward the city attorney's office.

Callie doesn't have an office, just a cubicle, so she's visible as soon as I turn the corner toward the city attorney's wing. Her brown hair is tied back in her signature low ponytail, and she's wearing a beige sweater and jeans. Casual. Nice. She's on the phone and gestures for me to wait.

A few moments later, she ends her call. "All right," she says to me. "Give me the number."

I grab my phone out of my purse, pull up recent calls, and show her. "Here you go."

"Colorado area code," she says, more to herself than to me. "We can trace the number, but it won't do us any good."

"Why not?"

"Because it probably won't amount to anything. Whoever we're dealing with is . . ."

"Is what? This is Pat Lamone. How many numbers do you think he has?"

Callie chews her bottom lip.

"Callie . . . what are you thinking?"

"I'm thinking I need to talk to Donny. Right now."

"You will not. You will *not* leave me hanging like this. That's not fair, Cal."

"It's just . . . I feel like our problem is almost converging with the Steels' problems. Has Brock told you anything about what they're going through yet?"

"No."

The thought jars me more than a little. Brock and I aren't serious. We've had all of two dates, maybe four or five if you count all the times we've been thrown together. There's absolutely no reason why I should think he'd confide in me about all his family issues. Still, it irks me. I want to be involved. I want to help him if I can.

I've got to get out of that mind-set. I have my own issues to deal with—naked photos of me potentially spread across social media.

"Sorry," Callie says. "I've got to talk to Donny. I'll only be a minute, Ror." She rises, leaves her desk, and walks into Donny's office without knocking.

What now? I plunk my ass down in her chair, which is surprisingly comfortable with good lumbar support. Several manila folders are splayed across her desk, and her computer is open to—

I wrinkle my forehead. The computer is open to the county page. She's looking up properties. Properties here. In Snow Creek.

The property displayed on her screen? It's owned by Carmelita Mayer—the same property where Pat Lamone is currently renting a room.

But even that isn't the most interesting thing about the house.

There's a lien on the property, held by the Steel family.

Held, specifically, by something called the Steel Trust.

What the heck is she researching?

She returns a few minutes later. "Donny has to talk to Dale and to Brock."

"What for?"

"I gave him the number, and he's going to work on tracing it. Then I asked if I could tell you what was going on with his family."

"I don't want to pry," I say.

No lie. I'm not nosy or gossipy. What I *do* want, though, is to help Brock if I can. I don't know why I feel that way. After all, we've only had a couple of dates, and I have my own issues to contend with.

"I know you don't, but to tell the truth, Ror, I'm aching to confide in you. But I have to respect his wishes. Dale didn't answer when Donny called, and apparently Brock is in Wyoming today with his father."

I raise my eyebrows. "He is? He didn't bother telling me."

Callie's cheeks blush a little. "I'm sorry, Ror."

"Don't be."

"Is there anything I can do?" my sister asks.

I stand and return her chair. "Yeah. You can tell me why Mrs. Mayer's property has a lien on it held by the Steel Trust."

CHAPTER TWO

Brock

I'm going to puke.

Seriously, I'm going to upchuck right here in the middle of my father's pickup as we drive to Wyoming looking for dead bodies at GPS coordinates. As if that isn't reason enough to lose the contents of my stomach.

Lamone.

My father didn't just say *Lamone.*

"He claims to be a grandson," my father continues.

"Let me fucking guess. His first name is Pat."

"Patrick, yes." Dad turns and stares at me, but then he moves his glance back to the road. "How the hell do you know that?"

I gulp audibly. Do I tell him what's going on with Rory and Callie? I don't exactly have their permission.

"Where's the guy live?" I ask.

"He's in Snow Creek. He's been there for a while...a couple of weeks at least."

"What about his father or mother? Which side is related to the Steels?"

"His mother's side, apparently. That's about all we know right now."

"Pat Lamone went to school with Callie and Rory Pike," I say.

"Yeah, he'd be about the right age. His parents lived in Snow Creek, but they moved after his junior year."

"Yeah."

"You know this guy?"

"Callie and Rory do."

"Yeah, they probably do. They went to high school with him."

"Have you talked to Brad? Brad would've been in high school then."

"That was the year he was homeschooled," Dad says. "Remember?"

Right. My brother was in a bad riding accident the week after school started his freshman year. Actually broke his back and couldn't walk for nearly a year. Mom homeschooled him that year. After Mom's laborious education and his doctors' rigorous physical therapy, Brad went back to school the next year knowing more than any of his classmates and physically stronger than they were as well.

Damn. I'd forgotten all about that. Funny how the worst years of your life crawl into a corner in your mind and you ignore them. It happened to Brad, not me, but it was hell on all of us.

Will all of this someday be one of those memories that we never think about?

And is that part of the reason Dad and my uncles chose not to tell us about all the shit that went down twenty-five years ago?

"Okay," I say. "Brad wasn't in school at all that year. Pat Lamone left after what would've been Brad's freshman year. So Brad wouldn't know Pat at all."

"No. Maybe he knew of him. It's a small town. Oh ..." Dad sighs.

"What?"

"Diana was a freshman that year as well. Maybe she knows him."

Oh, God. Diana knows him all right. He freaking poisoned her, except she doesn't know that. Only Callie and Rory know that, and they told me.

"I know of him," I say quietly.

"How? They moved right after his junior year. You were still in middle school. Sure, you probably heard the name here and there, but how did he make any kind of impression on you at that age?"

He didn't.

I only know because of Rory.

"You going to answer me sometime this century?" Dad raises his eyebrows, still watching the road.

I draw in a breath. This is my father. The man who I trust with my life.

Also the man who has been lying to me—even though it's lying by omission—my whole life.

I love my father. I love him with everything I am.

But I can't break Rory's confidence.

No.

"Donny mentioned him," I say. "Apparently Mrs. Mayer's house, where he's renting a room, was vandalized while she was out of town. He filed a report with Hardy Solomon, and Hardy told Donny."

"Oh?"

"Yeah, he named Jesse Pike and the rest of his band as the vandals, but all of them except Dragon had an alibi. So apparently Hardy dismissed it."

"Maybe it was Dragon by himself," Dad says.

"No. Lamone named four masked men."

"If they were masked, why did he think it was Jesse and the band?"

"Because..." I swallow. "Because..."

God, I can't do it.

Dad slows the truck down, pulls over to the side of the highway.

This isn't going to be good.

"Brock, what the hell aren't you telling me?"

"I made a promise, Dad. It's not my story to tell."

"I'm your father. You can tell me anything."

"I want to. It's just... Rory..."

"This has something to do with Rory? And Callie?"

I nod. I can give him that much at least.

"Rory told me in confidence," I say.

"If it has to do with Callie, then Donny knows."

I nod.

"All right. Maybe Donny will tell me." Dad grabs his phone.

He can try, but he'll fail. Donny won't speak of it until he has Callie's permission.

"Hey, Don. Sorry to bother you at work. Brock and I are on our way to Wyoming to check out those coordinates."

Pause.

"Yeah, I'm going to put you on speaker."

"Hey, Brock." My cousin's voice comes to the line.

"Hey, Donny."

"I just gave your cousin some news," Dad says. "I'm going to need to know what you know."

"What news is that?" Donny asks.

"We got a name from our people. The name of a grandson.

An alleged grandson of your great half uncle."

"Oh?"

"Yes. A man named Pat Lamone."

Donny's phone clatters to his desk. Seriously. I hear it happening. Then the noise of him scrambling to pick it up.

"Did you just say Pat Lamone?" Donny asks.

"I did. And apparently your fiancée knows the man, according to my son here."

"Brock . . ."

"Hey, I didn't tell him anything. I said I couldn't say anything until I talked to Rory. He decided to call you because he figured if it involved Rory, it involved Callie, which means you know."

"I do."

"Listen, Donny," Dad says. "If this Lamone is truly a relative of ours, and if he's a bad seed, I need to know."

"Has he taken a DNA test?" Donny asks.

"Not that I know of, and of course we will insist upon that. But here's the thing. We're talking three generations descended from a half sibling, so a DNA test may not be conclusive."

"How the hell can't it be conclusive?" Donny asks.

"Because we all have second and third cousins walking around that we don't even know about, and this is a descendant of a half sibling on top of that."

"Right," Donny says. "That makes sense."

"Brock won't tell me what's going on with this Lamone guy without Rory's permission."

"I may be able to help you out there," Donny says. "Rory's here. In the office with Callie."

My heart jumps. Just the mention of Rory's name, and my heart responds.

"All right," Dad says. "Can you ask them? Get their permission for Brock to talk to me?"

"I'll try. Hold on a second."

Shuffling, as Donny moves out of the office.

How long will we have to wait? I have no idea. And what is Rory doing in the city attorney's office anyway?

Get over yourself, Brock. She's probably just visiting her sister. It's lunchtime. Which means—

"Hey, I'm back," Donny says. "Rory and Callie are here with me, and they've given me permission to tell you about what's going on with them and Pat Lamone."

My heart beats faster just knowing Rory is on the other end of the line. Damn.

"Have you told them who Pat Lamone allegedly is?" Dad asks.

A throat clear. Then, "I have not."

"Donny"—Callie's voice—"what are you talking about?"

"Rory? Are you there?" I ask.

"Hi, Brock. I'm here."

She has the voice of an angel. A worried angel.

Dad clears his throat. "Rory, Callie. I don't know what's going on with you and Pat Lamone right now, and we'll get to that, but we have reason to believe he may be a Steel relative."

Gasps come through the phone.

Two gasps, and I know which one came from Rory.

Already I know her that well.

"There's no reason for anyone to be freaked out yet," Dad says. "We haven't figured out if it's real or not. But that's the claim."

"Oh my God." From Callie. Then, "Rory, are you all right?"

My nerves contract into spasming twitches.

"Rory?" I yell. "What's wrong with Rory?"

"I'm fine, Brock." But she doesn't sound fine. Her voice is shaking.

"Damn all of this." I rub my arms against the tension. "I don't want to do this over the phone."

"Oh, you're going to do it over the phone, Brock," Donny says. "You and Uncle Joe don't drop a bomb like this on me and the women without finishing it."

He's right, of course. I'd never let him get away with the same.

"Who wants to tell the story?" Dad asks.

A pause, and then Rory's voice.

"I was the adult in the room back then. This falls on me."

I hear the trembling in her voice, and in my mind's eye, I can see her bottom lip. She's probably chewing on it. The lovely rosiness is gone from her cheeks, and she's probably feeling as nauseated as I am right now. Probably more.

I listen, wishing I could hold her in my arms as she goes through, in a robotic tone, everything she told me the other night.

Dad goes rigid.

Rigid and red-faced.

More rigid and red-faced at each point in the story.

The hairy buffalo that was drugged with angel dust.

Diana's poisoning, the reward offered by our family.

Callie inadvertently overhearing Pat and Jimmy talking about drugging the punch.

Callie and Rory coming up with an idea to claim the reward.

Rory—my beautiful Rory—putting herself in harm's way to get the confession.

Then—

16

Rory, along with Callie, lured by Brittany Sheraton, getting poked with something. Drugged. Passing out.

The two women waking up, surrounded by X-rated photos of themselves.

Finally, Lamone's return to town, his antics since then.

Rory goes silent.

"Are you okay, sweetheart?" I ask through the phone.

No reply.

Then, "She's okay." Callie's voice.

God, I need to be holding her. I need to be telling her this is all okay. That I'll fix it. That I'll move heaven and earth to fix it if I have to.

Dad finally speaks. "All right."

"We're really sorry, Mr. Steel," Callie says. "We knew who poisoned Diana all those years ago, and we didn't come to you."

Dad lets out an angry growl. Yeah, it's a growl. This is Jonah Steel when he's mad. Red with rage. The Jonah Steel that has to be talked down by his calmer brothers.

Except they're not here.

But *I* am, and I'm not going to let him blame Rory and Callie for this.

"Dad, they had no choice."

"No choice?" Dad growls again. "We would've protected them."

"Uncle Joe"—this from Donny—"they had no reason to believe we would've protected them. They were kids."

"*I* wasn't a kid." Rory's voice. It's soft and distraught.

"I'm not going to let you do this," I say. "We've talked about this, Rory. You were barely eighteen."

"I wasn't a kid," she says again.

I turn to my father and glare at him. *Don't you dare*, I tell him with my eyes. *Don't you fucking dare go after her.*

His lips are pursed, his jaw tense.

He's angry. Yes, he's angry, and he has a right to be. But damn it, if he goes after the woman I love, I'll never forgive him.

Then I drop my jaw.

I did not just think that word. The L word.

Doesn't matter. All that matters right now is Rory, and I need to protect her from my father's rage. And yes, it's rage. I see it everywhere.

"Dad," I say, "this isn't about Diana. She had already recovered by the time Rory and Callie even knew. It doesn't matter."

"Uncle Joe"—from Donny through the phone—"Brock is right. You *know* Brock is right."

"We're talking about your sister," Dad says to Donny through clenched teeth.

"Yes," Donny replies, "and trust me, I was plenty pissed off when I first found out. Diana's fine. There were no long-term effects, and like Brock said, Diana had already recovered by the time the rest of this happened."

Dad sucks in a breath. "Callie could've come to us when she first heard the confession."

"This was ten years ago," Donny says. "They wanted to have proof. Don't you see? There was no proof."

"We would've found the proof," Dad says.

He's right. We would have. We would have manufactured it if necessary. But that doesn't matter now.

"If this fucking degenerate is a relative," Dad grits out, "I will personally see to it that he never gets a penny of Steel money."

Good. Now we're back on track.

I nod. "I'm with you there."

"Me too." From Donny.

"Give me a minute," I say. "I need to talk to my dad."

"Sure," Donny says.

I press the mute button.

"You need to apologize to them," I say to Dad. "To Rory and Callie."

"I don't need to apologize to anyone."

"Callie's going to be a member of this family, and Rory—"

Rory what? God, I fucking love her. Crazy as shit, but I do.

I clear my throat. "Rory is her sister. They were kids, Dad."

"They were trying to get our reward."

"Yeah. *Everyone* wanted that reward."

He doesn't reply.

"You can't blame them for this. They were fucking kids. You know it, and I know it."

"But Diana..."

"What Pat Lamone did to Diana is unforgivable. I agree with you. He's not going to get a penny of Steel money, even if he is entitled to it. But Diana recovered. Diana recovered before Rory and Callie had the proof. And you have to understand, once Lamone took those pictures of them—"

"They still should've come to us."

"Dad, are you listening to yourself? Two young women were violated. *Violated.* Along with Diana. They are victims of this just as she is. They were drugged, put in compromising positions, and photographed. They were *violated*."

That finally gets him. His jaw softens...but not quite enough.

"But they were respon—"

I draw in a breath, force myself not to yell. "No, Dad. Go there, and I won't forgive you. You will not say they put themselves in that position by Rory seducing Pat and getting the confession. You absolutely will *not*."

He nods then.

He knows. That would be taking it too far.

"You're right, son. I'm sorry."

"Callie's going to be a member of this family," I say again.

"I know. The Pikes . . . They're good people."

"Yes. Don't forget that. Don't forget that Callie and Rory were children."

He opens his mouth, but I stop him.

"Don't tell me she was eighteen. Don't tell me that. You know as well as I do that an eighteen-year-old and a seventeen-year-old aren't all that different. It's simply an arbitrary line, Dad, and it has to be drawn somewhere."

"She wasn't a child. Not in the eyes of the law."

"No. And believe me, she knows that. She's punishing herself so much for this."

"You really care for her, don't you?"

"I do. Very much."

Dad sighs then, and he turns to look at me. I don't know what he sees on my face, but the tension in his countenance visibly lessens.

"I'm ready. I'll apologize."

"Thank you." I take the phone off mute. "Don? You still there?"

"Yeah. What the hell are you doing?"

"He was telling off his old man," Dad says. "And I hate to say it, but rightfully so. Rory, Callie, I apologize. This isn't your fault."

No response from either of them.

"They're both pretty upset, Uncle Joe," Donny says.

"Again, rightfully so." Dad rakes his fingers through his hair. "You girls don't know me very well, but Brock and Donny do. I'll do anything to protect this family, but this happened ten years ago, when you were kids. Before you say anything, Rory, you were a kid."

I smile at Dad, thanking him silently.

"That's kind of you to say, Mr. Steel," Rory says, "but there's a part of me that will never forgive myself."

"I know where you're coming from," Dad says. "Believe me. There are things in my past I may never forgive myself for. But try to forgive yourself. Please. And call me Joe."

CHAPTER THREE

Rory

"All right," I say, my voice shaking. "I'll try."

"I mean it, Rory. You too, Callie. Call me Joe. You're family now."

I'm not technically family, but Callie will be soon.

I'm worn out. Exhausted. Washed, wrung, and hung out to dry.

I feel weakened yet also fortified.

Telling the story to the Steel family patriarch took everything in me, but it also gave me strength. His first inclination was to berate me, which is of course what I expected.

Diana Steel was the family jewel back then—the first daughter born to this generation of Steels. And she was perfection. The three Bs—beautiful, brainy, and built.

Why I'm still considered the most beautiful woman in Snow Creek is beyond me. Diana Steel eclipses me in everything.

Brock. I need Brock to hold me. I want to bury myself in his hard, strong body.

But he's not here.

I have only myself from which to draw strength.

"Are you okay, sweetheart?" Brock's voice comes through the line.

"I'm fine."

It's a lie, and both he and I know it. But he's on his way to Wyoming with his father, presumably on business. I can't allow him to worry about me.

Funny.

Just last night, I almost went to bed with Dragon, and just this morning, I almost accepted a date with Davey. I'm glad I didn't do either of those now.

I want to see how it turns out with Brock.

Sure, he was drunk as a skunk last night. But who did he call? He called me.

I stop myself from absently touching my abdomen. Callie knows I may be pregnant, but Donny does not. I don't want to give him any reason to suspect.

Donny and Brock are talking through the phone line now. Words surround me, get into my brain, but I don't make any sense of them. I'm in my own thoughts now.

Callie leads me to a chair and helps me sit down across from Donny's desk.

"It's okay, Ror," she whispers.

"I know."

Part of me does know.

Part of me knows the Steels will help us. Not just Donny, and not just Brock, but we have the power of the Steel family behind us now.

Can Pat Lamone really be related to Brock?

I can't even freaking believe it.

Donny finally ends the call and looks toward Callie and me.

"Are the two of you okay?"

"We're good," Callie says, rubbing my hand.

"Sorry about Uncle Joe."

"It's okay," Callie says. "You had the same first reaction."

"Brock didn't react that way," I say. "When I told him the story, all he did was comfort me. Tell me it would be okay. He didn't berate me for not coming to the family with the information."

"He loves Diana," he says, "but she's my sister, not his. It hit a little closer to home for Dale and me. Plus, Brock seems to have found his soft spot."

I meet Donny's gaze. "Soft spot?"

"My cousin and I are alike in some ways, different in others. Sure, we were both womanizers in our day—"

"In your day?" I say. "I think Brock is still a womanizer."

"Maybe," he says. "I'm not sure what's going on between the two of you, and it's not my business. Brock never really had a soft spot before, other than his family. He loves Diana nearly as much as I do, and if he had heard the story from anyone else, I think he would've gone as ballistic as his father."

"You think?" Callie says.

"I know. I know Brock. I taught Brock everything he knows about women, and I've spent the last several years watching him in action. He's an expert at leaving emotion at the door. I didn't think he had a soft spot. Not until now."

I warm inside . . . and I welcome it. An imaginary blanket drapes itself around my shoulders, and I find my strength once more.

"I'm glad your uncle knows," I say. "We never wanted to go to anyone for help, but you know what? It feels good that your uncle knows."

"I agree," Callie says. "Maybe it's time to stop hiding from this."

"I just don't want . . ."

"That won't happen," Donny says. "I swear to you. Those pictures will never see the light of day."

"Callie told me that you hired someone to search Pat's room at Mrs. Mayer's."

"I did. It's supposed to happen sometime today. Mrs. Mayer is still out of town, so once Lamone goes to work, my guy will go in."

A brick lands in my gut. I don't know why I'm feeling like this. I want the place to be searched. And Callie and I basically stormed our way into Doc Sheraton's house while Pat was there and searched every crevice. Of course, we didn't know how to do a thorough search.

"Donny," I begin, "do you think—"

"Already done," Callie says. "He's going to search Doc's place too."

Damn, that girl can read my mind.

"Donny knows we were there," she continues. "Donny knows we searched. Brittany and Doc Sheraton are still in Wyoming, so our guy—"

"*Our* guy?" I lift my eyebrows.

"I mean, the Steels' guy."

"You'll be a Steel before you know it, baby," Donny says.

"Whatever," I say. "I shouldn't have made that comment."

Callie squeezes my hand. "But yeah, the guy's going in, and if there's anything to be found in the doc's house, he'll find it . . . if Lamone hasn't removed it after our ill-advised foray."

"Yeah. We probably shouldn't have done that."

"No, you shouldn't have," Donny says, and then, looking at Callie, "and you, Ms. Would-be-Lawyer, should've known better."

He's not angry with her. There's a twinkling glint in his eye.

Callie sighs. "I know."

"Don't blame her," I say. "It was my idea. I barged my way in, and Callie just followed."

"I'm not blaming either of you," Donny says. "None of this is your fault. You were put in this position."

I open my mouth—

Callie stops me with a gesture. "Stop it. Don't go there, Rory. You were what, five days past your eighteenth birthday? None of that matters. We've been through it *ad nauseam*. Stop blaming yourself."

She's right. I promise myself I won't mention my age at the time again. At least until tomorrow.

"I'll be getting a report tomorrow if everything goes as planned," Donny says. "If he can't get in, he'll let me know, and he'll get to it as soon as he can."

I breathe in. "Okay."

"In the meantime, I have a meeting this afternoon, so I've got to prepare for it."

"Anything I can do to help?" Callie asks.

"Yes, just stop worrying. We'll take care of this. All of this. I promise you."

Callie nods, and she and I leave Donny's office.

"Walk out with me, will you?" I say to Callie.

"Sure."

We leave the second floor, walk down the stairs, pass reception, and end up outside on the sidewalk in front of the building.

"The Steels are so strong," I say.

"They are," Callie agrees. "Every single one of them."

"I wish there was something I could do to help. Not just for Brock but for the whole family."

"I think the best way you can help is to be there for him."

"But I don't know what's going on, Cal. Brock said there's some shit going down with his family."

"There is. Some big shit."

"I feel so selfish. They're taking this away from us, bearing our burden for us, Callie. All the while, something huge is going on that I don't even know about."

"Brock will tell you when he's ready."

"I'm not so sure about that. I'm not so sure that Brock and I . . ."

"You heard Donny. Brock found his soft spot."

"I know. But last night . . . He and I . . . Well, let's just say it wasn't pretty."

"What happened?"

"You know what happened. I might be pregnant. And I swear to God, I did *not* neglect to tell him about the condom on purpose."

"I believe you, Ror. I know you didn't."

"But then he got drunk, and I went over. I took care of him. But before that . . ."

"What?"

I close my eyes, for some reason thinking it won't be as bad if I can't see my sister when I say it. "Before that, I almost left with Dragon."

"Rory . . ."

I open my eyes. Callie's own eyes are wide, her jaw dropped.

"I said *almost*, Cal. I didn't do it. But I was so upset, and if Brock hadn't called me . . ."

"Thank God he did."

"Yeah, but then this morning, I got a phone call from the counselor I talked to at the family-planning place in Grand Junction."

"Oh? Surely you're not still thinking about—"

"No. I mean, I might be pregnant, so I'm not shopping for sperm. She called to apologize because we kind of left things on a sour note. But it was my fault, not hers, so I apologized to her. And then . . . she asked me out."

"Okay . . ."

"I considered it, Callie. I even told her I was interested, except that I was seeing someone else and had to talk to him first."

"And . . . *are* you interested?"

I sigh. "No. I mean she's perfectly lovely, and I am attracted to her. And believe it or not, I'm also attracted to Dragon."

"Really? Dragon?"

"You don't think he has something? That darkness?"

"Oh, yeah, he's good-looking. Totally. But there's just something not quite right there."

"Well . . . I wasn't really looking past his handsomeness last night . . ."

"I see."

"And this woman from the sperm bank, she's also gorgeous. And bisexual, which is a good thing. She would understand me."

"But you just said you're not really interested."

"I'm not, Callie. And damn it, I should be."

"Don't tell me you're really falling for Brock."

"I don't know. I think . . ." Crap. Do I really need to say the words out loud? "I think . . . that I *am*."

CHAPTER FOUR

Brock

Dad and I reach the first set of coordinates—rather, as close as the roads get us. He pulls the pickup over to the side and fiddles with his phone.

"Is this our property?" I ask.

"Yeah," Dad says, his forehead wrinkling.

"Okay . . . What's wrong, then?"

"This particular tract of land is rented."

"To whom?"

"Dr. Mark Sheraton."

"The vet?"

"Yeah. He owns a tract adjacent to this tract. He had a house built, and he does business there."

"I suppose he doesn't make much as a small-town vet."

"Well . . . he could make a lot more than he does."

"What do you mean by that?"

"About ten years ago, Uncle Bryce and I made the decision to bring all our veterinary care in-house. We probably should've done it decades ago, but our family has always tried to support our local community as much as possible."

"I guess I knew that. I just never thought anything about it."

"Yeah. We have one full-time and one part-time

veterinarian on our staff and payroll. We take good care of our livestock, but with the sheer number of animals we have on our property, it just didn't make sense to have the town veterinarian coming out so often."

"And financially?"

"Financially it benefits us, yes. But that wasn't the main consideration for taking the business away from Doc Sheraton."

"What *was* the main consideration?"

"As I said, we've always liked to support our local community. But we're not the only ranch close to Snow Creek. We're the biggest, by far, but we felt Doc Sheraton was spreading himself a little too thin. We paid him a lot of money every year to take care of our livestock, but he couldn't always get out there as quickly as we needed him to."

"Did you offer him the job?"

"As our veterinarian on payroll? No, we didn't."

"Why not?"

"That's a long story."

"You can tell me now or later. Right now I suppose we need to check out this coordinate."

"Yeah." He clears his throat. "Suffice it to say, for now, that we chose a brand-new veterinarian right out of that school in Fort Collins, armed with the newest techniques specifically geared toward cattle and horses. Specifically grass-fed cattle bred for meat consumption."

"Makes sense."

There's more to the story. I know my father too well. Plus, he said it was a long story.

Did he and Uncle Bryce have a problem with Doc Sheraton?

I've always considered Doc Sheraton to be a good guy, but now? Knowing that his daughter had a part in what happened to Rory and Callie all those years ago? I'm not sure. I'm not one to blame the parent for the sins of the child, but I can't discount the fact that kids who commit crimes usually haven't been raised perfectly.

Doc Sheraton is a widower, though, so he had to raise his daughter alone. He probably wasn't there for her as much as he should've been through no fault of his own.

Who knows? Just another piece to this puzzle that is becoming more convoluted every day.

"So this land, then," I say to Dad. "It's under lease to Doc Sheraton?"

"It is. When he asked if he could rent it, after buying the adjacent tract, Uncle Bryce and I agreed. We felt kind of bad for not offering him the job on our payroll."

"I see."

"It was a rational business decision," Dad continues, "but like I've said a million times before, we've always wanted to support the local community. And we didn't support Doc Sheraton this time."

About ten years ago...

Those are the words my father started this conversation with.

Ten years ago.

Around the same time Pat Lamone and Brittany Sheraton drugged Rory and Callie and took those incriminating photos.

I file that information in my mind for future reference.

At the moment?

We need to figure out why these particular GPS coordinates were left in an envelope for Donny in a safe-deposit box he never rented.

"Let's take a look," Dad says.

"Okay. How do we get to the exact coordinates?"

We're parked on what appears to be vacant land.

"No freaking clue," he says. "Let's drive the perimeter of this tract."

"How big is this tract?"

"Several hundred acres."

"Then we have to go to the exact point of the GPS coordinates."

"Yeah," Dad says, "except I'm not exactly sure how to get there. There are no roads here."

"Fuck. Seriously?"

"Seriously. As far as I know, it's a tract of vacant land. Why Sheraton wanted to rent it is beyond me."

"For grazing maybe?"

"He doesn't raise cattle or horses."

"He raises dogs," I say.

Guard dogs, specifically. Doc Sheraton may well have provided the dogs for whoever is behind all of this.

"Right," Dad says. "Dobermans and Rottweilers. He trains them as guard dogs."

"He doesn't need our land for that."

"No. But Bryce and I didn't give it a thought at the time."

"No, you didn't. You were feeling guilty about not supporting him as a local veterinarian."

"Yep."

Something is rotten here. I sense it already. "I wonder . . ."

"What?" Dad says.

"What if we rented a helicopter or a small crop-dusting plane? Flew over to see what he's got on this land?"

"Not a bad idea, son, but I'm thinking it's best to drive the perimeter and look that way. These coordinates were given to us for a reason. And on those first coordinates, you and your cousins found evidence of rotting flesh, and then you left. By the time you returned, whatever might've been in that attic was gone. If we fly a plane or helicopter over the next set of coordinates, we will alert someone."

My father's right.

He usually is.

"All right. Let's drive the damned perimeter."

CHAPTER FIVE

Rory

I said it.

I said the words.

I'm falling for Brock Steel.

"Rory..."

"I know. I may be pregnant with his child. Which is of course what I wanted. But damn it, Callie, I don't want it this way. This baby—if it even exists—deserves to be part of a family. A family with two parents. I don't know how Brock feels about me."

"You're a soft spot."

"Those words are Donny's, not Brock's. Is it even fair to talk to Brock about a relationship when so much else is going on with his family that I don't even know about?"

"First things first," Callie says. "When is your period due?"

I pull my phone out of my pocket and check the calendar. "A week and a half."

"Okay. There are pregnancy tests now that you can take, like, five days before you miss your period."

"That's still a week away."

"I know."

"I should talk to Brock."

"Yeah, you probably should."

"Why? Why did I get into this?" I let out a sigh. "You never fall for the rebound guy."

"Good advice," Callie agrees. "But this is still new, Ror. Maybe you are falling for him. But maybe you're not. Maybe you're just infatuated with the rebound guy."

"Maybe."

But I already know this isn't mere infatuation.

This is something more. Something so much more.

What if he's not feeling anything, though? What if Donny's wrong, and I'm not Brock's soft spot? Even if I am, what does that even mean? A soft spot doesn't mean love.

"You want to get some lunch?" Callie asks.

"Is it still your lunch hour?"

"I've got a few more minutes. I can just check with Donny."

"He's not going to mind."

"I know." Callie smiles dreamily as she sends a quick text. "Normally I don't use my relationship with Donny to get extra time for my lunch hour, but today, I think you need me."

I smile. "Thanks, Cal."

Her phone rings with the text.

"He's good with it. Where would you like to eat?"

"Wherever."

"Come on, Ror. We're going to get through this. I promise."

Callie is certainly upbeat today. As I look at her, I wonder why she ever thought of herself as an ugly duckling. Does it truly go back to Pat Lamone's words all those years ago? Just another reason to hate the bastard. My sister is beautiful. Not just beautiful but radiant. Her hair is a shade lighter than mine, and her eyes a golden amber compared to my brown. She has a lovely figure, and she can wear button-down blouses.

She's gorgeous, and I'm so glad she found a man who sees that and appreciates it.

"Since you don't care," she says. "Let's go over to Lorenzo's. I feel like a meatball sub."

I nod and walk with my sister the few blocks to the Italian place. Once there, we get a table, and our server approaches us.

"Well, hi there," she says, sounding bubbly.

Oh, God. It's Sadie... Sadie... I can't remember her last name. Sadie who was all over Brock with her black hair, blue eyes, and flat chest the other night at Murphy's. She's still flat-chested, but I'd be lying if I said she didn't look pretty in her checkered waitress dress. Damn her, anyway.

"Hi," Callie says.

"Remember me? We met at Murphy's. Sadie McCall?"

McCall. That's it. Sadie McCall.

"Of course," Callie says in that dry way of hers. "How are you?"

"I'm just dandy," Sadie says. "Could you refresh me with your names again?"

"Sure." This time I speak. "I'm Rory Pike, and this is my sister, Callie."

"Of course. Pardon me for not remembering. I've met so many people in such a short time since I've been here."

Right. I'd be willing to bet she remembers Brock's name. This is a small town. Really, how many people could she have met in such a short time?

Plus, in small towns, people usually remember each other's names. But she's new. I'll give her the benefit of the doubt. Okay, I won't give her the benefit of the doubt, but I'll pretend like I am.

"Not a problem, Susie," I can't help saying.

"It's Sadie." She shows her dimples as she points to the name tag on her lapel.

Callie gives me the stink eye.

Yeah, I deserve it. Mean girl isn't my style.

"I'm so sorry, Sadie." This time I smile and do my best to make it look real. "Could we get some water please?"

"Of course. The bus person should've brought it by now. I'll get that right away. Do you know what you'd like to order?"

"Meatball sub for me," Callie says.

"One meatball sub. Check. And you?"

"I don't know." I sigh. "I think I'll just have a salad. And a side of garlic bread."

"Perfect." She pencils some notes on her pad. "I'm about to take a break. Do you mind if I join you?"

I'm having déjà vu.

Didn't a waitress take a break with us just a few weeks ago? Yes. Her name was Nora.

"Uh...sure," Callie says.

Damn it, Callie...

"Wonderful. Let me just put your order in and make sure you get those waters."

I'm shooting darts at Callie with my eyes.

"What did you want me to say?" Callie asks.

"I don't know. Maybe...no?"

"She's new in town. We can't be rude."

"Didn't we just go through this a couple of weeks ago with that other new waitress? Nora?"

"Right. I forgot about that."

"Of course you forgot about that."

"What's that supposed to mean?"

"You're head over heels. Everything is falling into place

for you, Cal. But if you recall that day with Nora, she was after Donny."

"Oh..."

"Callie, you're usually quicker than this."

"You're right. Sorry, Ror. I totally wasn't thinking."

"Right. You weren't thinking that lovely Susie there was all over Brock the other night."

Callie opens her mouth to respond, but before she does, Susie—er... Sadie—returns with our waters and sits down with us.

"Thanks for letting me join you. It's so difficult meeting new people."

Okay, that's a lie. Meeting new people in a small town is strikingly easy, and didn't she just say she's met *so many new people*?

"Not a problem," Callie says. "We met another waitress this way just a few weeks ago. Her name is Nora."

"Not Nora Bates? She's my roommate."

This just keeps getting better and better.

"Maybe," Callie says. "I don't know her last name."

"Blond? Very bubbly?"

"That's her," Callie says dryly.

"Déjà vu," I say softly.

"Excuse me?" Sadie says.

"Nothing. Where are you from, Sadie?"

"A suburb of Denver. Broomfield. I did two years of community college, and I have an associate's degree in hospitality."

She's young, then. Younger than both Callie and me. Possibly even younger than Maddie.

A perfect age for...

38

Brock.

"How old are you?" Callie asks.

Nicely done, Cal.

"I'm twenty-four. How old are you?"

Twenty-four. Older than I pegged her for. In fact . . . she's Brock's exact age.

"Twenty-six. I'm starting law school in January."

"That's wonderful! And you?" Sadie says to me.

She's asking me for my age, which I'm not ashamed of, except that I'm four years older than Brock, who she clearly has her sights set on.

"I teach music here in town," I say, deliberately dodging the age question. "Piano and voice."

"Wonderful," she says.

Right. Wonderful.

"So tell me all you know about the Steel family," Sadie gushes. "I met one of them the other night, when we met at the bar."

"Right," I say. "Brock Steel."

"He's positively delicious. A great pool player too."

"All the Steels are good at pool," Callie says.

"Are they? They must be good at everything."

"Callie is engaged to a Steel," I say.

"You are? Oh my God, which one?"

"Donny. Donovan." Callie waves her left hand.

Sadie grabs her hand and gawks at the ring. "This is positively gorgeous. Donovan, you say? He's the blond one. Nora has quite a thing for him."

"Well, he's taken," I say dryly.

"Of course he is. You are absolutely the luckiest woman in the world."

"I won't disagree with you there." Callie smiles.

"How about you, Rory? Are you seeing anyone?"

How am I supposed to answer that?

"She is," Callie says. "Brock."

"You are? He didn't say anything to me that he was seeing anyone."

"Well, they're quite an item," Callie says.

"Callie... Actually, we haven't been seeing each other that long."

"I'm certainly glad you told me," Sadie says. "But we just saw you the other night at Murphy's, and he didn't act like you two were together."

"She just said they haven't been seeing each other that long," Callie says.

"Oh. I guess I'll stay away from him then. There's certainly no shortage of hot Steel men."

"For sure there's not," I say.

For sure there's not? Those words aren't even in the right order. What the hell is wrong with me?

I discreetly look at my watch. Only five minutes have passed? Her break is probably for at least fifteen. Ten more minutes of this torture.

"Do you two know all the Steels?" Sadie asks.

"Our family owns a ranch adjacent to theirs," Callie says.

Thanks a lot, Callie.

"So you've known them a long time, then?"

"Yeah, forever." Those words from me.

"That's so great. So you're engaged to Donny. And he's... the son of Jonah?"

"No, he's Talon's son," Callie says. "Brock is Jonah's son."

"Awesome. What other delicious men are there to choose from?"

"Donny has a brother, Dale," Callie says. "But he's married."

"Such a shame," Sadie gushes.

Callie continues. "Brock has a brother as well. Brad. He's been in a relationship for the last two years."

"There's another blond one though, right? Nora was telling me."

"Yeah. Henry Simpson. He's the son of Marjorie Simpson, née Steel, and he's also in a relationship. He has a brother named Dave, dark hair and blue eyes. And that's it. The rest of them are women."

"Is Dave seeing anyone?"

"Dave's a womanizer," I drawl.

"That's not a bad thing," Sadie says. "Reforming a womanizer is fun."

Is it? I meet Callie's gaze. She just reformed a womanizer. She can take this one.

But to my surprise, she says nothing.

"Dave Simpson it is, then. I guess he's my only shot."

"Your only shot at what?" Callie asks.

Good for her. Callie's going to make Sadie say it.

"At a Steel, of course."

"Snow Creek has its share of hunky cowboy men," Callie says. "The Steels aren't the only family in town."

"They're the only family that matters. They own this town, don't they?"

"Don't believe everything you hear," Callie says.

"But I thought—"

"Rumors," I say. "They're abundant in a small town. My sister's right. Don't believe everything you hear."

CHAPTER SIX

Brock

It takes about a half hour to drive the perimeter. Nothing of note is visible from the car in the road.

"Now what?" I say to Dad.

"We have a couple of choices," he says. "We can walk through on foot, walk in a few miles and see what there is to see. Or we can go see Doc Sheraton. Check out his land."

"He may not be there."

"All the better," Dad says.

"If he has a home there, a road has to go in."

"Exactly."

"What if he's there? I think he's ... Dad, I just remembered. He and Brittany are here in Wyoming. Rory mentioned it."

She mentioned that when she told me she and Callie had searched Doc Sheraton's house while Pat was there, house-sitting.

"Hmmm ..." Dad says.

"What?"

"Let's go talk to them, then."

"Is that the best way to handle this?"

"I don't know. Do you have another idea?"

"You heard the story that Rory and Callie told you. Brittany Sheraton was involved with what Pat Lamone did to them. In fact, whatever they drugged Rory and Callie with was probably from a veterinary office. And it's quite possible..." My mind races.

"What aren't you telling me, son?"

"I don't know. This is just conjecture, but Donny and I, when we met with that nurse, Donny asked if atropine—the stuff Uncle Tal was poisoned with—had a veterinary use. It does."

"Yeah, it does. But that doesn't mean..."

"Doesn't it? I mean, at this point, don't we have to take every clue we have to try to piece them together any way we can?"

Dad grips the steering wheel with white knuckles. "You're right, son. I think Uncle Bryce and I... I think we've gotten a little complacent in our old age. We thought the bad years for the Steels were over. Apparently we were wrong. Dead wrong."

"Dad, I like Doc Sheraton. I always have. But honestly? How well do we really know him? If his daughter is capable of drugging other girls and helping to photograph them in compromising positions, what kind of man is he? Really?"

"A widower. A single parent. A small-town vet." Dad sighs. "A small-town vet who lost a lot of his business when Uncle Bryce and I made a decision ten years ago."

Wow. Total zinger.

Guilt. Dad and Uncle Bryce felt guilty, so they let Doc Sheraton rent the property adjacent to what he owned here in Wyoming.

Doc needed a side hustle. He trains guard dogs.

Still... Why does he need our property?

If we go to Doc Sheraton now, start talking to him...

But he doesn't have anything to do with us. I can't even

believe it. Except that... If Dale, Donny, and I are right, and whoever is using our property for nefarious purposes uses guard dogs...

But of course they could get their dogs anywhere. We can't assume they got them from Doc Sheraton. He's not the only person in the area who trains guard dogs.

But now... With Pat Lamone possibly being a relative? My God, it's all converging...

It's all converging in a way that makes me want to hurl.

So many questions.

Did Pat Lamone have any idea he might be a relative ten years ago, when he poisoned Diana? If so, that's certainly not the way to make nice with the Steel family to get part of our fortune. Pat Lamone is no brainiac, but he's not *that* stupid.

But... he *is* back in town now. Right around the same time that Donny and Callie became an item. And right around the same time Uncle Talon got shot.

"Are you thinking what I'm thinking?" I say to Dad.

"All I'm thinking, Brock, is that we have a lot of little pieces of evidence—"

"*Little* pieces of evidence?"

"Wrong word. Sorry. And *insignificant* certainly isn't the word I want either."

"No, I'd say they're damned significant. Especially the one about your brother being shot."

"Unrelated... Seemingly unrelated pieces of evidence," Dad continues, "that may not be so unrelated after all."

"What is the common thread?"

"The common thread seems to be my esteemed half uncle. William Elijah Steel."

"Steel? Not Pat Lamone?"

"It seems to all come back to him. I mean, look at everything. We've got the stuff Brendan Murphy uncovered under his floorboards, including a birth certificate for William Elijah Steel."

"Yeah, but the rest of the stuff has nothing to do with William Steel. It has to do with our family and the lien we hold on Murphy's."

And liens we hold on the rest of the freaking town, but I'm not ready to tell Dad that Callie and Donny have done that research.

"Right," Dad says, "but it does have to do with the Steel family. Then we have Talon's shooting. Talon's poisoning. The fact that someone had access to the atropine, which does have veterinary uses. We have the Steel property, and our family being implicated in"—he swallows—"something truly evil."

"Right."

"Then we have the GPS coordinates. Left for Donny by who knows who, along with an orange diamond ring that apparently once belonged to my mother, and which is now missing again."

"True."

"Someone left us these coordinates for a reason. And Doc Sheraton happens to rent this particular parcel of property."

"And Doc Sheraton trains guard dogs, and guard dogs are most likely being used by whoever..."

"Right," Dad says.

"So it's all related, somehow. Who the hell is getting past our security, Dad? We've been so focused on other things, but someone left that glasses case in Donny's mirrored cabinet, and someone took the orange diamond ring from Uncle Talon's safe."

"And the Monarch Security logs from those times just happen to be missing."

"Have you and Uncle Bryce found a new security company yet?"

"We're working on it. But we have to keep Monarch in place for now. We can't just stop being monitored."

"True."

"I've known those people at Monarch for years. I can't believe they'd..."

"Dad," I say, "if they were compromised, they were given a lot of money."

"Who has more money than we do?" Dad asks. "No. It's not money, son. My old man may have been an asshole and a liar, but he taught me well. Only one thing trumps money."

"And what's that?" Though I already know the answer.

"Life, son. Someone's life was threatened."

I nod.

"And if whoever is doing this knows what they're doing, they didn't threaten one person's life. They threatened the lives of their loved ones. That's what will really get you."

"You think?"

"You're young, Brock. Unmarried, and you have no children. But I can tell you this for sure. If someone threatened my life, I'd fight like hell. But if someone threatened *your* life? Your brother's? Your mother's? All three of you? I'd roll over so fast you wouldn't see it coming. I would do *anything* to save your life."

I regard my father, and even though he's looking forward, driving, I see the truth in his eyes.

He would gladly do anything to spare the lives of each one of us.

As much as I am harboring anger at my father—anger for keeping our family's history from us—I see him for who he truly is at this moment.

A man. A man with sun damage to his skin and callouses on his hands from working outside. A man with wrinkles around his eyes, silver threading through his thick dark hair. A hard-working man who loves his family beyond anything else.

A man who would sacrifice everything for us.

A man who maybe has made mistakes, but he made them for the noblest of reasons.

"So someone at Monarch..."

"Someone high up," he says. "They ~~got~~ to someone high up. Not the CEO of the company. He's single. Has no loyalty to anyone but the Steels. We're his paycheck. Uncle Bryce and I made sure of that years ago."

"How long have you been using Monarch Security?"

"Forever. Your grandfather contracted them when I was just a baby. When I was threatened."

My jaw drops. "What?"

"I don't know the details, Brock. If I did, I'd tell you. There's no use hiding any of this from you now. All I know is that when I was just an infant, someone threw a rock through the window of the main house, right into my nursery."

My flesh goes numb. Someone threatened a child? A baby?

But why am I surprised? Whoever's behind our current situation used an innocent baby to deliver drugs.

Dad continues, "My father got a state-of-the-art—for that time—security system, and he financed— Oh my God..."

"What?"

"He financed Monarch Security. Made sure they were

always at the top of the heap of what's going on in security. He fucking financed them, Brock. How could I have neglected to consider that?"

"You had a few other things on your mind. Are you saying our family owns the company?"

"No. It would be a lot simpler if we did. But we are their major client."

"What does it matter, then?"

"My father. He had a lot of enemies. He—"

"What, Dad? For God's sake, what?"

Dad pulls the car over to the side of the road and turns to me, his face stern.

"Brock, we have a problem."

CHAPTER SEVEN

Rory

"Thank God," Callie says under her breath once Sadie's break is finally over and she has to go back to work.

First thing she does is bring our lunch.

She smiles. "It was positively fabulous talking to the two of you. I hope we can talk again sometime."

I flash a smile, and I hope it looks sincere. "Sure."

Callie doesn't flash a smile. But that's just Callie. She simply nods.

"Geez, Cal," I say. "You might be a little nicer. After all, it's my guy she's after, not yours."

"Your guy?" Callie lifts her eyebrows.

"I don't know. I don't know what the hell he's feeling. But . . ."

"I know. You can't help who you fall for."

"It's ridiculous. I've got an amazing bisexual woman who's interested in me, and I'm hung up on an alpha Steel guy."

"It's kind of cool, when you think about it," Callie says.

"How exactly?"

"What if you and Brock work out? Then you and I will both be with one of the Three Rake-a-teers. Can't you just see it? 'The Pike sisters nab the Rake-a-teers.'"

I roll my eyes. "Doubtful that will happen."

"You don't know."

"He's twenty-four years old," I say. "He's so young. He's not really interested in an old maid like me."

Callie laughs out loud. "You're the only one who thinks you're an old maid, Ror. You're twenty-eight, drop-dead gorgeous, and every man and quite a few women in Snow Creek would love to have you."

"I don't see them lining up."

"You're usually in a relationship, and now that you're not, Brock Steel is into you. No one's going to try to take you from Brock Steel."

"I don't belong to Brock Steel," I say. "Even though—" I stop.

"Even though . . . what?"

I sigh. "Even though . . . a big part of me wants to belong to Brock Steel. Okay? I said it."

Callie twists her lips into a sly smile. "You didn't say anything I don't already know."

Callie's phone buzzes with a text. "It's Donny. I've got to get back."

"Can't you even finish your lunch?"

"Unfortunately, no." She waves to Sadie. "I'm going to need to box the sub, please."

"Sure. I'll take care of that for you." Sadie takes Rory's sandwich away.

"What's going on?" I ask.

"I'm not sure yet. He just said he needs me to come back right away."

"I hope it's nothing bad."

"I hope so too, Ror. I'll fill you in as soon as I can."

Sadie returns with Callie's sandwich in a bag.

"Thanks, Sadie," Callie says.

"Not a problem. I hope to see the two of you again soon."

Callie waves goodbye, still not smiling, and leaves.

"You okay?" Sadie says to me. "I hate eating alone."

"I don't mind."

Not the first time I've eaten alone, and it probably won't be the last.

"Is there anything I can get for you?"

"Nope, I'm good. I'm just going to finish up. You can go ahead and bring the check whenever."

Sadie smiles and bustles off.

I add a little salt to my salad and get ready to take a bite when—

"Oh, for God's sake . . ." I mutter under my breath.

Seriously? My ex did not just walk into this restaurant.

Except that she did.

Raine Cunningham. Her hair is covered in a red bandana, but otherwise she looks fresh-faced and pretty, as she always does. Her jeans fit in that slightly loose way that she likes, and she's wearing a T-shirt and denim jacket. But it's all put together in a way that works for her. Raine is the kind of person who can put on sweat pants and still look like she's ready to go out on the town. You can't be the town beauty expert and look unkempt.

And already, she's seen me.

It would be totally okay with me if she chose to ignore me. But Raine is not a rude person. We didn't end on the best of circumstances, but she's not going to be disrespectful.

I don't mind eating alone, but eating alone in front of my ex? Not really on my bucket list.

She walks toward the table. "Hi, Rory."

"Hi, Raine. What are you doing here in Snow Creek?"

"I had a few extra boxes at the salon that I needed to grab from Willow. Then I thought I'd head over here for some of Lisa's lasagna before I drive back to Denver."

Ask her to join you, Rory. You're eating alone, and it will look really bad if you don't.

"Why don't you join me?" I say. "Callie was here, but she got called back to the office."

"Oh . . . Well . . . Sure."

Damn. I shouldn't have asked. She's looking for a way to get out of it, but now she can't because she's not a rude person. She takes Callie's vacated seat.

"I'll grab our waitress." I wave to Sadie across the room.

Sadie arrives promptly. "Hi there. Will you be joining Rory?"

"Yeah. I guess so," Raine says.

"What can I get you?"

"Lasagna, please. And an iced tea."

"You got it." Sadie sets my check down. "Here you go, Rory."

"Yeah, thanks."

Thank you, Sadie. Now I won't get roped into paying for Raine's lunch, and she won't get roped into paying for mine. Perfect.

I pull my credit card out of my purse and slap it on top.

"You're paying already?" Raine asks.

"Yeah. Like I said, Callie had to leave early, so I just went ahead and asked for the check."

"That's good. Now we don't have to bother her for separate checks."

"True."

And...we've effectively run out of things to talk about. It's strange, really. Raine and I used to stay up late into the night talking. What did we talk about? At the moment, I can't remember a damned thing.

"So how's everything going in Denver?" I ask. "Are you getting set up at the spa?"

Her eyes brighten then. "It's actually pretty amazing, Rory. The place is so classy, and the decor is fabulous. Plus, all the therapists are great, and we trade services. So I'm getting all the massages I can ask for, and all I have to do is color hair or do a rebase. It's heaven."

"I'm happy for you. I was talking to Willow the other day, and she only does hair. There's going to be a lot of clientele here who will be missing your manicures and facials."

"Really? Willow only does hair?"

"Well, she's from LA. She had lots of hair there."

"Honestly? I'm doing mostly hair now myself. The spa has nail techs and aestheticians. I'm the only one that does all of it. I love doing hair, but I miss the other stuff."

"I'm sure you can probably take a few appointments here and there."

"Probably. Honestly? I can deal. The money is phenomenal."

I nod. That's not shocking at all, given that she's in Denver now at a top-notch salon and spa rather than a tiny salon in Snow Creek, Colorado.

"I'm happy for you, Raine." I already said that, but it's true. This was the right move for her, and the timing was also impeccable.

"Thank you. It was the right decision. For so many reasons."

I nod again. She doesn't have to elaborate. We both know.

"So how are you?" she asks.

"Good, actually. Callie is engaged to Donny Steel, as you know, and I'm actually seeing his cousin. Brock."

"You and Brock Steel?"

She cocks her head, and her lips . . . I think they're trying to smile but not quite getting there. She doesn't look unhappy. Or jealous. She just looks . . . like she doesn't get it.

Which, of course, she doesn't. She's not bisexual. She likes only women, all the time.

And that—the fact that she doesn't understand me—led to our breakup more than anything else.

"Yeah. Brock Steel."

"Great. I'm happy for you."

"Thank you. He's a good guy."

"But isn't he one of the Rake-a-teers? I believe you're the one who coined that term."

"I did, and he is. I didn't say we were serious or anything."

"Oh. I see."

Except it's clear that she doesn't see. But that's okay. We're no longer together.

"How about you? Are you seeing anyone new?"

"Not yet. I haven't had a chance to breathe, with getting my book up and running at the new place. I'm so lucky that they already have such an established clientele. Since I own a share of the business, I get first dibs on new appointments."

"How do the others feel about that?" I ask.

"It doesn't really matter how they feel. I own the place."

That means they don't feel great about it. This is classic Raine. She has her ideas, and she doesn't budge—hence her lack of understanding about my bisexuality.

"That's great," I say. "You'll be rolling in the bucks before long."

"I know. This is actually what I always wanted. I needed to get out of Snow Creek."

Raine grew up here like I did. She's several years younger than I am, but she didn't come out until a few years ago. I was her first real relationship, which is probably a big part of why she couldn't accept the fact that I like both women and men.

Snow Creek is a small town, and our LGBTQ population is tiny. In Denver, she won't have any problem meeting another lesbian. This was a good move for her.

"So . . . You and Brock Steel . . ."

Interesting. I figured we had laid that subject to rest.

"Like I said, we're not serious."

"You think it could get serious?"

I hope so.

I might be carrying his child.

The words hover in the back of my throat.

But I don't say them.

"I wouldn't mind," I say. "He's more than just a womanizer. He's actually a really good guy."

"All the Steels are pretty good people," she says.

Interesting perspective for her, and it makes me think . . . "Hey, I have a question for you."

"Yeah?"

"Did you know that the Steel family had a lien on the salon building here in town?"

"Yeah, I think I recall something like that on the paperwork when I bought it."

"And you didn't think anything of it?"

"My dad was helping me with all of that," she says. "I

figured if he didn't mind, I didn't mind."

"Oh."

"Why do you ask?"

"Just curious."

"How did you even know that?"

"Callie and Donny have been doing some research."

"Why?"

"I don't know. Steel family stuff, I guess."

She seems to buy my response, thank God. I may have just said something I shouldn't have.

Sadie brings the lasagna, and Raine digs in.

Which means we don't have to talk.

And that's fine with me.

I finish up my salad and garlic bread, drain my water glass, and stand. "I need to get back to work. It was great to see you."

"You too, Rory. Have a great day, okay?"

"You do the same." I force a smile, and then I realize it's actually not forced.

I'm totally over Raine, and I'm totally in love with Brock Steel.

God help me.

CHAPTER EIGHT

Brock

My dad never laid a hand on Brad or me when we were kids. There was never a threat of physical punishment.

But if we got our father angry enough, he put his fist through a wall, not unlike I did in his office recently.

And then?

He'd make us fix it.

I fixed a lot more holes in drywall than Brad did. Brad was the good son. He knew when to stop shooting off his mouth to our father.

So did I. I just chose not to.

Dad would get a look on his face—his features would go rigid, almost to stone. His lips would tremble slightly—very slightly—and pent-up rage would ooze from him. It was so palpable, sometimes I swore I could see it. The truest sign, though? His cheeks. They'd go from ruddy to blazing red, like a flare of fire.

Red Joe, Uncle Talon and Uncle Ryan used to call it.

When Brad and I saw Red Joe emerge when we were kids, we knew it was time to shut up.

Because if we didn't?

We'd be spackling up drywall later.

Like I said, Brad was better at it than I was.

Right now? As my father turns to me?

I see the beginnings of Red Joe.

Brock, we've got a problem.

There's no drywall in the truck, but there are a lot of things he could put a dent in.

I can stay quiet and see what happens. Or I can ask the obvious question.

"We've got a lot of problems, Dad, but I can see you're angry. Which problem are you talking about?"

I ready myself—ready myself against the eruption that'll spew out in seconds.

So I'm more than surprised when it doesn't.

Instead, he sighs.

"My father. Your grandfather. He made the Steel family what it is today."

"I know that."

"I've turned a blind eye to things over the years. Things I never thought would matter in the long term. After all, my siblings and I are all innocent. We were children when our father did what he did."

I cringe inside. "Wait… You're not telling me that the Steel family is built on dirty money, are you?"

"No. Nothing that can be proved anyway."

My heart beats rapidly. "Nothing that can be proved? What the hell is that supposed to mean?"

"Fuck," he says. "We got complacent. Bryce and I got complacent."

"Complacent about what?"

"Not so much complacent as… We just decided to keep some things to ourselves."

"Meaning…"

"Meaning that we didn't let Talon and Ryan in on everything. We didn't let our wives in on everything."

I curl my fingers into the palms of my hands.

Cool it, Brock. Don't go off. Don't go Red Brock on your father.

"In on *what* exactly?"

"Over the years, things popped up. Nothing that implicates any of us directly but that indicates that my grandfather and father may not have always been aboveboard in their dealings."

"Will that affect the family now?"

"No, not in any way that will matter. Not legally. Our money is our money, and it's all clean."

"All that means is *they* may have laundered it."

"No. Not that we can trace. But my father and my grandfather... Sometimes they used coercion to get what they wanted."

I feel sick. If my fingernails were slightly longer, they'd be drawing blood in my palms. "What kind of coercion, exactly?"

"Stories have come out of the woodwork over the years about my grandfather, George Steel, and my father. Stories about them holding people at gunpoint, forcing them to do certain things."

"But nothing illegal." I shake my head. "What the hell am I saying? Holding people at gunpoint *is* illegal. It's assault with a deadly weapon."

"It is. And you're right. It's illegal."

My father's voice has an edge to it—an edge I recognize, and I wish I didn't.

Red Joe has held someone at gunpoint in his life. God, I don't want to know anymore.

"What else?" I ask. "Anything else illegal?"

"No, not that I've been able to ascertain. And mind you, I have no proof of this. Like I said, they're stories that have come out of the woodwork over the years—stories I've shared with Uncle Bryce and no one else."

"Why Uncle Bryce?"

"Uncle Bryce and I have been best friends our whole lives. He and I share a closeness that..."

"What? What kind of closeness? Why would you share something with him but not with your brothers?"

"Well, first of all, Bryce *is* family. He *is* my brother. He's married to Marjorie. My sister. And he's the chief financial officer of the company, and I'm the chief executive offer. We work together closely."

"I know all this, Dad."

"Right. I'm not sure how to explain it, Brock. I've told you about Uncle Bryce's father. About what a psychopath he was. I was there when Tom Simpson ended his life. I was the last person who saw him alive. I'm the one who had to tell Bryce that his father was dead. And I'm the one who had to tell Bryce...who his father truly was."

I gulp.

"Tom Simpson was a good father to Bryce. So this was hell for him."

"What about Aunt Ruby? Her father was one of the three as well."

"Right, but that was different. Aunt Ruby never had a good relationship with her father. It's a long story, but he tried to molest her when she was only fourteen or fifteen. Aunt Ruby ran away. She lived on the streets for years."

Oh God. I'm really going to puke now.

"The good news is that Aunt Ruby's father didn't actually

complete the deed. She got away. But Aunt Ruby always knew who her father was. Bryce did not."

My bowels clench. "I think I'm going to be sick."

"Believe me, Brock. I've been there and then some."

I can't say anything. If I do, puke might spew out of my mouth.

"My point is," Dad continues, "Uncle Bryce and I have a bond that in some ways is closer than the bond I share with my brothers. Tom Simpson was like a father to me as well. And my own father... Damn. My own father did not molest children. He did not kill people. He was a better man than Tom Simpson."

My father stares straight ahead now, straight to the mountains through the front window of the truck.

Is he trying to convince himself more than me?

"Obviously my grandfather did some bad things, but at least they didn't include abusing children."

"Tom Simpson did more than abuse children, Brock. He killed children. He killed his own nephew."

God. Bowels clenching. Stomach churning. I swallow. Swallow again. "His nephew?"

"Yes, his nephew on his wife's side. The little boy's name was... Damn. What was his name? How ridiculously comfortable have I gotten in my fucking life that I can't remember a tortured little boy's name?"

I'm starting to feel sympathy for my father, but I'm feeling anger as much as anything. Anger that he kept all of this from us, left us unable to deal with it, and now everything's creeping back.

"Luke. That was his name. Luke Walker. He was Bryce's cousin on his mother's side." Dad rubs his temples.

"Dad..."

"Yeah?"

"What does all this mean? You, Uncle Bryce..."

"Uncle Bryce and I have an understanding. We... We had a friend. Well, he wasn't really a friend. He was a kid in school who got bullied. Uncle Bryce and I hated bullies, so we came to his defense. We tried to befriend him, and we invited him on one of our camping trips with Bryce's father."

Oh God. Already I know this story isn't going to end well.

Dad pauses, and just when I'm convinced he's not going to share anything more—

"The kid... He died on that camping trip. Or so Bryce and I were led to believe. It wasn't until later, nearly thirty years later, that we learned what actually happened."

"Do I want to know?"

"If you're old enough to ask the questions, son, you're old enough to hear the answers. I've told you this before."

I swallow. Swallow back the nausea that threatens to erupt out of my throat like freaking Mount Vesuvius.

Do I want to know? Is it even important to what's happening now? Only Dad can tell me.

"Is what happened in the past, on that camping trip, important to what's happening to our family now?" I ask.

"I don't know. I honestly don't know, Brock. I wouldn't blame Justin Valente—that's his name, although he goes by Cade Booker now—if he came after our family."

"So the kid, this Justin kid. What happened?"

"Uncle Bryce's father found him on the shore of the river where we were camping. He told us that he was dead. That he must've gotten up, gone to the river, and drowned."

"And then was washed up at the shore? That doesn't make any sense."

"Uncle Bryce and I weren't even ten, Brock. We believed what we were told. We found out later that Justin hadn't died. Tom Simpson had taken him, abused him . . ."

"To sell him into human trafficking?"

"No. He kept Justin as kind of a . . . plaything."

I swallow, but to no avail. I open the door of the pickup, lean my head out, and dry heave a few times. It hurts like hell, but nothing comes up.

"Get it out, Brock," Dad says. "Just get it out."

"There's nothing," I choke out. "Nothing's coming out."

"Dry heaves are the worst."

Something in Dad's voice . . . He knows. He's been where I am, learning this for the first time.

I get my salivation under control—sort of—and close the door of the truck, turning to Dad.

"So what happened to the guy?"

"Uncle Bryce and I found him twenty-five years ago. He was kind of under our noses the whole time."

"Wait, are you saying he was living as a free man?"

"Sort of. I think he was a victim of Stockholm syndrome. He had always been under Tom Simpson's thumb, and then, when Tom died, he was a little bit lost."

"I can't even imagine. How the hell does that happen?"

"Hell if I know, Brock, but it does."

"What happened to him?"

"He left the United States with another one of Tom Simpson's victims. And again, this all happened twenty-five years ago."

"Have you heard from them since?"

"I haven't. And Bryce and I chose not to reach out to them. We had already decided that if either of them came to us, we would give them what they asked for without question.

But they never came to us."

"I don't see how this could be related to what's happening now."

"It may not be."

"I mean . . . You parted on good terms, right?"

"As good as can be expected. But I think there was part of Justin that still blamed Bryce and me for what happened to him. I know we were only kids, but we were the ones who invited him on that camping trip. We were the ones who befriended him, tried to help him with the bullies at school, and we inadvertently delivered him into the hands of the biggest bully in Snow Creek."

My head feels like it's about to explode. I grab two fistfuls of my hair, yank a little, and then just grab my head, push on it, as if somehow that will keep it from rupturing.

"How the hell did we get on that tangent?" Dad says.

"You were explaining the bond between you and Uncle Bryce."

"Right." Dad sighs.

"I can't, Dad. I want to go home. I can't go see Doc Sheraton. I need time to process all this."

"I agree with you. If Doc Sheraton is somehow involved in whatever is happening here, we can't alert him to the fact that we may know."

He starts the engine, and the truck rattles to life.

"What now, then?"

"We go home," Dad says. "Then we send our guys out to search Doc Sheraton's property. People who can stay hidden when they need to. People who are trained for this."

I swallow, nod, stare straight ahead out the windshield.

And I wonder how . . .

How in God's name did this all happen?

CHAPTER NINE

Rory

I'm back in my studio, and after a couple of afternoon lessons, I decide to begin the dreaded job of organizing my music. I've been putting it off forever. Now that I've got all the boxes out of the apartment across the hall, I can finally get everything in some semblance of order. I always imagined my studio would have shelves and shelves lined with music books, opera scores, and everything in between.

So now I'm going to. In fact, I think I'll build my own bookshelves too—wooden bookshelves to house my music and my books.

All right here in my own little studio.

Maybe if I get my own place, I'll move some of it there. Maybe, if I get a big enough place, I can actually have a studio and I won't need to rent this little place over the salon.

I start to unload the first box when my phone dings with a text.

I need you. Can you come over?

From Brock. I hastily look at the clock on my phone. Wow. Nearly six o'clock. Have I been working on my books and music that long?

I haven't eaten since lunch at Lorenzo's.

Of course he's not offering me dinner. He just asked if I could come over. He's going to at least have to feed me.

I text him back.

I'm starving. Can we get dinner?

I get a response almost immediately.

I'll cook. Just please come. Please.

Two pleases?

He must really need me.

Since I'm in love with the man, I'm going to go. If nothing else, I'll get a meal out of it.

I get to a good stopping point and then lock up my studio and walk down to my car. A little less than a half hour later, I'm meandering up the driveway to the guesthouse where Brock lives.

I get out, and then I stand at the doorway for a few moments without knocking.

Last time I came over here, Bryce was stinking drunk on tequila after having nearly thrown me out of the place for having sex with him without a condom.

Yet here I am. Unable to stay away from him. Coming when he calls.

He did say please.

Twice.

I raise my fist to knock on the door.

A tail-wagging Sammy smiles—that tongue-hanging doggy smile—at me through the window next to the door.

"Hey, girl," I say through the glass.

Then I jerk when the door opens before me.

Brock stands there in nothing but jeans again. No shirt, bare feet, hair a mess.

I inhale.

Nope. No tequila on his breath or oozing out his pores. I don't smell any alcohol at all.

"You all right?" I ask.

He threads his fingers through his disheveled hair. "Come in. Please."

The third please.

Something's definitely wrong.

"Thanks for coming," he says.

"What do you need, Brock?"

"I think you know."

"Yeah, I think I know too. But I'm starving. I need something to eat."

I expect him to grab me and smash our mouths together, but he doesn't. Instead he takes my hand and leads me through the foyer into the big country kitchen in the back.

"No filets mignons tonight," he says. "I didn't have time to plan."

"That's fine. What are we having?"

"Burgers."

"With . . ."

"How should I fucking know? A salad maybe?"

I roll my eyes, walk to his refrigerator, and open it. "What do you plan to make a salad with? Shredded cheese?"

"I don't know."

"Do you have any green vegetables, Brock? There's nothing in the refrigerator."

"I've had my mind on other shit."

"So have I, but I do manage to get my greens." I close the refrigerator door and walk to his pantry. "You've got some potatoes in here. We can make oven-baked fries."

"Do you know how to do that?"

"You said *you'd* cook."

"I will. But I've never made oven-baked fries. I've never made regular fries. What the hell is the difference?"

I grab a couple of potatoes. "For God's sake. Get the damned burgers on the grill. I'm too hungry to wait for fries. I'll put these in the microwave, and we'll have baked potatoes. Do you at least have butter or sour cream?"

Without waiting for a response, I open the refrigerator again. No sour cream, but he does have butter. I suppose it's too much to hope that he has salt and pepper too.

I turn. He's standing there, gawking at me.

"What are you waiting for? Put the damned burgers on the grill."

He nods then, takes the plate of burgers from the counter where I assume they've been thawing, and walks out to the deck.

I scrub the potatoes and look for some olive oil, but when I don't find any, I rub bacon grease on them, cut tiny slits in the top, and then set them on a plate to microwave for five minutes.

They won't be as good as oven-baked potatoes, but they'll do.

Since Brock has nothing green in his refrigerator, I resort to the pantry again.

I find a few Mason jars filled with peaches. I grab one. I assume these are Steel peaches from the orchard. Marjorie probably canned them. I can't imagine that Brock did. After searching through several drawers, I find a jar opener and pull the seal off the peaches. The glorious orchard-fresh peach smell wafts up to me.

For a moment, it's August, and the peaches are ripe on the trees.

Hamburgers, baked potatoes, and canned peaches.

Good old comfort food.

I grab some ketchup and mustard out of the fridge, but since there are no greens, there will be no lettuce on the burgers. The shredded cheese will have to do, along with a few slices of onion that I quickly cut from an onion I find in the pantry.

I slice open the buns—from Ava's bakery, of course—that I find in the breadbox.

There. All set for when the burgers are done.

Except for drinks.

I pour two glasses of water, add ice, and set them on the table.

Will Brock want something else to drink? Will he wonder why I'm not drinking alcohol?

I absently touch my abdomen.

I won't know for another week at least.

Until then, I can't drink.

I'll do a preemptive strike. I grab a bottle of Fat Tire out of the refrigerator—seriously, he has beer but no greens—and set it at his place. When he asks me why I'm not having one, I'll just say I'm not in the mood.

Simple enough.

A few moments later, when Brock hasn't returned, I walk onto the deck—

"Brock!" The scent of charred beef hits my nose with a vengeance. "What are you doing?" I run to the grill, open the lid, and flip the burgers. Flames erupt.

"Shit," he says.

"Where's your mind today? These are ruined."

"I'm sorry. Let me get a few more from the freezer."

"You stay here. I'll get the burgers. I'll grill them."

Sammy is running around the yard, chasing after something invisible.

And Brock? Brock is not here. And that concerns me.

I head back to the kitchen, grab the burgers out of the freezer, bring them to the deck, and place them on the grill. I close the lid and set the timer on my phone for four minutes.

Then I stand next to Brock, watch Sammy running around the yard happily.

He's definitely not himself. Usually, when something is bothering him, he grabs me and kisses the air out of my lungs.

Tonight though?

His mind is somewhere . . . dark. Somewhere very dark.

My timer goes off, and I flip the burgers. I set the timer for two minutes.

Once the burgers are done, I transfer them to a plate. "Come on," I say to Brock. "Everything's ready."

He follows me in, and I place a burger on a bun for him, add some of the shredded cheese and a bit of onion. Does he even like onion? Too bad now. He's getting some. If I'm eating onion, so is he. We'll cancel out each other's onion breath.

Though I'm not sure, at this point, that my breath matters. He hasn't so much as touched me since I got here.

I place a potato—cut open and steaming with butter, salt, and pepper—next to the burger, and then I add a few canned peaches to complete the meal.

"Sit down," I instruct him.

He sits down, his eyes glazed over. I shove the plate in front of him.

"Thank you," he murmurs.

I didn't come over to cook dinner, but I don't mind. I'm no gourmet, but I can certainly handle burgers and microwaved baked potatoes.

But if Brock and I have any future at all, he's going to have to learn how to eat vegetables.

CHAPTER TEN

Brock

I'm a piece of shit.

I told Rory I'd feed her, and what do I do? I burn the fucking burgers. An idiot can make burgers, but I burn them.

But she's not complaining. She made the burgers, made some baked potatoes, and opened a can of Aunt Marjorie's peaches.

I invited her here, and I have nothing in my kitchen, but she managed to make a meal out of it.

I don't deserve her.

I should let her go.

Let her walk away unscathed.

She's got her own issues, and I can't drag her into mine.

But here's the kicker. Her tormentor—Pat Lamone—may be related to me.

Fuck it all to hell.

She's a wonderful woman. She's not trying to get me to talk, which I appreciate. Though I suppose I should speak up at some point.

She squirts some ketchup on top of her burger and takes a bite of it.

She's so beautiful. Even chewing her food, she's so fucking beautiful.

Her hair is in a ponytail. I'm not sure I've ever seen her wear a ponytail. It's a high ponytail and makes her look young. Like she's back in high school, walking on the homecoming court.

Finally, she speaks.

"I don't know what's going on with you, Brock, and you don't have to tell me. But I've been thinking… About that recital you scheduled for me."

There's a chill back to reality. I totally forgot about that.

"I appreciate it, but I just don't think I can get a program ready in less than two weeks."

"It's okay. I understand."

"Can you get your money back? On the cinema?"

"Probably. But instead of getting it back, why don't we just push it back a few weeks? Make it a Christmas recital."

She swallows the bite of burger she just took. "Brock…"

"For God's sake, Rory, would you please just let me do this for you? It's the only thing good I've got going in my life right now."

Her lips turn down to a frown.

Fuck. I just insulted her.

"I didn't mean it that way. I mean *you*. You're in my life, and you're good."

She wipes her lips with her napkin, takes a sip of her water. "Nice save."

"Rory…"

She takes another bite of hamburger, chews, swallows. "Sure. I get what you mean."

Except she doesn't. She *so* doesn't get what I mean. She's everything to me. Every fucking thing. And even though I forgot about that damned recital, when she brought it up, something inside me ignited. I want to do this for her. I *need* to do this for her. But she's right. Neither of us has the time to put it together in two weeks. There's just too much else going on.

Will pushing it back two or three weeks make a difference? I have no idea. The Steel family is kind of going down the toilet right now. I feel like we all have metaphorical toilet swirlies.

"Jesse . . . Jesse asked me to go on tour with the band," she says.

"When?"

"Next weekend. Or the weekend after. I can't remember. First I told him no, but now I'm thinking about it."

"Why? Why would you think about it when you can prepare your own performance?"

She twists her lips a little, takes another sip of water. "I just thought it might be good to get away."

"What about your students?"

"My students will be fine. It's only for a long weekend, and it's not the first time I've had to cancel lessons. They'll continue their practice while I'm gone, and then we'll continue our lessons when I return."

"Okay, then. What about . . ."

Us. What about us?

But after the way I've treated her . . . Maybe she doesn't think there's an *us* anymore.

"What about *what*, Brock?"

"Me. You. You and me."

"What *about* you and me?"

Damn. She's going to make me say it. I don't think I'm ready to say it, and I damn well know for sure she's not ready to hear it.

Turns out I don't have to say anything, though, because

she keeps talking.

"You behaved atrociously the other night. You accused me of not reminding you to put on a condom on purpose."

"Yeah. That wasn't my best move, and I'm really sorry."

"Then, you call me, and I come over here thinking you're lying dead somewhere, but you're only drunk as a skunk. You dropped the phone and didn't bother telling me."

"I passed out, Rory. I *couldn't* tell you."

She huffs. Takes another sip of her water. "And now you still want me to do this recital?"

"Yeah, I do. It will give us both something to focus on."

"Don't you have *enough* to focus on? With running a ranch and all?"

"Yeah, I have my work, just like you have yours. Then we also have the shit that's going on in our lives. The recital is something...different. It's not work. It's for fun."

"Producing a recital sounds fun for you," she says dryly.

"Well, it's a challenge. It's nothing I've ever done before."

"Let's get honest about this right now, Brock. You don't know anything about music production, so all the work is going to fall on me. *Me.*"

"No. That's not what I want."

"Who's going to put together the program? Me. Who's going to find an accompanist? Me. Who's going to stage the performance? Me. Your only contribution is monetary."

"No, I'll produce."

"What the hell do you think producers are? They're deep pockets."

Is she correct? Hell if I know. I produce beef, not music.

I sigh. "Fine. We can cancel the damned thing."

She opens her mouth. Closes it. Opens it again.

"Do you have something to say, Rory?"

I see it in her eyes. A big part of her wants this recital. A really big part of her.

And damn… A really big part of me wants to give it to her.

"No," she finally says. "I have nothing to say. I need you to do some talking."

"About what?"

I instantly regret the words.

I know exactly what she wants to hear.

"I'm so sorry," I say. "I wish there were something more I could say. I behaved horribly. And I'm sorry."

"What happens if I *am* pregnant, Brock? What happens then?"

"Can't we just wait and see what happens? Deal with it then?"

From the look on her face, I can see clearly that's not what she was looking for in a response. But it's all I can give her right now.

She's ready for a baby.

I'm not.

God, I do love her, though. I love this beautiful woman. I never expected to fall in love, not at my age, at least. Sure, marriage, a family—they were all down the pike for me.

I figured maybe in my midthirties.

Not at twenty-four.

Not when…

Not when my family is being upended at every turn.

If only I could confide in her, tell her. But do I really want to lay that on her? When she's going through her own shit?

No, I do not.

"Fine." She purses her lips. "If you don't mind, Brock, I think I'll be going."

I widen my eyes. "Actually, Rory, I do mind."

"Let me rephrase that, then. I'm going." She stands, takes her plate, which consists of a half-eaten burger, a potato, and peaches that weren't touched at all, to the sink.

In an instant I'm behind her, my body touching hers, my dick hard and pressing into the small of her back.

Probably not what she needs right now, but my dick responds to her.

"Please don't go," I whisper in her ear.

She stiffens, throws her food down the garbage disposal.

I hate wasting food. My mom drummed that into my head early on. People are starving, so we don't waste food.

"I thought you were hungry," I say to her.

"Turns out I'm not." She turns off the garbage disposal. "If you'll excuse me, please."

I don't move.

I place my arms around her on the counter so she's trapped.

"Excuse me, Brock," she says again.

"Please, Rory."

She seems to relax then, soften a little.

"Please what?"

"Please don't go."

She says nothing more, but she doesn't attempt to move.

I can't help myself. I press my lips to her neck, inhale her soft and silky fragrance.

"Rory . . ." I rasp.

She turns then, turns to face me, and now my hard dick is pressing into her abdomen. "Brock, please tell me what you want."

"You know what I want."

"I'm not talking about that. We could go to bed right now. We'd both have a hell of a good time. Then we could forget for a few minutes what else is going on in our lives."

"I think I've proved I can last more than a few minutes."

She pushes me away then. "For God's sake, Brock. Could you just be serious?"

I could grab her. I could kiss her hard. She'd respond. She and I both know this.

But I don't want to take the easy way out with her. I don't have it in me anyway, not after today. Not after what my dad and I discussed.

I walk to the table, grab my bottle of Fat Tire that I haven't touched until now, and take a deep draft.

I'm not going to get drunk. I'm still not over last night. But the smooth ale coats my throat, eases the dryness.

I face Rory. "I won't lie to you. I want you to come to bed with me. But you're clearly not in the mood."

"Who says I'm not in the mood?"

I stalk toward her. "Okay, then—"

She puts out her arms to stop me. "Just because I'm in the mood doesn't mean it's a good idea."

"It's always a good idea."

"Not at the moment, Brock. Not at this freaking moment."

"Just tell me what you want. Please."

"Why should I have to spell it out for you? You're a grown man. A grown, intelligent man."

"Are you going to make me say it? With everything else that's going on, are you going to make me say it?"

She wrinkles her forehead. Is she truly that clueless about how I feel about her?

Of course she is. I offered to produce this recital for her. I told her no one would hurt her on my watch.

But I also treated her poorly last night.

Very poorly.

I've apologized, but I know enough about women—from my mother—to know that a simple apology of words, while it may be enough for the long term, won't suffice in the short term. Women take time to get over things. It's how they're wired. Men are different.

Men can have a knock-down, drag-out and then be ready to fuck a minute later.

Yeah, we're wired a lot differently.

"Say *what*? What are you talking about, Brock?"

"I'm done talking," I say.

Then I do what I've been fighting. I crush my mouth to hers.

CHAPTER ELEVEN

Rory

I don't want to love this kiss.

With everything in me, I want to push him away, tell him we're over.

But I can't.

His kisses are that powerful. That drugging.

And this one? It's the most powerful and drugging kiss to date.

I feel like he's marking me. Branding me.

Branded by Brock Steel.

Oddly, the thought isn't anathema. On the contrary, I like it. I like it a lot.

Why wouldn't I? I'm in love with this fool.

His teeth clash with mine, and his abrasive stubble abrades the skin on my cheeks and chin. And all I can think about is his hard dick pressing into my belly.

My nipples are so hard, I feel like they're poking straight into his chest. And my pussy . . . God, that tingling between my legs is so intense . . .

I'm wet. So damned wet.

I've had a lot of sex in my life, but no one gets me wet the way Brock Steel does.

How could I have considered going to bed with Dragon

Locke? Going out with Davey Haynes?

No one else will satisfy me now that I've had a taste of Brock Steel.

It's over for me. It's this man or no one.

Sure, there are parts of him I don't like. But the heart wants what it wants.

I may not like every part of him, but I'm completely in *love* with all of him.

So I respond. I respond to his kiss with my own brand of passion and desire. My groans meet his groans, and when he grabs my ponytail and yanks it, exposing my neck, our mouths part with a smack, and he slides his tongue over my throat.

"God . . ." comes out of me.

"So fucking beautiful," he growls against my flesh.

I think I say something then, but I'm not sure what the words are. I only know that this is leading to the bedroom. This is leading to naked bodies thrashing together.

And I don't have the will or the desire to fight it.

I love this man, and I want to be with him.

"Need you," he grits out.

"Yes. Me too."

"No. I mean now. I need you now."

In sheer seconds, it becomes clear what he means. My shoes and jeans and panties lie on the floor, and I gasp at the cold against my ass when he sets me on the counter.

Within another second, his jeans and underwear are around his thighs, and his dick is inside me.

I don't want to stop. He fills such an aching emptiness. But—

"Brock."

He thrusts.

"Brock . . ."

He thrusts again.

"Brock!" I push at his chest.

His eyes are wide, crazed. "What? What is it?"

"Condom, damn it. Condom!"

"Fuck." He pulls his jeans back up and shoves his hands in the pockets. "Fuck," he says again when his pockets turn up empty. Without snapping his jeans, he walks out and returns a moment later, fully sheathed.

Then he plunges back into me.

And again, I'm filled.

It's different, though. There's a barrier between us—a barrier I don't want there. Besides, if I'm already pregnant, what does it matter?

But he can't blame me this time. I told him to get a condom.

Part of me was hoping he would say screw it and continue without one.

But he didn't.

That saddens me.

He continues thrusting, and yes, it feels good. The way his massive cock stretches me every time. It's amazing. Soul crushing.

But something was lost.

It's not as raw and heart-wrenching as it was before he put on the condom.

I close my eyes, lean my head back as he continues.

I want desperately to recapture the rawness of when he first entered me.

But I already know I'm not going to have a climax. I'm thinking too much.

Not a problem for Brock, though. He plunges into me deeply, and I feel him. I feel the contractions as he spurts—not into me but into the condom.

He groans. "Damn, Rory."

I open my eyes.

Beads of sweat emerge at his brow, and the hair around his face is slightly damp.

He's beautiful, of course. He's Brock Steel. His lips are red and swollen from our kisses, and his eyes are glazed over from the orgasm.

Yes, he's beautiful.

But something was definitely missing this time.

So much I want to say to him, but he'll go running away if I do.

"I think I'll go on the pill." I lift my eyebrows. I'm not sure where those words came from.

"I'd love that, sweetheart."

"Would you? Of course you would because it means you get to fuck me without a condom. I know enough about male anatomy to know it feels a hell of a lot better that way."

"Wait, wait, wait… You said the words, Rory. And yeah, of course it feels better. Do you feel as much when you pet your dog with a glove on?"

I push him away and hop off the counter. "I'm not going on the pill, Brock."

"Then why did you say it?"

Why did I? To please him. I said it to please him, not myself. And I'm not going to be that woman. I'm not going to be that woman who sacrifices a little part of herself to please her partner.

Still, I'm not sure how to answer his question, so I wing it.

"To see what your reaction would be."

"What did you *think* my reaction would be?"

"Pretty much exactly what it was."

He shakes his head then. "I give up. I freaking give up, Rory. I don't know how to please you."

"I'm just like any other woman."

"But you're not. You're—" He rakes both hands through his hair. "You're not. You're beautiful and you're bright. You light up the whole fucking room. And I'm—"

"What? You're what?"

"Damn it!" He snaps his pants and paces throughout the kitchen. "I got drunk over you, Rory. I don't do that."

"You got drunk because you thought you might have gotten me pregnant," I say.

"Christ! Don't you hear what I'm saying to you?"

"I hear it very well. I'm not the one in an orgasm-induced haze right now."

"Oh, sweetheart… Damn, you know how to cut me like a knife."

His words gut me, but I continue. "Why does that surprise you? It was just a fuck, Brock. You didn't do anything to make me come."

"This is so not how I wanted tonight to go. I wanted to… I wanted to make it right between us, Rory. I wanted to…"

"I don't know what the hell you're trying to say."

"Don't. Don't make me say what I'm not ready to say. Don't make me say what you're not ready to hear."

"I'm ready to hear whatever you have to say."

My heart speeds up. What does he think I'm not ready to hear?

I'm ready to hear whatever.

Now, the part about him not being ready to say? That I believe.

"I'm not a guy who gets serious," Brock says. "Sure, in the future. I want all of that. A family, kids, everything my parents have. But right now? I don't want that."

"Yeah, you've made that pretty clear."

"No, I'm not making myself clear. Don't you see? This wasn't supposed to happen to me. Not yet."

"For God's sake, Brock. Would you spit it out? I don't give a shit that you're not ready to say what you want to say. I can guarantee you I'm ready to hear anything you have to say. I'm a grown-up."

He rubs his forehead, his temple, his stubbled jawline. "God, you can slice into my heart like no woman I've ever known."

I soften then. I don't want to hurt him. I never wanted to hurt him. Or anyone, for that matter. I'm not that kind of person.

Sure, I'm angry with him. But I also love him. I don't want him to hurt because of me. I find my jeans and panties and put them on. Brock is still pacing around the kitchen. I go to him. I take one of his hands, entwine his fingers through mine.

"I'm sorry," I say. "I don't have any intention of going on the pill, and I shouldn't have said that."

"No, you shouldn't have."

"But Brock, you're not being honest with me. What exactly is it that you want to say?"

CHAPTER TWELVE

Brock

I love you.

I love you so damned much, Aurora Maureen Pike.

If only the words weren't caught in my throat.

"Rory..."

I touch her then. I trail my fingers over the softness of her cheek. Then I trace her lips, her beautiful red lips still glistening from the kisses we shared.

I'm going to do it. She may not return my feelings, but I'm going to say it. I'm going to say those three words I've never uttered to another human being.

I clear my throat.

And I pause.

She rolls her eyes then. "I don't have all day for this."

"Damn it." I kiss her lips. How soft they are. "I..."

She draws in a breath. Lets it out slowly.

"I love you, Rory. I fucking love you."

Her beautiful lips form an O.

Is this really a surprise to her?

Hell, why shouldn't it be? It's a big surprise to me. Except that on some level, it's not. It's almost as if it's always been with me, and Rory brought it to the surface. Fate brought her to me, and I fell so deeply in love with her.

I've put myself out there. I've given her love, and—

Her lips tremble. "Really?"

"Of course *really*. Do you think I said those words for my health? I've never said that to anyone before, Rory."

"You haven't?" She swallows.

"No."

I don't bother to ask her if she has. I know she has. She was with Raine for over a year. And I know she had two other serious relationships—one with a man and one with a woman— before Raine.

"I don't know what to say," she says.

"Say whatever you feel, Rory. I'm not going to ask you to say it back. I know you don't feel—"

She presses her fingers to my lips. "But I do feel it, Brock. I never thought in a million years that *you* would."

"You mean..."

"Yes. I love you too. I'm in love with you, and trust me, no one is more surprised than I am by that fact."

My jaw drops.

Rory loves me? The most beautiful woman in Snow Creek loves *me*?

The woman who has her pick of not just all the men in Snow Creek but also all the women? She chose *me*?

"Oh my God, Rory." I pull her into my arms, kiss the side of her neck. Revel in the feel of her against me.

"I never imagined..." she says.

"God, neither did I."

"Brock..."

"Yeah?"

"I need you to let go of me for a minute. Because there's something we need to talk about."

I reluctantly let her go. "All right."

She sits back down at the table and motions for me to join her.

"I am totally in love with you," she says.

"Sweetheart, that makes me the happiest man alive."

"But we're in two different places, Brock. I'm ready for a child. You're not."

I nod. I can't help myself. I'm not ready. "Rory... If you're pregnant, I'm going to be there. I love you, and I will love our child."

Her face softens then, and she glows. Damn, the woman glows.

"But if I'm not pregnant..."

"If you're not pregnant, I'm still in love with you. Our relationship will grow, and one day... I hope we *will* have a child."

"So you're saying... You're saying this is a forever love for you?"

"What other kind of love is there, Rory?"

My heart nearly falls into my stomach. *Is* there another kind of love for her?

Maybe there's a reason I've never said I loved anyone before. Maybe because love itself is forever for me but not for her. I hate the idea of her ever having loved another when I haven't.

"I've been in love before," she says, "and I've found that it's not forever."

"I see." But I don't see. I just feel a thick nausea that wants to consume me.

"But let me be honest with you," she says. "What I feel for you is stronger. Stronger than anything I've ever felt before. It frightens me, the intensity of it."

I cup her cheek. "It frightens me too."

"It's just... I have been in love before, so I know this is different. If you've never been in love before, then what if... What if this isn't really love for you, Brock?"

"How can you say that? I've never said those three words to anyone. This is something I've truly never felt, and it's... It's something I never imagined. Right now, I can't imagine being with anyone but you, Rory. Why do you think that's going to change?"

"I don't necessarily think it's going to change. But you and I both know that you're young and you're kind of a playboy."

"I am young. But I'm no longer a playboy. I haven't been able to think of anyone but you since we started this, and that's never happened to me before."

"My God... How can I love you this much? You're so not who I thought I'd end up with." She breaks into her dazzling smile.

"However much you love me," I say, "I love you just as much or more. You're everything to me, Rory. Every fucking thing."

"So if I'm pregnant..."

"If you're pregnant, we deal with it. We become parents. But if you're not... I'd like to wait a little while. If that's okay with you."

"Relationships are a two-way street. I know that. So we'll come to some kind of compromise. I mean, it's not like we're engaged or anything."

"We're in love. Right now, let's just concentrate on that."

She closes her eyes and exhales. Then she opens them. "All right. With everything else going on in both our lives, I think being in love and concentrating on that sounds perfect."

And with those words, I love her even more.

I stand then, take her hand, and lead her to my bedroom.

We undress each other slowly, and then we lie naked on the bed, and we kiss each other. We kiss for a long time.

I grab a condom from my nightstand drawer, sheath myself, and then I slide into her slowly. And we make love that way. Slowly and seductively.

And this time ... I make sure she comes.

★ ★ ★

I jerk awake at the sound of my phone. Rory lies in my bed, sleeping soundly.

What the hell time is it anyway?

Four thirty a.m.

Who the hell is calling me at this hour?

I grab my phone. It's Dale's number.

"Dale, what is it? Is everything all right? Is it Uncle Talon?"

"Dad's fine," Dale says. "I'm sorry to alarm you. I've got Donny on the line as well."

"Don?"

"I'm here." Donny's voice.

"Why are you calling so early?" I demand. "If everything's okay, I don't understand—"

"I didn't want to wait," Dale says. "Remember the guy Aunt Ruby referred me to? The one who was going to check out those bones we found?"

"Yeah." I stifle a yawn.

"He got back to me. Just now. He didn't want to wait, and I don't want to wait either."

A feeling of impending doom settles in my stomach. With everything that's been making my stomach and bowels react lately, I've been keeping Pepto-Bismol in business.

Damn.

This can't be good news.

"What is it?" Donny asks.

"He was able to do some analysis on the bones. We were right. They're old. Really old."

"Okay," I say. An odd wave of relief settles over me. If they're old, they can't belong to anyone we know.

"His analysis shows that the bones are around sixty years old. And they belonged to a female."

"How can he tell it was a female?" From Donny.

"From extracting the DNA from the bones. It's a female. And there's no way to tell exactly how old the female was when she died, but he's estimating around twenty years old."

I gulp. "A twenty-year-old female? Sixty years ago? With her bones on our property?"

As disgusted as I am, another wave of relief consumes me. At least it wasn't a child, though a twenty-year-old woman is still a child in some ways. But at least she got to grow up.

God. Has it truly come to this? Where something that isn't as horrific as it could be is *good* news? I need to get a grip.

"That's right," Dale replies.

"That's horrible," Donny says, "but why was it so necessary to call this early?"

"Because..." Dale pauses slightly. "The guy did some other research. And what he found is truly frightening."

CHAPTER THIRTEEN

Rory

It's a damned good thing I'm an actress. I should get an Oscar for what I'm about to do.

I'm driving Cage's van, the one he uses for the band. Jordan convinced him to let us borrow it. I'm not sure what excuse she gave him, but it sure wasn't the truth.

I drive by the school, where I know Pat Lamone and his buddies are hanging out. I roll down the window on the driver's side. "Hey, guys."

"Hey, hot stuff," Pat says.

Hot stuff. I totally want to hurl.

"Get in," I force myself to say.

"You talking to me?"

"Yeah, I'm talking to you. Get in."

He raises his eyebrows at his friends. "Now that's an invitation I'm not going to turn down."

He walks around to the other side of the van, opens the door, and takes his position in the passenger seat. "What's going on with you tonight?"

Do it, Rory. Just do it. Say it. *"I'm feeling kind of horny. How about you?"*

"I'm always horny around you. Have you changed your mind about us?"

Hell, no. *"I'm not really in the mood to talk,"* I say.

"Damn…" He smiles a lazy smile. *I see it out of the corner of my eye while I keep my gaze glued to the windshield.*

You can do this, Rory. You have to do this.

The condom Callie and I stole from our brother's dresser drawer sits in the ashtray. I grab it and toss it to Pat. It lands in his lap.

"Just in case you're not prepared."

He drops his jaw.

Then I grab a bottle of Coke from the cooler between the two seats. A very special bottle of Coke. I unscrew the cap and hand it to him. *"Drink up. I don't want you getting dehydrated."* *I shove the van into gear and start to drive away.*

"Where are we headed?"

"I don't know. Feel like a drive?"

"Not really. You want to know what I feel like?"

"Oh, we'll get there. I thought we'd drive for a while. Work up…you know."

"Nice," he says.

"Could you hand me a Coke?" I ask, gesturing to the cooler.

He nods and takes a big sip of the bottle I gave him.

Good boy.

Then he reaches between the seats, grabs another, opens it for me, and hands it to me.

"Thanks." Dazzling smile time. I take a sip.

He takes another sip of his.

Good. He needs to finish his Coke before we park.

"I'm so thirsty." I take a few more sips.

He follows suit.

Yup. I knew I could get him to drink the Coke if I drink one with him.

Pat Lamone is such a lemming.

Earlier, Callie and I ground several Benadryl tablets into powder and mixed them in the Coke that I gave Pat. It should be enough to put him to sleep, but I need to drive around awhile, make sure he finishes the entire bottle.

I can do it.

We thought it all through.

I'm going to call Callie and Jordan, and they'll know exactly what's going on once we get to the parking lot.

I make small talk with Pat, which turns out to be pretty easy because Callie, Jordan, and I came up with a bunch of topics that we knew he would talk about—baseball, his friends, and the big one—himself.

We drive along the outskirts of town, getting nearer to my family's property.

"You're heading onto the Steel property," Pat says.

"Am I? Just driving, you know."

"Damn Steels."

I hide my surprise at his comment. "You've got something against the Steels?"

"They own this goddamned town. They think they're all that, you know?"

I've heard the rumors, but the Steels have always been nice to my family. We own property adjacent to theirs.

"They've got money for sure," I say.

"They've got more than money."

I'm not sure what he's talking about, and I don't rightfully care. I have one objective tonight—to get him to confess to spiking that punch—and then Callie and I can collect the Steels' reward.

Finally, he finishes his Coke. By the time we drive back to the parking lot Callie and I decided on, the Benadryl will begin to kick in. I need to work quickly.

I roll into the parking lot and snag a space. I grab my phone. Callie's number is already queued up, so I can tap a single button without Pat knowing.

In the back of the van, a mattress waits for us. Time to go to work.

"You want to get in the back?" I ask.

"Hell, yeah!" In mere seconds, Pat has leaped over the cooler and is on the mattress, waiting.

So that was easy. I place the call and then join Pat on the mattress, where I set my phone on top of the cooler. Pat is so involved in trying to get laid that he doesn't notice. Everything's going as planned. Now if I can get through the next fifteen to twenty minutes without vomiting . . .

"Not too many cars here tonight," I say.

"Just as well." Pat turns to me, meets my gaze. "No one to bother us."

I smile. A big one, despite wanting to gag. This is the biggest acting challenge of my life. "I know. I've been looking forward to this." I rake my gaze over Pat. "God, you look hot."

"Not as hot as you, baby."

"Tell me something," I say.

"What?"

Big smile again, and I raise my eyebrows, lick my bottom lip. "I'm dying to find out what was in that hairy buffalo homecoming night. I've never had such an amazing high."

He shrugs. "Probably just some Everclear."

Sorry, Lamone. You're going to have to do better.

This time I bite my lower lip and then curve both lips into a sly smile. "No, it was more than that. I've drunk my share of Everclear."

He narrows his eyes. "God, you're fucking hot."

"So are you." I giggle—the kind of cheerleader giggle that I know will turn him on. I try not to hate myself for it.

Then I move toward him, brush my lips over his.

And try not to hurl.

He grabs me, runs his tongue over my lips, and . . .

I open. I open for his kiss.

Mind over matter, Rory. Just do it.

He sweeps his tongue into my mouth, and for a moment, I wonder if he can taste my tonsils. Is this how he kisses? Or is he just kissing me this way? So he can go tell his juvenile friends that he shoved his tongue down Rory Pike's throat?

Doesn't matter. None of it matters. This is an acting job, nothing more.

Then his hand . . . He's groping one of my breasts. I knew it would happen. I knew it . . . still . . . I feel so cheap. So used.

But I'm here to do a job. I resist the instinct to brush his hand away. He squeezes. Hard. Does he really think that feels good to me? A moan escapes his throat. Then a louder one. A full-fledged groan.

I force myself to sigh softly, to make him believe I'm enjoying myself. A few more minutes pass, and then his kiss gets noticeably less forceful. I take the chance to pull away and inhale.

"Getting tired?" I ask.

"A little. But believe me, I have enough energy to make you happy." Pat yawns.

Nice. The Benadryl is working. Except now I have a window of about five to ten minutes to get him to admit to spiking the hairy buffalo.

Pat is gazing at me—well, not at me, exactly. Rather at my chest.

I smile again. "You can't stop looking at my tits, can you?"

"Baby, no one can stop looking at your tits."

"Here." I take both his hands, place them on my breasts.

Yeah, I really should get a freaking Academy Award for this.

He squeezes them again. Hard. "I want to suck on them, baby. I want to pinch them until they're red."

"Easy. We'll get there, stud."

Pat closes his eyes, continues squeezing, but then the pressure of his hands lessens.

I pull him into a lying position. "Come on. Lie down here with me."

He yawns again and then turns to face me.

I touch his cheek. "I wish I knew who spiked the punch. Then I could find out what they put in it. Get some more of that for myself."

He smiles lazily. "I can get you some stuff."

I trail my finger over his chest to his abdomen, coming perilously close to the bulge beneath his jeans. I hope I don't have to go there, but if I have to, I will.

"Can you? Wow, that would be great. So you know what was in the punch, then?"

"Sure, I do, baby. After all, I'm the one who fucking spiked it."

Okay, he earned it. I grab the bulge. "You did that? How?"

He groans and closes his eyes. "I can do anything. Don't you know that right about now?"

All I know is that I want to throw up.

He's fading. The Benadryl will take him any minute now, but I may as well see if I can get more information out of him.

"Why do you suppose Diana had a reaction?" I say. "No one else did."

"I don't know," he says, "but the Steels... They get what they fucking deserve."

★ ★ ★

I jerk awake.

My heart is pounding, and I feel sick. Really sick.

God, that night. Whoring myself out to Pat Lamone to get information. Thank God he passed out before...

I shiver at the thought.

But the memory. The dream.

It's like it happened yesterday.

Only... I'm more alert now. And something he said triggers me.

The Steels get what they fucking deserve.

Oh my God.

Pat said he spiked the punch.

And I'm sure he did.

But I think... I think he may have poisoned Diana Steel on purpose.

Even then, he had something against the Steels.

Did he know? Did he know then that he might be a relative?

I turn to grab Brock—

But he's not there. Sammy's not at the foot of the bed either.

"Brock?"

It's four forty-five. Even Brock doesn't get up this early.

I get out of bed, find my jeans and shirt, and pull them on quickly. "Brock?" I leave the bedroom.

I find him in the kitchen on the phone. Sammy is scratching at the door to come in. I open the door, and she comes racing in and laps up some water from her bowl.

"Brock? What's wrong?"

He motions for me to be quiet.

CHAPTER FOURTEEN

Brock

Rory stands before me, her eyes wide, her hair falling out of her ponytail that she didn't take down before we fell asleep.

My God.

I love her so much.

I can't believe I've fallen in love.

And she loves me back. This wonderful woman loves me back.

Part of me...

Part of me almost hopes she's pregnant.

Except that my heart is pounding out of my chest at the moment.

Because of the words my cousin just uttered.

He did some other research. And what he found is truly frightening.

"Don't leave us in suspense," Donny says, his voice cracking a little.

Rory kisses the top of my head. "I'll leave you alone," she says softly.

"No. Please. Stay."

"What?" Dale says.

"Sorry. I was talking to Rory."

"Brock..." Dale's voice.

"No," I say adamantly. "I'm tired of keeping this from her.

I . . . She and I . . ."

Rory takes a seat across from me at the kitchen table and widens her eyes.

I smile at her.

"We're in a relationship. Rory and I are in a relationship."

"You are?" Dale says.

"Don't sound so surprised."

"I'm not surprised." This from Donny. "If I can be turned, anyone can. The Pike sisters are magical."

"You're not kidding," I agree.

"Yeah, yeah, yeah." From Dale. "Whatever. I'm happy for you. But you guys, this shit is truly scary."

"All right," I swallow. "Go on."

"Turns out there was a woman, a young woman, who was apparently a friend of our grandmother's. Her name was Patricia. Patricia Watson."

"Yeah?" Don says.

"Yeah. She disappeared. While she was in Snow Creek with her boyfriend. They were in college. In fact, Patricia—Patty she was called—was our grandmother's college roommate her first year."

"Just her first year?" I ask.

"Our grandmother only went to college one year. She became pregnant with your dad, Brock. And she left school, went to the Steel ranch to live. Married our grandfather."

"Okay. Are you suggesting that these bones belong to this Patty?"

"There's not really any way to know without having a sample of Patty's DNA. But everything else seems to point to that fact."

"Who would want to kill an eighteen-year-old girl?" Donny says.

My blood is running cold. "Really, Don? After what we've recently found out about our esteemed family, you're asking that question?"

"Anyway, it sparked a memory in me," Dale says.

"What do you mean?" I ask. "You weren't alive back then."

"I know that, numbnuts. But do you remember that old guy who worked with Uncle Ryan back in the day?"

"I don't," I say.

"No, you wouldn't. You were too young. But Donny might remember."

"I don't know," Donny says. "A lot of guys worked around the ranch."

"Yeah, maybe you don't remember. But I spent a lot of time with Uncle Ryan. That's how I got my interest in wine. Anyway, there was this old British guy. Apparently he was the first winemaker at Steel Vineyards."

"British guy?" I say. "What the hell does a British guy know about wine?"

"This British guy knew about wine. He lived on the ranch, but then he went back to England years later. I was probably twelve or so."

"Okay."

"Anyway, his name was Ennis. Ennis Ainsley. He also knew our grandmother from college, and that's how he met our grandfather."

"What's this got to do with our dead girl's bones?"

"Ainsley never married," Dale says. "He trained Uncle Ryan to run the winery, and then when Uncle Ryan took over, he stayed around for a few years on the ranch. But I remember him talking about the one true love of his life. Her name was Patty."

"The one who disappeared," I say.

"Yes. Probably. Uncle Ryan might remember her last name. Ennis and Patty were visiting Snow Creek, were here to see our grandparents, and apparently Patty disappeared."

"Was she killed?" I ask.

"That's what we need to find out. We're going to do some research. Her parents are most likely dead by now. They'd be in their hundreds. But you know who *is* still alive?"

"Ennis Ainsley?" I ask.

"Yes. Ennis Ainsley is still alive, and he lives in London. He's eighty-eight years old."

"That's way too old to fly him over here."

"Yes, it is," Dale agrees. "Which is why we're going to have to go to him."

"Drop everything and fly to London?" I say. "With everything else going on?"

"We don't all have to go. Only one of us."

"I'll do it." My words surprise myself.

But getting the hell out of Colorado? Sounds like freaking paradise to me.

You can't escape your problems, but when we're talking about rotting human flesh, my uncle being poisoned, finding out your family really *does* own the damned town, and still no leads on the whole Brendan Murphy situation... Oh, and the best of all. Finding out Pat Lamone is probably a long-lost cousin...

I just want a fucking break.

Even if the break entails talking to an old man about his one true love who disappeared sixty years ago.

"You sure?" Dale asks.

"Yeah. I'm pretty sure. I'll take Rory with me."

"Have you told Rory everything?"

"No... But I'd like to. With your permission of course."

"You've got mine," Donny says. "I let Callie in on everything without even checking with you guys first, so I won't stand in your way."

"You're truly serious about her?" Dale asks.

I regard her as she sits across from me, her beautiful brown eyes heavy-lidded, and her lovely lips in a soft smile.

"Yeah. Totally. Believe me, I'm as surprised as you are. Plus, she's Callie's sister. The Pikes are good people. She can be trusted."

Rory lifts her eyebrows at me.

"In fact, she's sitting right here. At my table."

"At five in the morning?" Donny says.

"Yeah. I'm not sure why she's up."

"I had a dream," Rory says.

"Apparently she had a dream that woke her," I tell them.

"All right," Dale says. "You and Rory go to London. Find out what you can from Ennis Ainsley. In the meantime, I'll talk to Uncle Ryan about it. He knew Ennis well."

"All right." I sigh and run my fingers through my already messed-up hair. "Anything else?"

"You mean other than all the other bullshit we've got going on?" Donny says.

"That's exactly what I mean. After all, just when you think it can't get any hairier . . ."

"It does," Dale says. "It always fucking does."

"Send me all the documents you got from the guy about bones," I say. "And anything else you have on this Ennis Ainsley and Patricia Watson."

"Will do. They'll be in your email within a few minutes."

"All right." I draw in a breath. "I guess I'm going to London."

CHAPTER FIFTEEN

Rory

I drop my jaw.

I guess I'm going to London.

Why the heck is Brock going to London?

He ends the call and meets my gaze. "So how much of that did you actually understand?"

"The part where you said you and I were in a relationship." I smile as the warmth of a sheepskin blanket envelops me. "Other than that... I have no clue what you're talking about."

"Well... You're going to wish you didn't after we get on with the conversation. I have my cousins' permission to tell you everything."

"You mean everything Callie already knows?"

"That, and whatever else there is."

I swallow. "Maybe I'd better put some coffee on."

"Yeah. Coffee, definitely. In the meantime, how'd you like to go to London?"

"You really want me to go with you?"

"Of course I do. Have you ever been there?"

I roll my eyes. "You're talking to Rory Pike, Brock. I've never been anywhere, except a few trips to New York for auditions back in the day."

"Then I'd love for you to come with me."

"But I have work. Students."

"Didn't you just say you were going to a gig with your brother next weekend or something?"

I open my mouth, and then I close it.

"You didn't have any problem taking a break from your lessons when that was the issue," he says.

"I probably can't go. I did tell him I'd do the gig."

"But first you told him you wouldn't do the gig."

"It's all a big mess," I say. "Maybe I'll go. Maybe I won't."

"All right." He draws in a breath. "Here's what we'll do. I have to go to London. And I have to go soon. As soon as I get the information from Dale, I need to get in contact with this old man in London. Ennis Ainsley. I need to tell him that we're going to come see him, that we have some questions. I need to do that as soon as I can, which means I have to tell my father that I'll be leaving for several days, and Rory, I really want to do this, and I really want you to go with me."

"I understand why *you* want to go."

"Do you?"

"Of course I do. Even though it has to do with ... Actually, what *does* it have to do with?"

"It's family stuff. More family bullshit. And I will tell you everything."

"Still," I say, "it's a trip to London. Which in its own way is kind of an escape from everything else that's going on."

"Bingo."

"I'd love to go with you. I'd love to see London. But will there even be time for that? You're going on business."

"Sweetheart, I will make the time to show you all the sights in London. That I can promise you."

"All right. Jesse's going to kill me."

"Why? Because you're doing the whole push me, pull you thing?"

"Push me, pull you? Is that from *Dr. Doolittle*?"

"Yep. One of my favorite books as a kid."

"You're kidding. Mine too."

"Makes total sense for me because I love animals. Why for you?"

"I love animals too. Dogs especially. Why do you think I want to be a mom so bad? I love babies of all kinds."

He smiles then. My God, he's so good-looking.

"You are perfect in every way, Aurora Maureen Pike."

"And you, Brock… What's your middle name anyway?"

He rolls his eyes. "Promise you won't laugh."

"Oh, no. I do not promise that at all."

"It's Alistair. After my mother's grandfather."

"That's not so bad," I say. "I was thinking you'd say Eugene or Maurice or Aloysius or something."

"Nope. Still, it's not something I advertise. I don't even use my middle initial. My signature is simply Brock Steel."

"Well… Brock Alistair Steel, you are amazing and magnificent, and I'm completely in love with you."

His features soften. My God, he's even more beautiful.

"Anyway, the push me, pull you thing," he continues. "I've been feeling that since I kissed you that night of Uncle Talon's welcome home party. Something was pulling me toward you, and I was trying to push you away. I was feeling more than I wanted to feel, even then."

"And now?" I say.

"Now I'm all in, Rory. I'm not going to try to push away these feelings any longer. I'm all in."

I warm all over. "I'm all in too, Brock. And yes. I will go to London with you."

★ ★ ★

"You're fucking kidding me," Jesse says.

"I'm really sorry."

"For Christ's sake, Ror. I should be mad as hell at you, but I can't be. I wish I could go to London."

"You will, Jesse. Someday. I'll make it happen."

He scoffs. "How exactly are *you* going to make it happen?"

"I don't know, but I will. In the meantime, I'm making an executive decision."

"What's that?"

"Brock and I are producing a recital for me. It's going to be sometime before Christmas at the cinema in town."

My brother furrows his brow. "Say what?"

"I don't have all the details yet, but when I do, I'll fill you in. I'm going to need your help with sound and lighting, and … I want you to sing with me."

"You want the band at a Christmas recital?"

"I don't want the band, Jesse. I want you."

"I don't sing opera, Ror."

"I know you don't. But you have a beautiful voice for musical theater. We can do some duets. I was thinking 'A Little Priest' from *Sweeney Todd*. 'The Song That Goes Like This' from *Spamalot*."

"As long as you don't make me sing 'Baby, It's Cold Outside.'"

"Gross. We're brother and sister."

"Exactly."

"But yeah, we can find some arrangements of holiday duets as well."

"Rory, I've probably wrecked my voice over the years singing rock and roll."

"I'll get you into shape. I'm a voice teacher, by the way."

"I know that. But Ror ..."

"I'm not taking no for an answer. In fact ..."

My mind is racing. Brock has connections, right? Maybe he could get some agents to come to the recital.

"What?"

"I can't make any promises yet. Just trust me. You want to be part of this, Jess."

"So you're bailing on me for a gig, and now you want a favor?"

"Yes, but in the end, I think you'll realize that I'm doing *you* a favor."

He scoffs again. "Okay. Send me the material as soon as you've got it. When is the recital?"

"I don't have a date yet. Brock set it before Thanksgiving, but we're going to change that. First of all, I don't have time to get something together by then, and second of all, he doesn't want to interfere with Ryan and Ruby's big Thanksgiving anniversary thing."

"Their anniversary is Thanksgiving?"

"Apparently."

"All right. Send me the information. And Ror? Don't you dare call me back tomorrow and say you want back on the gig."

"Dude, tomorrow I'm going to be in London."

Enough said.

CHAPTER SIXTEEN

Brock

The Steel family doesn't own a private jet.

The cost outweighs the benefit. We're ranchers. We do most of our business in the USA, and mostly in the West. So we fly commercial—first class of course, but commercial.

Rory's eyes are as big as dinner plates when we board the British Airways aircraft and sit in our first-class pods with lie-flat seats. Last-minute airfare was exorbitant but of course pennies to my family.

Dad wasn't happy I was leaving, but when I told him I was researching the bones we found on our property, he relented. The work gets done, even if I'm not there. We have a vast stable of employees, all who are well-trained to take over pretty much everything we do.

Everything except what Dad and Uncle Bryce do. They run the entire company.

Dad and Uncle Bryce.

God . . . So much to unpackage there.

But for the next couple of days, I'm going to focus on showing Rory London. The only time I'm going to let my brain think about my family will be when we talk to Ennis Ainsley.

Rory hasn't said much since I brought her up to date last night.

We sat on the deck, Sammy and Rory's dog, Zach—she brought him for a visit—between us, each getting loves and pets and scratches behind their ears, as I told her the story.

She had to get up a few times, go inside.

I asked her later if she was getting sick. She said no. That she just had to be alone for a minute to recap everything and wrap her head around it.

I'm not even sure I told her all of it.

"And Callie knows all of this?" she said.

"According to Donny, she does. They're engaged now. They have no secrets."

"I don't want us to have any secrets either."

I widen my eyes.

"No, I'm not asking for an engagement ring, silly. You're so funny, Brock. I can see from a mile away that you want to run away screaming when you think about commitment."

"Actually, you're wrong," I said. "I do want to go running away screaming, but not at the thought of committing to you."

She laughed then. We both laughed, because sometimes, when things seem insurmountable, all you can do is laugh.

Now we sit, hand in hand, in posh first-class seats on the plane.

The flight attendant brought me a beer and Rory a Diet Coke before takeoff.

"My nerves are a mess," Rory says, taking a sip.

"Welcome to the club."

"Oh, no. I mean because of the flight. I've never flown overseas before. What if we crash and plunge into the ocean?"

I smile at her. "You're safer up here than you are in your own car. You know that, right?"

"Yeah. I mean, but . . ."

I kiss her cheek. "I promise you that you're safe. Just like I promised I would keep you safe from Pat Lamone."

"Yeah. Except now Pat Lamone may be your long-lost cousin."

"All that means is that we share a relative somewhere on our family tree. It doesn't mean I owe him any loyalty. He sure as hell doesn't feel like he owes me any."

"That's for sure."

"He said something to Dale or Donny a while back. I can't remember which one. Probably Donny because it involves Callie. He said he wouldn't put it past your family to have started that fire themselves."

She gasps. "Just when I thought he couldn't sink any lower."

"Yeah. He's pretty much proved how low he can go."

"You know, Callie said something a few weeks ago about him and the fire. She said what if Pat started that fire?"

"At this point, I wouldn't put anything past him," I say. "But . . . I'm not sure he has any beef with you guys. I mean, it's high school drama, right? What brings him back now?"

"Callie thought he may have gotten wind of her dating Donny and thought he could get some Steel money for the photos."

"Yeah, that made sense at one time, but now? It's so much bigger. If he thinks he's a Steel, and that he's entitled to part of our fortune, I could see him having a bone to pick with us. Like setting our land on fire. But why yours?"

"I don't know. Maybe it was easier access. I mean, you guys lost stuff in the fire too. Maybe that was the ultimate goal, but it didn't work out that way due to the way the winds blew."

She has a point. You can't plan a fire. Mother Nature

always has its own ideas.

Then she gasps and clasps a hand to her mouth.

"What?" I ask.

"I can't believe I forgot this. Remember yesterday morning when I said a dream woke me up?"

"Yeah..."

"I was going to tell you about what I remembered, but then it got lost in the shuffle with the old bones and planning an impromptu trip to London and all." She shakes her head.

"What is it, sweetheart?"

"When I was with Pat that night in Cage's van—the night we... God, I hate even thinking about it—he said something that I'd forgotten until I had the dream, and I didn't think anything of it at the time, or even afterward, until now. Now that Pat is claiming to be a Steel relative."

My skin chills. "Uh-oh. What is it?"

"I asked him why Diana was hospitalized from the hairy buffalo but no one else was, and he said he didn't know. But then he said something like, 'the Steels get what they deserve.'"

Icy shards scatter across the back of my neck. "What?" I grit out.

"I know. Callie, Jesse, and I talked about this one night a while back. We were wondering if Pat somehow poisoned Diana on purpose. It was just a theory at that point, but now... with this new memory..."

"You're saying he poisoned Diana directly?"

"I'm saying I wouldn't put it past him, especially now that we know he thinks he's a Steel. Maybe he knew about his alleged lineage then. I mean, isn't it strange that only Diana was hospitalized with drugs in her system? We all drank that stuff, and he admitted to spiking it, but I think he spiked Diana's particular drink with something else. If he'd put the PCP and meth in the punch, it would have either been diluted enough not to make anyone sick, or we'd all have been hospitalized."

Shit. Shit, shit, shit. "Do you know how much Diana drank?"

"I have no idea," Rory says. "Diana was a freshman, and I was a senior. We didn't hang out. But there were people there who drank cup after cup of that stuff, but Diana was the only one who ended up in the hospital that night."

"Jesus Christ…" I wipe the emerging sweat from my forehead with my hand. "Is it possible he knew then? Is it… Fuck."

"I wish we could just forget about the stuff for a few days," Rory says.

"Sweetheart, you have no idea."

"I'm sorry I didn't tell you about this sooner," she says. "It was purely a theory at the time, but now that I remember what he said that night…"

"The Steels get what they deserve…" I echo.

I can't. I just can't with this. Rory and I are on a plane to London. Fucking London, where I was hoping, other than talking to Ennis Ainsley, we could actually spend some time together seeing the city and not ruminating on Pat Lamone and everything else.

So damn it, that's what we're going to do.

I meet her gaze. "We're going to put this on hold. Just for now. Just for London. That's my plan."

"Can we, Brock?"

Her eyes are so big and brown, and I love her so much. I'll promise her anything in this moment.

"Yes, we can, and we will."

"I *would* like to see London. I mean, I wish we could enjoy it without this stuff always hanging over our heads like a rain cloud. I feel like one of those cartoons, where a rain cloud follows the person around. Or like Charlie Brown when he always gets a rock in his Halloween bag. It's like bad luck is everywhere."

I smile then. "This isn't bad luck, Rory. Not for you and not for me. It concerns my parents, but not even my parents. My grandparents mostly. My great-grandparents and my grandparents brought all of this to fruition."

"But it *does* have to do with us, Brock, because we're caught in it now. We're the ones whose lives are being upended. We're the ones who will ultimately suffer and pay the price."

"I'm pretty sure there's nothing my money can't buy," I say. "You have my word. If it takes every last penny, I *will* protect you."

She squeezes my hand. "But I don't want you to have to, Brock. That's my point. You and I didn't do any of this. Well . . . I did. I'm the one who seduced Pat Lamone, drugged him with Benadryl, and got the confession out of him that put this in motion."

"That doesn't make any of this your fault."

"Doesn't it? Pat would say he's the victim."

"Because you gave him Benadryl? I'd love to see him prove that. You and Callie are the victims, Rory. You're the ones who got drugged and put on display in photographs. You were violated. Maybe you weren't raped, beaten, or anything like that, thank God, but you *were* violated. I won't let you make light of it."

She squeezes my hand again. "You're so understanding."

"I'm just a man who loves you. You must love me, because

you're still here after hearing everything that's going on with my family."

"I'm glad you confided in me. I hate the thought of you going through this alone. I'm glad to be here with you. This is where I belong, at your side, bearing any burden with you."

I kiss her cheek. "I didn't think it was possible, Rory, but I just fell in love with you a little bit more."

CHAPTER SEVENTEEN

Rory

We arrive at our hotel around noon London time. I'm sleepy, though not horribly so. Being able to lie flat during the long flight helped, and both Brock and I were able to get some shut-eye.

Still, I'm learning the meaning of jet lag quickly. A nap sounds like heaven. I yawn and lie down on the bed when—

"Nope. No, you don't."

"Just a little nap, Brock."

"You can't. We have plans this afternoon. We're going sight-seeing."

"Right after my nap."

"I already ordered a pot of coffee," he says. "Room service will be bringing it up momentarily. You can't succumb, Rory. If you do, you'll never get on London time."

"Do I *need* to get on London time? We are only going to be here a couple days."

"Yeah, you do. It only takes one day of caffeine. You'll be fine tomorrow. We're meeting Ennis for tea."

"Don't the English take tea in the afternoon?"

"Yes. We're meeting him at four o'clock."

"If that's not until tomorrow, then there's plenty of time for me to take a nap today."

His eyes twinkle. "If you insist on going to bed, it's going to be up to me to make sure you do *not* fall asleep."

I smile.

In a moment he's next to me, lying on the bed, and I'm in his arms getting kissed passionately.

"I haven't paid nearly enough attention to your tits lately," he says. Then he moves on top of me, pushes my shirt up over my chest, kisses the top of my breasts.

In another second, my bra is gone.

"How'd you do that?" I ask.

"Ancient secret."

"Part of the Brock Steel experience?" I laugh.

"I'll never tell ..."

"I swear, Brock, you have skills I never imagined existed."

"You have some pretty awesome skills of your own, Rory Pike."

He clamps his mouth onto my nipple then, while plucking the other with his fingers. Jolts of electricity spark through me as he tugs and munches.

With a movement so fluid I'm not sure when it happens, Brock moves to gentleness, licking the tips, kissing my areola.

Then back to munching, as if he can't decide whether he's savoring beluga caviar or chomping on beer nuts.

And damn ... It's hot.

I slide my hands down his back, pull his shirt up so I can feel his warm muscled skin.

He groans and drops the nipple from his lips. "God, your touch, Rory."

"I know what you mean."

He sucks on my nipple again, and then he moves to the other while he replaces the fingers of his other hand on this one.

My nipples are so hard. So hard and hot, and I swear I can feel each movement in my pussy.

"Brock, my nipples. Feels so good."

"Sweetheart, it feels good to me too. I'm so hard for you right now. But I swear to God, I could spend the whole day on your nipples alone. They're perfect. Dark red-brown and fucking perfect."

He bites one, the shock arrowing straight to my pussy.

It's crazy how much I want him. More than I ever imagined wanting anyone of either sex.

Brock Steel is in a class by himself.

It doesn't matter whether he's male or female.

He's Brock.

He's Brock, and I love him.

All those other times I thought I was in love? It was puppy love at best. This? This goes beyond passion, beyond desire, way beyond lust.

It's an emotional connection I've never conceived before.

If you asked me before, I'd have said I know what love is. I'd have said sure, I've been in love.

Now? I know I wasn't. I know that real love—true love—is something that can't be described, but when you find it, you know.

But until you find it? You assume. You assume the love you feel is real.

He lets my nipple drop then, and he groans. "Need to be inside you."

He undresses so quickly he seems to be naked in a flash. Then he unbuttons my pants, and I wriggle out of them as fast as I can.

Then a condom.

I get it. I do.

He rolls it on, and then he climbs atop me and thrusts inside.

I gasp at the beautiful invasion.

Always so complete with Brock. Even the first time, I felt it. I should've known then. What is the difference between intense physical chemistry and intense emotional love?

I'm not sure anymore. I think, with the right person, it's all important. You can't tell where one ends and the other begins, because it's a complete thing in its own right.

He fucks me slowly at first, and I grab his shoulders, dig my fingernails into his flesh.

"Harder," I say.

"Oh no, I have to keep you awake, so I'm going to take my time."

I sigh then. I can't be angry. How can I be angry at him for wanting to prolong this physical contact between us?

Though I wouldn't mind an intense and hard fuck right now.

But he slides in and out of me slowly, going deep and then withdrawing, tickling my pussy lips with the head of his cock.

And then deeply again. Balls deep, so I feel his sack pushing against my perineum.

Damn, it's all so hot.

He continues his slow strokes for a moment, and then he withdraws completely.

I whimper at the loss, but before I know it, he's turned me onto my side, still hovering, and then he slides back into my pussy while gripping my ass cheek.

It's a different feeling, this angle. Something I've never felt before, something that exists only between Brock and me. Well … me. He's probably done it this way many times.

Doesn't matter. He's in love with me. He's said those words only to me.

Part of me wishes I could take back all the other times I said it. Not because I didn't feel it at the time, but because I know now that *this* is love.

This is true freaking love.

"You've got a great ass, Rory." He gives it a light slap.

A tingle pops through me—as if all the cells in my body explode like popping candy.

Just a slap.

No one has ever slapped me before.

I never even thought about it, but damn… Those tiny tingly pops…

It wasn't even a hard slap, just a little pat, really.

"Do that again," I say.

"Sure, baby." He slaps my ass cheek again.

Again the tingly little pops. I could so get used to this.

Still he's giving me long, slow strokes, and again, I'm wanting hard and fast.

But he's way more experienced than I am, and I want to know everything he has to offer me.

"Feels so good," I say. "It's … different at this angle."

"Feels different to me too, sweetheart. And it would feel…"

"What?"

"Never mind."

I close my eyes then. I'll ask later what he meant. Right now, I want to revel in the pure completion.

He continues his slow strokes in this position, but then he withdraws again, and he slides me from my side onto my stomach.

Without spreading my legs, he hovers on top of me, slides between my cheeks, and embeds his cock in my pussy.

"Oh . . ." He groans. "So snug this way."

He's right. It is tight. Another position I've never tried with a man. It's not altogether comfortable at first, but I relax into it. And I find . . . that it's amazing as hell.

I am tighter this way, and he seems larger, which should scare me, but it doesn't. Such a good slow burn.

Yes, I'm beginning to relish the slow. Sure, I'd still like a good hard and fast fuck, but this has its own merit.

He pulls out then, pushes back in. "Makes you so tight," he grits outs.

"Yes." My voice is but a murmur as my cheek is embedded in the pillow, but my body is on fire.

A flare of flames.

He continues, slowly . . . so achingly slowly . . .

Then, just when I'm sure he must be ready to pop, he withdraws once more, slides me onto my other side, and repeats the second position, gliding between my ass cheeks while gripping the one on top.

"Fuck . . ." he groans.

And it's just as amazing as it was the first time, only slightly different. Of course it is, because his cock is touching my pussy in a different way.

"Different . . ." I sigh.

"Fuck, yeah. I get to feel every part of your pussy this way with every part of my cock, and damn . . . I wish . . ."

This time I know what he's thinking.

He wishes he didn't have to wear a condom.

Maybe I'll rethink the pill issue. Except I can't think about it now. All I want to think about is—

Smack!

His palm comes down on my other butt cheek, and it's the same tingly pop, as if each tiny cell in my body is exploding on its own under my skin.

"Oh my God," I say.

"I know, right?" His voice is low. "God, you feel good, sweetheart."

Again with the slow thrusts, delicate sliding in and out.

And no longer am I wishing for the hard and fast strokes. I've settled in. I'm loving the slow.

I close my eyes, and I feel something nudge my asshole. My instinct is to jerk, to wince, but I trust this man. I trust him, and I want what he wants. So I ease into this new sensation.

His finger. He's massaging it with his finger, and my God... With the slow and languid strokes... It all works together.

"Such a sweet little ass, Rory Pike."

I sigh into the pillow.

"One day..." He continues to massage it lightly, poking his fingertip in slightly, but not enough to hurt me.

"One day," he says again.

Yes, one day he's going to fuck me in the ass. Another thing I've never experienced, but I'm sure he has.

I've been fucked many times, by men, and by women with a strap on. But no one has ever gone into my ass.

And now I know why I never let it happen. I was saving it for Brock.

"Is there anything?" I ask.

"Anything what, sweetheart?"

I sigh, my eyes still closed. "Is there anything that can be just... *ours*?"

He pulls out then, and I wish I hadn't said anything.

"No, back inside me. Please."

"Okay." He slides in, holds himself balls deep for a moment, and then begins his slow stroking again.

"Talk later," I say.

"Of course, sweetheart."

He doesn't go back to my asshole, but that's okay, because he withdraws, moves me over to my back, and then spreads my legs, positioning himself between them. "I'm going to lick your pussy now, Rory. I'm going to lick you and lick you until you can no longer stand it. You're going to come. And then you're going to come again. You're going to come and come and come, until you beg me to stop."

I want to say something, but all that comes out is a soft moan.

And then his mouth is on me. His teeth pulling at my labia, his tongue sliding into my slit. And then his lips around my clit, and two fingers slide inside me—

"Oh my God!" The orgasm catapults me into oblivion.

Such beautiful, sweet oblivion.

"That's it, sweetheart. God, you're so beautiful, Rory. When you come like that. Your whole body gets pink. Such a gorgeous shade of pink, the same as your cheeks."

"Mmm…"

"Your nipples are hard. So gorgeous and hard. Play with them, sweetheart. Play with them while I eat you."

Seemingly of their own accord, my hands trail from up my abdomen to my breasts. I cup them a moment, squeeze them lightly, and then trail my fingers over to my nipples. I jolt when I touch myself.

Or is it from the amazing oral I'm getting from Brock?

Who cares?

I squeeze my nipples gently, reveling in the hot flares that shoot through me. I strengthen my fingers, tug harder on the nipples.

"Fuck, you're hot," Brock says against my clit.

And with those words, I jump into my second climax.

CHAPTER EIGHTEEN

Brock

I grew up on good food. Prime beef, succulent fruit fresh from our trees.

And pussy? I've been eating pussy since I was sixteen.

I swear to God, Rory Pike tastes better than the sweetest pussy and the ripest peach combined.

I could eat her forever and never tire of that tartness—that tartness of a sour cherry, combined with the sweetness of an orchard peach, and that perfect spiciness that's unique to her.

And God, how she responds.

She gushes. Gushes for me. She's so wet, so ready, all the time.

And that luscious cream on my tongue... Delicious.

I have to keep myself from fisting my condom-covered cock as I eat her. If I do that, it may be over before I can get back inside her.

I had to force myself to go slowly as I fucked her. She wanted me to go fast, and damn, it was so difficult not to acquiesce to her request.

But that will come later.

Right now, I'm going to get a third orgasm out of her, and then I'm going to get a fourth.

She clamps around me, around my two fingers that are

deep inside her pussy massaging her G-spot.

As I start to feel her come down, I attack her clit again. I lick the tip, slide my tongue around it, and then close my lips over it and suck gently.

Gently is all it takes for Rory. This woman is so sensitive to clitoral stimulation and G-spot stimulation.

She's a freaking wet dream.

I'm good at what I do. I'm experienced, I love doing it, and I'm damned good. But I swear to God, I can pull an orgasm out of Rory Pike easier than I've ever pulled an orgasm out of any woman.

Is it because the two of us are so great together? Is it because she's just that sensitive? Or is it because I love her and she loves me?

I slide my tongue over her, capture her clit between my lips.

"Yes!"

And there's number three.

I watch with amazement as her body responds. As it turns pink at the beginning of each climax and then softens to a light rose.

And then—

I pull a fourth out of her . . .

And then a fifth . . .

"Brock, no more. I can't . . ."

Do I take pity on her? Or do I force her into a sixth climax?

I'm good at giving women multiple, but I'm not sure I've ever gotten anyone to six before.

"One more," I say between gritted teeth. "One more, Rory. One more."

I fuck her hard with my fingers then, poke her G-spot, massage it more harshly.

I slide my tongue between her folds, over her clit, down to her asshole, and then back to her pussy to suck up all the cream she's giving me.

Then—

Her clit. I tug on it harder than usual.

"No, no, I can't— Brock! God, Brock!"

Bingo.

Number fucking six.

I remove my fingers, let her body do its work as she flows in and out of the haze of orgasm.

I kiss her pussy, and then I move forward and plunge into her.

Even with the damned condom, being inside Rory is like being in heaven.

That one time… That one…

God, I want that.

But now, I'll settle for what I do have. Me. Rory. The two of us together, our bodies joined. In London.

She moans beneath me, and I fuck her hard. I fuck her fast. I plow into her, tunneling through her with all the force inside me.

She moans beneath me, screams my name, and it never sounded so sweet as it sounds from her lips.

Brock! Brock! Brock!

God, I love her.

"I love you, Rory. I love you."

I jam into her, releasing.

And everything around me falls into place. For this blessed, timeless moment, my family's problems, Rory's issues, everything…

It all stops existing.

An invisible bubble encases us, protects us, keeps us safe from life's problems. From anyone who seeks to harm us.

And I embrace it.

I embrace this moment with my love.

★ ★ ★

Reality has a way of poking its head in when it's not wanted. This time, it's in the form of my phone.

I hear the damned ring from the pocket of my jeans on the floor of our hotel room.

I don't want to answer it. I want to stay deep inside her, stay in this dreamlike state forever.

But . . . reality.

I withdraw, try to ignore her whimper, move off the bed, and pull my phone out of the pocket of my jeans.

"Yeah," I say without bothering to see who's calling.

"Mr. Steel?"

"Yes, this is Brock Steel."

"This is Mr. Havisham, Mr. Ainsley's butler. He'd like to meet you and Ms. Pike today for tea instead of tomorrow if possible."

"We just got in," I say. "Four o'clock is only an hour away."

"Mr. Ainsley sends his apologies," the butler says, "but his personal physician just rescheduled his monthly appointment to tomorrow afternoon."

"Yeah. All right. I'll make that work."

"Mr. Ainsley thanks you."

I end the call. Rory is still lying on the bed, her body flushed with pink, her eyes closed, her hair strewn on the pillow like a dark-brown curtain of silk.

I hate to disturb her. But this way, at least, she doesn't get her nap.

I pull on my jeans and sit on the bed. "Sweetheart..."

Her eyes pop open. "Hey."

"You have to get up. Get dressed. Our coffee should be in the hall."

She yawns. "After what you just put me through? No way am I getting out of this bed."

"I'm so sorry, but that phone call—"

"You got a phone call?"

"Boy, you *are* in a climax-induced fog. Yeah, I just got a call. Ennis Ainsley wants to meet us for tea today. In an hour."

She jerks into a sitting position. "Are you kidding?"

"Believe me, part of me wishes I were. But then there's another part of me that wants to get to the bottom of all this right away, so I'm actually happy about it."

"Hey, I'm with you. Let's find out what the old guy has to say. I sure hope they delivered that coffee."

I rise, walk to the door of our suite, and open it. Sure enough, a room service cart sits outside holding a pot of coffee, two cups and napkins, cream and sugar, and an assortment of scones.

I grab a scone and take a bite. I'm suddenly famished.

I wheel the car in, pour coffee for Rory and myself, and then I dress.

Once dressed, Rory takes a sip of her coffee. Then screws her face into a frown. "I guess I see why the English drink tea."

"Really, is it that bad?" I take a sip. "Yeah, it's that bad."

My family loves coffee. And Jade especially. She's got us all hooked on dark swamp root.

I stir in a bit of cream. I don't normally take cream, but it will cool the coffee down so I can drink quickly, and it may also help the flavor. I take a sip.

"The cream will help," I tell Rory.

"Cream isn't really my thing, but I'll take your word for it." She pours cream in her own coffee, stirs it, and takes a drink.

She still makes a face, but then she takes another drink.

"Ugh. But at least we'll get tea with Mr. Ainsley, right?"

"Yes, and hopefully it will be good English tea. Unless he's a chamomile guy."

"Chamomile? Herb tea?" Rory shakes her head. "Not a good Englishman."

"I'm afraid we won't know until we get there." I finish buttoning my shirt. "Finish your coffee, because we need to go downstairs and hail a cab."

"Won't there be cabs right outside the hotel?"

"Probably, but we still need to hurry."

"Understood." She slides her shoes onto her feet and then walks into the bathroom.

I finish the terrible English coffee.

In an hour, we'll get some information.

Will it help us? I have no idea.

All I know is that I wish I were back in bed with Rory, safely enveloped in our post-orgasmic protective bubble.

CHAPTER NINETEEN

Rory

We are met at Ennis Ainsley's front door—the front door of a lovely large red brick mansion—by an honest-to-God tuxedo-clad English butler. He's tall, with a receding blond hairline, piercing blue eyes, and slightly crooked teeth.

"Mr. Steel, I presume," he says in perfect Queen's English. "And Ms. Pike?"

Brock holds out his hand. "Yes, I'm Brock Steel, and this is Rory Pike."

"I'm Mr. Havisham, Mr. Ainsley's butler. Please just call me Havisham."

He does not return Brock's handshake. Instead, he opens the door, and we walk in. Then he leads us into a sitting room.

I'd call it a living room, though it doesn't look like anyone lives here. It's pristine, with Queen Anne furniture—all in cherry wood and lavender-and-blue brocade.

"Please have a seat." He nods to the sofa. "Mr. Ainsley will arrive in a moment." Havisham leaves the room.

I can't help a tiny giggle. "I think we've just entered the twilight zone."

"That's a gentleman's gentleman if I ever saw one," Brock replies.

"Mr. Ainsley must have some money."

"I'm sure he does. Remember, he worked for my family for years. Decades even. I'm sure they set him up with an amazing retirement package."

Right. I should've known that. But I'm not a Steel. I'm a Pike.

An elderly gentleman enters the room. He has a shock of silvery-white hair, and he walks upright without the help of a cane. If this is Ennis Ainsley, he's eighty-eight years old. This gentleman doesn't look a day over seventy. He wears a blazer with leather patches on the elbows, blue jeans, and brown leather loafers. He's got a professor vibe going.

Brock rises. "Mr. Ainsley?"

The elderly man's eyes widen, and they're a searing blue. He must've been a handsome young man with all that hair. From its color, I'm guessing he was dark blond or light brown.

"My God," he says. "You look exactly like your father."

"Brock Steel." Brock holds out his hand. "Yes, I get that all the time."

Ennis takes his hand and gives him a hearty shake back. "You couldn't have been more than two or three years old the last time I saw you. You resembled him even then. I remember your brother had your mother's green eyes, but you? I could tell you were going to be a carbon copy of Jonah Steel. After all, you looked exactly like him at that age."

"Did I?"

"Oh yes. He was the apple of your grandmother's eye, that one. Her firstborn. She called him her little dove. A child born out of love if there ever was one."

"Oh?"

"Didn't you know? Your grandmother became pregnant with your father before they were married."

Brock nods. "I only recently found out."

"I didn't mean to open any wounds," Ennis says.

"No wounds at all. I'm here, and I wouldn't be if not for my grandparents and their"—he smiles—"horniness."

That gets a cackle out of Ennis Ainsley. He turns to me then. "You must be Ms. Pike. My goodness, you're a pretty thing."

My cheeks warm. "Yes, I'm Rory Pike. And thank you."

"Thank you for seeing us," Brock says.

"Not at all. I'll be happy to help in any way I can." He gestures to the sofa we just rose from. "Have a seat, and Havisham will be in with our tea momentarily."

Brock and I sit back down, and within a few seconds, Havisham returns with a tea tray.

"How do you take your tea, ma'am?" he asks me.

"Just as it is, thank you."

Havisham nods, pours a cup of tea, and then places several finger sandwiches on a plate and hands it to me. He sets my tea on a coaster on the coffee table in front of me. I inhale the fragrance.

Thank goodness. It's black tea, which means it will have a lot of caffeine.

Although, I seem to be wide awake now.

"And you, sir?" Havisham nods to Brock.

"Same."

Havisham serves Brock, and then serves Mr. Ainsley. "Will there be anything else, sir?"

"No, thank you, Havisham."

"Very well." Havisham bows and leaves the room.

Mr. Ainsley takes a sip of his tea and then sets the cup back on the saucer. "I won't bore you with any small talk," he says. "You said you wanted to talk about Patty."

"Yes." Brock clears his throat. "I'm sorry for your loss."

"It was sixty years ago," he says. "But I never met another woman like her. She was strikingly beautiful. Not the kind of woman I was normally attracted to. She had flaming red hair and piercing emerald-green eyes. Freckles across her face. But goodness, she was gregarious. Such a force to be reckoned with. To be honest, I wasn't her type either. She liked playboys. She liked to have her fun, that one. But somehow, we found our way to each other." He closes his eyes for a moment and then opens them. "The universe didn't give us enough time together."

"I'm so sorry," I say.

"Like I said, it was sixty years ago. But she was special. I dated other women from time to time after I lost her, but I never felt the same thing. So I never married. I gave my life to your family, Brock. I'm the one who taught your uncle Ryan how to make wine."

"I know. He speaks highly of you."

"I owe your family a lot."

"Do you know what ultimately happened to Patty?" Brock asks.

"For a long time, I thought she left me. But her parents didn't know where she was. Daphne—your grandmother— didn't know where she was, and they were best friends. Her parents told me she had decided to join the Peace Corps. But that didn't sound like Patty. Not that she wasn't a wonderful human being who might like to give to others, but she wouldn't have just left me without telling me. We had just confessed our love to each other."

"There's no record of any Patricia Watson in the Peace

Corps," Brock says. "My cousin Dale checked it out."

"That doesn't surprise me."

"We believe she was killed," Brock says.

Sixty years later, and Ennis Ainsley still acts surprised. Then he chokes up. "I always wondered myself. In fact, part of me always knew. I put it in the back of my head and refused to think about it. But to hear it said with such finality… Even now, I don't like to think of her suffering."

"I understand. I hate to bring up painful memories for you, but we need your help."

"Of course. Whatever I can do. Your family has taken wonderful care of me over the years."

Brock clears his throat. "Is there any way that you have anything that once belonged to her? Something that might have some DNA on it?"

"I had a few of her belongings, things she left in her suitcase after she disappeared. We were in Snow Creek at the time. But would any DNA still be viable after all this time?"

"To be honest, I don't know," Brock says. "But if you were staying with her at a hotel, it's likely there was a hairbrush in her belongings. It might have a hair on it with the root intact."

"But again… Would it be viable after all this time?"

"It may or may not be. I just don't know. But there's another possibility as well, perhaps a handkerchief or pair of panties that might have a"—he clears his throat again—"a drop of dried blood."

I wrinkle my nose. Is he talking about menstrual blood?

"Dried blood after all these years?"

"It's a shot," Brock says. "Just a shot."

Ennis sighs. "I sent most of her belongings back to her parents. I couldn't bear to look at it after she left, and remember… The story back then was that she joined the Peace Corps, and that she left without telling me. I didn't think she loved me as I loved her."

"Did she say she did?" I ask.

Ennis nods. "She did. And I believed her. Foolishly. Or so I thought at the time."

My heart is breaking for this man. Such a long-lost love that he clearly never got over. How his heart must've broken when he thought she left him for the Peace Corps without even saying goodbye.

"You said you sent most of it back to her parents," Brock says. "What did you keep?"

"Only a few things. Her perfume, and a few other things I couldn't bear to part with."

"Anything else?" Brock says.

"Honestly, I'd have to look. Where might I have put all that stuff?"

"So you still have it," I say.

"Of course. Somewhere. The only things left from the woman I thought was the love of my life. I could never bear to part with them."

"So they're here? Somewhere in this house?" Brock says.

"All of my earthly belongings are here. But this was all so long ago, and my memory isn't what it used to be."

His short-term memory, he means. His long-term memory seems to be completely intact. He remembers everything about his long-lost love. I can see it in his watery blue eyes.

He never got over her.

I glance at Brock, his strong jawline, his broad shoulders, his dark hair that feels like silk from the Indies.

If he left me today, I don't think I'd ever get over him. I never felt that way about Raine or any of the others.

"I kept the stuff from Patty in an old shoebox. It was in Colorado with me for a long time, and I assume it got packed up with everything when I moved back here to England."

"Do you remember seeing it get packed?"

"No. I didn't see anything get packed. Your family handled all of that for me. They're such good people."

Brock glances down at his lap. I know what he's thinking, as if I can hear his thoughts in my own head.

They're such good people.

Brock is wondering if they truly are.

"I'm not sure I ever unboxed some of those things," Ennis continues.

"The last thing we want to do is cause you any pain," I say, "but would it be possible for Brock and me to have a look?"

Ennis takes a sip of his tea. "Of course. I'll do anything I can to help you find out what actually happened to Patty." He picks up the bell sitting next to him and rings it.

Havisham arrives quickly. "Yes, sir?"

"Havisham, Mr. Steel and Ms. Pike would like to look through those boxes I have in storage in the basement. Could you make sure they have everything they need?"

"Of course, sir. Will they be staying for dinner?"

"Dinner is at seven," Ennis says. "You are certainly welcome to stay."

Brock looks down at his watch. "It's a little after four thirty now. Thank you so much for the invitation. If we could take a look at the items, perhaps we will be done by seven, and we would love to join you for dinner."

"Absolutely," I say. "Thank you for your kindness, Mr. Ainsley."

"Please, call me Ennis, my dear," he says. "And there's no need to thank me. I owe the Steel family so much. The pleasure is truly mine. Havisham, please show our guests to the basement."

CHAPTER TWENTY

Brock

This is truly the basement that hell forgot.

Dark and dank and more than a little eerie.

I half expect the ghosts of owners past to emerge from the stone walls.

Rory and I sit in front of a stack of cardboard boxes, an electric heater buzzing next to us.

Rory rubs her hands together in front of it. "I didn't expect it to be freezing down here."

"This is an old house. I wonder if it's been in Ennis's family for decades. Maybe centuries."

"I doubt it," Rory says. "I didn't get the impression that he comes from a lot of money."

"True. I didn't get that impression either. You're probably right. He purchased this house with money from his earnings from my family." I sigh. "You can say a lot about my family—and based on recent research, plenty of it isn't good—but they do take care of their own. Ennis was the first winemaker for Steel Vineyards, and now they're taking care of him."

"Why would he want to live in such an old house?"

"Because it's gorgeous," I say. "Big and beautiful and very English, I might add."

Rory laughs. "True." She scoots a box toward her. "I

guess we start." She takes one of the box cutters supplied by Havisham and slides it under the tape securing the cardboard.

I grab another.

"I should've known by how heavy this was," she says. "It's books."

"I suppose we don't need to look through them."

"I don't think a shoebox full of trinkets from a long-lost love is in here, but we may find some clue."

"What kind of clue?"

"I don't know. A flower pressed between the pages?"

I smile. "I never pegged you for a romantic, Rory."

"I never pegged myself for one either, but I definitely peg Ennis as one." She pulls out a book, opens the cover. "No inscription." Then she leafs through the pages. "And no flower between the pages either. No evidence here." She sets it aside and takes the next book.

She goes through four more books, until she gasps.

"Brock, this is one of your mother's books."

I take the book from her and smooth my fingers over its cover. "This was her first book." I open it. "Wow, it's a first edition."

"Maybe worth some money."

"I doubt it. I mean, my mother's a great author, and one of her later books did hit the *New York Times* list, but books on childhood trauma and psychology are rarely worth what, say, a first edition of *To Kill a Mockingbird* would be."

"Still," she says, "it's pretty awesome to see."

"We have first editions of all my mom's books at home," I say.

She reddens a bit. "Yeah, I guess I didn't think of that."

"This is her first book, though, and it was written before she met my father."

"So Ennis was still living in Colorado then."

"Yeah. We already knew that. He lived on our land for a while after he retired. But this book was written before my mom and my dad, which means she gifted it to him—" I stop, my mind racing.

"What?"

"Maybe she didn't gift it to him. Maybe he bought it."

"You think? Why would he be interested in a book on childhood trauma?"

I open the book. "There's no inscription. If my mom had given him the book, she would've signed it."

"You should be a detective," Rory says.

"I've just learned a lot from Aunt Ruby over the years. How to look for clues that you don't think would be clues."

"So . . . Ennis most likely purchased this book rather than getting it from your mom. Which means he has an interest in the subject. It doesn't necessarily mean he has any experience with childhood trauma."

"No . . . But he did have a good friend who had experience in childhood trauma. My grandmother."

"We could ask him about it," I say. "But it doesn't really have anything to do with Patty. Not on the surface anyway." Still, I set the book aside. I'm not sure why, but I feel like it may be important.

Rory continues going through the rest of the books. "Nothing in any of these books. No flowers, no love poetry, no letters."

"So you're no longer a romantic?" I gibe her.

"You know? I think maybe I am. I never thought I was until . . ."

I lift my eyebrows. "You met me?"

"Until I met the infamous Rake-a-teer." She smiles. "As much as I hate to admit it, I think you're right. I certainly didn't set out to fall in love with you."

"Sweetheart, I didn't set out to fall in love with you either."

"Maybe we're both romantics. Maybe we just never knew it. Maybe it just took the right person to turn us both into mush."

I grab her hand and squeeze it. "I love you, sweetheart, but do not ever refer to me as mush again."

She giggles, places all the books—with the exception of my mother's—back into the box, and grabs another.

Meanwhile, I'm still going through my box, which is mostly old clothes. Another dead end.

"Bingo!" Rory pulls out an old shoebox. "It even has Patty written on it in permanent marker." She begins to lift the lid.

But I stop her, placing my hand on hers. "Wait a minute."

"Why?"

"I feel like we should have a moment of silence or something. I feel like we're disturbing this woman's grave."

"I hate to tell you, Brock, but if those bones you found on your property are hers? Her grave was disturbed long ago."

She's right of course. But for some reason, I feel like this is a sacred moment. I'm not a religious person, but shouldn't we say a few words?

I'm being silly, I know. For all we know, the disappearance and death of Patty Watson has nothing to do with what's going on with my family now. With the dead bodies, the GPS coordinates left for Donny, the sudden reappearance and then disappearance of a ring that once belonged to my grandmother, and the various documents found at Brendan Murphy's place.

But perhaps we can at least give Ennis Ainsley some

peace. It's a long shot, but if there's something in this box that can tie those bones to Patty, he will finally be able to say goodbye.

I move my hand from Rory's. "Go ahead."

She pulls the lid off the box. The first thing she pulls out is a pair of white cotton panties. She grimaces. "I don't want to think of Ennis Ainsley as a dirty old man or a panty sniffer, but this is kind of . . . you know."

"He wasn't a dirty old man when he kept these," I say. "He was a dirty *young* man. Except that that's not such a dirty thing. If I lost you tomorrow, sweetheart, I would need something to remember you by, and . . . your scent would be on your panties. It's not like he pays to sniff women's underwear. This is a memento. Something that probably gave him a little bit of comfort at the time."

"If you say so." She sets the panties down and takes the next item from the box. "What do you know? It's an old cassette tape."

"Say what?"

Rory holds it up. "My dad has a few of these that were my grandfather's. They're audio recordings. There's writing on the top. It says *Patty's favorites.*"

"Music she liked?"

"Most likely. We can ask Ennis, although I don't know that we'd get any clues from her favorite tune." Rory pulls out the next item. "Here's the perfume he mentioned. It's called *Fresh and Light.*" She spritzes a little into her wrist and sniffs. "Ugh. Smells mostly like alcohol."

"Well, it's over half a century old."

She sets the perfume aside and pulls out the next item. "Eureka! It's a hair tie . . . and there are a few red hairs on it."

"Are you kidding?" My heart jumps.

"Nope." She hands it to me.

"This is a hair tie?" It's made out of a thin elastic type material, and it has two plastic balls on each end.

"Yeah," she says. "I had to think for a second, but yeah, it's a hair tie. First of all, it has red hairs on it, and second of all, I remember my mom talking about hair ties like this when she was a kid. She said my grandma would pull her hair back into a tight ponytail, and sometimes she'd lose hold of the tie, and the plastic balls would hit Mom in the head. She said it hurt like hell."

"And they don't make these anymore?" I ask.

"Why would they? They sound like torture devices to me. Besides, you've never seen one."

"Well, no, but I'm not a woman, and I didn't grow up with any sisters."

"Fair enough."

"But this could be a gold mine. I have no idea if these hairs are viable, but at least it's something. Is there anything else in the box?"

"Yeah," Rory says. "Take a look." She scoots the box over to me, and we both glance inside together. "I was right. Ennis was definitely a romantic."

Dried roses. The petals line the bottom of the box, but one or two of the buds are still intact.

"These are short-stemmed roses," Rory says. "For the thrifty romantic. Long-stemmed can sometimes be too expensive."

"Or one of them could've picked them," I say. "My mom picks roses all the time from her gardens."

"Could very well be. We'll have to ask Ennis."

"Let's put everything back in the box," I say. "I hope he'll let us take the stuff with us so we can have it all analyzed."

"What if he doesn't?"

"Then we have to respect his wishes," I say. "This is his stuff."

"Should we go through the rest of these boxes?" Rory asks.

"I don't think there's any need to further violate his privacy. We found the shoebox."

"I agree." She closes the box. "Havisham can come down here and retape these."

I grab the shoebox and help Rory to her feet. "How long have we been down here?"

She looks at her watch. "About an hour and a half."

"Still about half an hour before dinner, then," I say. "Maybe we can talk to Ennis now. This stuff isn't exactly good dinner conversation."

CHAPTER TWENTY-ONE

Rory

Ennis was napping before dinner, so we didn't have time to talk to him until dinner anyway, which is now being served in a formal dining room.

For such an affair, I'm expecting a four- or five-course dinner, but Ennis surprises us.

"I told Havisham to order from one of my favorite restaurants this evening. I wasn't sure the two of you would enjoy English food, so we're having Italian."

Actually, I would love to try a traditional English dinner, but we can go to a restaurant tomorrow evening.

Havisham serves us veal Marsala, broccoli with basil, and a side of spaghetti marinara, already plated. On our bread plates, he sets white bread with individual cruets of olive oil.

"We don't stand on ceremony here, regardless of Havisham's manners. Please. Dig in."

Brock smiles. "I think that's an American phrase."

"I lived in your country for the better part of my life," Ennis says. "Except for the accent, I'm more American than I am English now."

"We found the shoebox, Ennis." Brock dips his bread in some olive oil.

"Oh, good. I'm glad I still have it after all these years. Was there anything in there that can help you?"

"We think there may be." Brock clears his throat. "We'd like your permission to take the box and its contents back with us to the States."

Ennis frowns.

For a moment, I'm not sure he's going to allow us to take it, and this will have all been for nothing.

But then, "Of course. I knew when I let you look that I would have to part with those things. You do what you need to do, Brock."

"Thank you so much," Brock says.

"Yes, thank you," I echo. "Brock and I understand how much this stuff means to you, and we will return it intact if we can."

Ennis sighs and takes a sip of the Chianti next to his plate. "No. Don't worry about that. I don't have many years left in this life, and the more I've lived and the older I've gotten, the more I understand that *things* really don't matter. Things can be gone in an instant. What matters are people. Relationships." He swallows back a choke. "Memories."

His words touch my heart. Their truth flows through me, and even though my family lost its livelihood in that fire, I know we will survive. Because we are all here. We have each other.

No matter what Pat Lamone tries to do to Callie and me, she and I will survive.

And the Steel family? They will survive. They always do.

But Patty Watson? Beautiful, vivacious, redheaded Patty Watson? Her life was taken from her. And somehow her bones ended up on the Steel property.

Life is so unfair to some.

"Tell me," Ennis says, "how is Ryan?"

"He's good," Brock says. "Did you ever meet his daughters?"

"Only the first one, Ava. I returned to England shortly after she was born."

"You wouldn't recognize her now," I say. "She's the rebel of the Steel family. She wears her hair in this gorgeous pink color."

Ennis smiles. "Does she? Do you have photos?"

"I do," Brock says. "I have photos of all my family. I'd be happy to show them to you after dinner."

"I'd like that a lot."

"Ryan and his wife, Ruby, will celebrate their anniversary soon," Brock says.

"Yes, I remember. Thanksgiving. I always loved that American holiday. Imagine, a whole holiday devoted to being thankful. Sometimes we forget to express gratitude for all that we have. Sometimes we . . ."

I glance at Brock. He slightly shakes his head at me.

Silence, until—

"I'm sorry," Ennis says. "I get a little emotional about Patty, but it does help to remember all that I have to be thankful for. Tell me. How are Dale and Donny?"

"They're good," Brock says. "Dale is the master winemaker now."

Ennis smiles. "I knew he would be. Even when he was young, I could see he had the gift. He was so creative. So quiet and contemplative, but creative. And Donny?"

"The city attorney for Snow Creek," Brock says. "Aunt Jade retired."

"Did she?" Ennis chuckles. "I never thought I'd see that day."

Brock and I smile.

But Ennis's countenance changes, goes darker. "Your family has been through so much," he says. "Jade was a light for your uncle. A light he badly needed."

"So you were there when..." Brock doesn't finish.

"When Talon came home? When they solved the mystery of his abduction? Yes, I was there. I lived all of it. You see, I was there when Talon was taken."

Brock widens his eyes. "Of course you were. You..." He clears his throat. "You know more about our family history than I do, Ennis."

I stay quiet. This is a moment for Brock and for Ennis, and I'm out of the loop. Talon was taken? So much I still don't know.

Putting it all together... It's like...

I don't even know what it's like. Because I don't even know the full story.

Ennis takes a bite of veal, chews, swallows.

"I look forward to seeing the photos," he says. "And I look forward to hearing what you find out about Patty. Perhaps then... Perhaps then I can finally say goodbye."

★ ★ ★

Brock does his best to show me a good time the next day. We spend the day sight-seeing around London, and part of me loves it. Seeing Buckingham Palace, the changing of the guard, Big Ben, Westminster Abbey... All the sights. Even riding on the tube.

We stop and have a meat pie on Fleet Street. Brock knew I'd enjoy the nod to *Sweeney Todd*.

The part of me who's never been to England—heck, who's never been out of the United States—adores it and wishes we could spend more time here.

But the other part of me—the part that's consumed with what's going on in both of our families—just wants to go home.

We're both exhausted after traipsing around London all day, and our flight leaves early in the morning. Still, I want to try a traditional English meal, so Brock indulges me at a fine restaurant.

The result? After roast beef, mashed potatoes, green beans, and plain white rolls, I'm convinced English food is exactly what everyone says it is—starchy and carb-centric and filling.

And a bit plain.

Brock and I both enjoy the meal, though. He orders a pint of the restaurant's finest, served from draft, and I relent and take one sip. It's so good I can almost forget about the plainness of the meal.

We're both too full for dessert, so we head back to the hotel.

"You're quiet," Brock says to me back in our suite.

"I know. Thank you for a wonderful day. I loved every minute of it."

"Did you?"

"I did. Truly. It's just hard to keep my mind on what we're doing."

"I know." He sighs. "I swear to God, sweetheart, once all this mess is in the past, I'm going to take you on a trip all over the world. We'll come back here to London, and we'll enjoy it. Then we'll go to Paris. We'll go to Dubai. Barcelona. Athens. Prague. Every wonderful place. And we'll do it in style, and we'll do it worry-free."

I touch his cheek, loving how his stubble scrapes my fingertips. "I don't think anyone is ever truly worry-free, Brock."

"Maybe not, but this *will* end, Rory. I promise you. It will end. I'll make sure of it. I'll help my family get through whoever or whatever is trying to take us down, and I'll help you and Callie through the mess with my so-called half second cousin. It will end. I promise you that."

I fall into his arms then. Our lips meet. Our lips meet in a kiss that takes us away from the horrors we're both going through.

A kiss that promises a new dawn.

We stand there, fully clothed, kissing.

For a long, long time.

CHAPTER TWENTY-TWO

Brock

A few days later, I head to Grand Junction, Ennis Ainsley's shoebox in tow. I asked Rory to come with me, but she said she had to make up some of the lessons she missed while we were gone.

She doesn't have to work. I'll take care of her, but I know better than to suggest that to her. She'll go straight for my balls. Neither of us are ready for any kind of commitment. Not while so much is still up in the air regarding both our families.

I'm going to see Aunt Ruby's old colleague—the same one who checked out the bones for us.

He works out of his home, and I drive up to the tiny brick ranch house on the outskirts of the city. I take the shoebox, exit the car, walk up the pathway, and knock.

The door opens, and a gray-haired man stands before me. "Brock Steel, I presume?"

"Yes."

"I'm Gordon Jackson. Come on in."

Gordon Jackson is wearing joggers and a T-shirt, no shoes or socks. I enter, and a miniature schnauzer barks at my heels.

"Go on, Theo," Jackson says.

I bend down and give Theo a few scratches behind his ears. "He doesn't bother me. I love dogs."

"Well, you've done it now," Jackson says. "Now that you've shown him you'll pet him, he won't leave you alone."

I chuckle. "That's okay."

He glances at the box. "That's the stuff?"

"It is."

"Follow me. We'll take it down to my lab."

We head through a short hallway to a door. Jackson opens it. His lab is apparently in his basement. We walk down twelve steps, and he flips the light switch.

And I stop my jaw from dropping.

This is a lab all right. There's equipment down here that I don't recognize. I may have wandered into a secret government complex.

"Let's see what we've got here." Jackson takes the box from me and sits down on the stool in front of what looks like a workbench but is much more intricate.

"Have a seat." He gestures to the stool next to him. Then he puts on a pair of glasses, except they're not glasses. They have something like jewelers' loupes attached to them, so they're clearly some kind of magnifying device. Then he straps on some white rubber gloves.

He pulls out the first item, the perfume. Examines it. "You're not looking for fingerprints?"

"No," I say.

"Good, because most of these are old, except for a few that appear very new."

"That would be my girlfriend and me. We're the ones who found the stuff and brought it back from London."

"Got it." He looks at the perfume bottle from all angles. "Definitely nothing on here that I could get DNA from."

Next he pulls out the cassette tape. He examines it the

same way, looking at it from every angle with his magnifiers. He sets it down after a few moments. "Nothing here either."

"No. We figured our best bets were the hair tie or the panties."

He carefully pulls the hair tie out of the box. "I don't want to disturb anything that is attached to it. You do have some hairs here. But if they're over sixty years old . . ." He shakes his head.

"We know. It's a real long shot."

"It is." He examines the hair tie and carefully extracts the hairs from it, looking at them closely. Then he removes the magnifiers from his face and turns to a microscope.

He examines each hair under the scope. Then he sighs.

And I sure don't like the sound of that sigh.

"I'm afraid there's no viable root on any of these hairs. I thought we might have one, but under the scope, it's a no."

"What now?" I ask.

"Let me look at the panties, though I doubt there will be anything there."

"Okay."

He takes the panties, puts his magnifying glasses back on, and examines them.

Minutes tick by.

He's not leaving any stone unturned, that's for sure. Either that or he likes touching women's panties.

Just when I'm sure he's about to tell me he has nothing—

"Here we go. One pubic hair." He pulls it out. "Damn. She was a real redhead."

I dismiss the ick factor. I don't give a shit what this man says. I just want to know if this pubic hair has DNA attached.

He pulls the hair from the panties with tweezers, removes

his glasses again, and turns to the microscope. He examines it for what seems like hours but is only a few seconds.

"Shit," he says.

"Bad news?"

"No viable hair root. I'm sorry."

I sigh. "Well, I guess that's it. All that's left in there are some roses. Dried-up roses."

He raises his eyebrows. "Any stems?"

"Yeah. Short stems."

"Another long shot, but let me see the stems."

I hand the box to him, and he puts his glasses back on and intricately examines the stems.

"I'll be damned," he says.

"What?"

"Right here, by the thorn. A tiny speck of blood."

A spike of hope shoots through me, until—

"That blood could be the Englishman's," Jackson says. "It may not be the girl's."

"Pretty much a fifty-fifty shot, though, wouldn't you say?"

Jackson removes the magnifiers. "True enough. But we still have limitations. The speck of blood is probably over sixty years old."

"And is that a problem? I mean . . . I don't know anything about DNA extraction."

"It'll be difficult," he says. "But we at least have a sample. Will we get anything from it? More likely we won't, but at least it's something I can try."

"So you have the DNA from the bones. All you need to do is match it."

"Right. And if the blood doesn't match, we know it probably belongs to the guy."

"Do you need a sample of his DNA?"

"No. Unless you need it for something else."

"No, I don't."

"All right," Jackson says. "Give me twenty-four hours. I'll be in touch."

"Thank you. You'll be compensated very well."

"I know, and I appreciate it. Tell Ruby I said hi."

"Will do."

I leave the stems with Jackson, but I take the rest of the items in the shoebox with me. Once everything is over, I'll return the entire box to Ennis.

"I'll see you out," Jackson says.

"Don't bother," I tell him. "Go ahead and start your work."

★ ★ ★

Back in Snow Creek, I stop at the cinema to talk to Jenny Mabel, the manager.

Jenny and I went to high school together, and she always blushes profusely when I talk to her. True to form, her cheeks are bright red when she comes out of her office.

"Hi, Brock." She looks at her feet.

"Hi, Jenny. Thanks for seeing me. I need to change my reservation for Rory Pike's concert."

"You do?" This time she looks at me, and she widens her eyes. "We were all really looking forward to that."

"Don't worry. We're not canceling. There's just some stuff going on right now, and Rory can't get the program together as quickly as we first thought. I'm thinking maybe mid-December?"

"Come on back to my office, and I'll take a look at our schedule."

Schedule? Really? The Snow Creek cinema has a schedule?

"Okay."

I follow her back to her office, which is the size of a large closet. She sits down at a tiny desk and taps on the computer.

There's no extra chair, so I stand.

"Yeah," she says. "Just as I suspected. We're planning a great big Christmas movie marathon beginning December fifteenth. We'll have all the oldies. *Miracle on Thirty-Fourth Street, It's a Wonderful Life, The Bells of St. Mary's . . .*"

"What about *Elf*?" I ask.

"*Elf*?"

"Yeah. It's a freaking classic."

She reddens further. "Okay. I'll see if we can get it."

I chuckle. "I'm kidding, Jenny. What if we booked Rory on the fourteenth?"

"That's a Thursday."

"So what?"

"Wouldn't you want her concert to be on a weekend?"

Jenny raises a good point. "What would it take for me to get the place on that Saturday night, the sixteenth, and then you start your holiday thing on Sunday?"

"We're not open on Sunday, Brock."

Of course not. Nothing is open on Sunday in Snow Creek. Sometimes small-town living really sucks.

"Saturday then." I smile. "Give Rory Friday, and start the Christmas classic marathon on Saturday."

"Well . . . I might be able to swing that."

"Friday would be great," I say. "A Friday evening, ending the workweek . . . Coming to see Snow Creek's most beautiful woman with the voice of an angel singing—"

Jenny frowns.

Yeah, not my best moment. Mentioning how beautiful Rory is.

"I'm willing to pay more." I smile. "Enough so you can probably get *Elf* for your Christmas movie marathon."

She taps on her computer. "All right. You can have Friday. I'll send you a contract. Sign it and send it back to me."

"You're a doll, Jen. Thank you."

Red cheeks once more, as Jenny stares at her computer screen. "You're welcome, Brock."

Rory now has over a month to plan her program, and I can get back to dealing with this other bullshit.

Man… I hope the blood on that rose stem belongs to Patty Watson.

But then… What if it does?

That means…

That means we have the bones of an innocent eighteen-year-old girl buried on our property.

And that can't mean anything good.

CHAPTER TWENTY-THREE

Rory

It's two o'clock, and I just finished my last lesson for the day. I tidy the studio and then take a glance out my window.

Brock is walking up the street, looking luscious as usual in Levi's, a black button-down, and black ostrich cowboy boots. What's he doing here in town? He's supposed to be in the city meeting with Ruby's DNA expert.

He disappears behind the building.

I finish, lock up, and head down.

Sure enough, Brock is standing by my car.

"Hey." I walk into his arms and give him a kiss on the lips.

"Hey yourself, beautiful."

"What are you doing here in town?"

"I went to see Jenny over at the cinema. I changed the reservation for your concert to Friday, December fifteenth."

"Thanks for that. That gives me a little over a month."

"I thought you'd be happy."

"Surely we can figure out all this other stuff in a month, right?"

He doesn't reply.

"Brock?"

"I don't know, sweetheart. I just don't know. There's so much going on. It may take a while to find the answers."

"We have to. We have to at least find out if Pat Lamone is really your cousin."

"Yeah, we will. Although DNA may not be entirely conclusive."

"It'll be able to tell you if he's a second or third cousin, right?"

"I don't know. He's allegedly descended from a half sibling, which makes it more complex. A lot of it is Greek to me. I mean, sure, I studied agricultural science in college, and I can tell you all the parts of a bovine. When it comes to human anatomy and DNA? Not so much."

"Yeah, me too. I definitely don't have a science brain."

"So we'll leave it to the expert. The hair samples from the hair tie weren't viable, and he found another hair on the panties, which also wasn't viable. But . . . he did manage to find a speck of blood on one of the rose stems."

"But that could be Ennis's."

"Exactly. It's a shot in the dark. But it's better than anything else we've got."

"When do we find out?"

"He says he'll try to have more information for me within twenty-four hours. I called Dale and Donny and my dad and gave them the info. Then I came over here to deal with Jenny and the cinema and to see the most beautiful woman in the world."

He brushes his lips lightly over mine.

Then he gazes at me, his dark eyes flaring with fire.

Already I know what he's thinking.

"Not here," I say.

"Why not? There's nobody around."

"This is Snow Creek. There's always someone around."

"Is Willow down in the salon?"

"No, not today."

"Then who else would be around? Who else could see us in this parking lot right now?"

"No way."

He kisses me then—a hard and passionate kiss complete with clashing teeth and sliding lips and mashing tongues.

And I'm ready.

I'm always ready for him.

I break the kiss, breathing rapidly. "Upstairs. Studio." I grab his hand and pull him through the back door of the salon and up the stairway.

CHAPTER TWENTY-FOUR

Brock

Rory fumbles with the key in her purse and then has trouble getting it in the keyhole.

I take it from her, have trouble myself, but I'm able to get it unlocked.

I shove the door open.

The studio is a small room, not that I expected it to be huge. An upright piano sits against one wall, and one bookshelf stands against the adjacent wall. It's filled with what I assume are music books, and more music books are stacked in neat piles against the rest of the wall.

Her bachelor and master of music degrees are framed and on yet another wall.

There's a piano bench and a small desk with a chair.

Not really anywhere to make love.

But that doesn't matter.

All I need is a fucking wall.

I'm so hard already, raring to get inside her.

"Take off your jeans, sweetheart." I unbuckle my belt, unsnap my jeans, and slide them down along with my boxer briefs.

My cock springs out, awake and ready.

Rory flips off her shoes, removes her socks, jeans,

underwear. I grab her then, hoist her into my arms, her back against the wall, right next to her music degrees.

I shove my cock into her.

She screams out, and I crush my lips to hers, silencing her.

I pump. I pump hard.

She pushes at my shoulders, breaking her kiss.

"Condom!" she gasps.

"Don't fucking care." I slam my mouth back down on hers and continue thrusting.

Do I want a kid? No, I don't.

Right now? I need to fuck Rory.

I need to feel myself inside her with no barrier. I can feel every ridge, every valley inside her tight pussy. I don't want to ever wear a damned condom again with this woman.

She feels like heaven. Indeed, heaven can't feel any better than this place between Rory Pike's legs.

I plunge, and I plunge.

Will she come? I don't know, but I—

She grips my shoulders hard, and I feel it.

Her contractions, her moans and screams coming straight into my mouth as our lips are still locked.

Yes, she's coming, and that's all I need.

My balls scrunch up, and the contractions begin at the base of my cock. And I—

I pull out. I pull out of her, and my come shoots onto her thighs.

Not what I wanted, not what I was planning, but old habits die hard.

"I'm sorry, sweetheart."

"It's okay. I understand."

Does she? She's not smiling, but she's also coming down from an orgasm.

"We'll think of something," I say.

"I don't like the idea of the pill. I don't like putting hormones into my body that aren't meant to be there."

"I get it. Maybe an IUD?"

She shakes her head. "No. I don't want a foreign object in me either. And before you say it, no shots and no messy jellies."

"All right, sweetheart. Diaphragm?"

She nods finally. "Yeah. You have to use spermicide, but only a little. I'll see my doctor."

A diaphragm isn't my weapon of choice, but really, it's no worse than a condom. It won't hinder either of our enjoyment of the act except she'll have to stop and insert it. Same as me stopping to put on a condom.

"Brock..."

"I know. You might be pregnant. When will you know?"

"My period is due in about a week."

I nod.

And part of me—that part of me that I try to ignore most of the time—almost hopes she *is* pregnant.

"Bathroom?" I ask.

She nods to the door on the opposite wall.

It, like the rest of the place, is tiny. Just a sink, toilet, and a small shower. She doesn't have any washcloths, only paper towels.

I moisten one as best I can, bring it back out, and wipe my come from her thighs.

She gets dressed quietly.

"Dinner tonight?" I say.

She nods. "That would be nice."

"My place?"

"Actually..."

"What?"

"How about my place?"

"Aren't you staying with your family?"

"Yeah. But . . . my mom and dad really want to meet you."

"Rory, we've met."

"I know, but Callie is bringing Donny for dinner tonight, and my mom asked if I'd like to bring you."

"And you're just telling me about it now?"

"Yeah. You were gone all morning, Brock. I was going to call you, but . . ."

"But . . . what?"

She sighs. "I don't know. It feels like it's too soon, in a way. This has happened so fast between us, you know?"

"It has, but it's kind of great."

She smiles then, and things seem okay between us once more. "I agree. It's pretty great, and I'd really like you to come to dinner tonight."

I caress her cheek. "Okay. I'll be there. What time?"

"Six thirty. Don't be late."

"Wouldn't dream of it."

CHAPTER TWENTY-FIVE

Rory

My stomach feels like a couple of people are playing Ping-Pong inside me. I don't know why I'm nervous. Heck, my mom was thrilled. Not only am I bringing home someone from the Steel family, I'm bringing home a *man*.

She loves me and supports me, but deep inside, she's always hoped I'd end up with a man instead of a woman.

I honestly never knew which one it would be—not until Brock.

He's my forever.

Callie has moved almost all her stuff into Donny's guesthouse. She hasn't slept at home the last two nights.

I miss her.

Since Raine and I broke up and I moved back into my parents' home, I got used to having Callie next to me, joined by our Jack and Jill bathroom.

She and I have always been close, and it was great having her to talk to. Now that I know everything that's going on with the Steel family, and Brock and I have declared our love, I have more to talk to her about than ever.

But I guess we will find our way.

"Rory!" Mom calls from the kitchen.

I hurry in. "Yeah, what do you need?"

"Everything's ready for the most part. But I want to use the good napkins. The table's all set. Could you get them out of the cupboard in the closet?"

"Cloth napkins?"

"This is company, Rory. We always use cloth napkins for company."

"Right."

Except we haven't had company in years, other than Uncle Scott, Aunt Lena, and the cousins. And we don't break out the formal napkins for them.

I grab the forest-green napkins from the closet, along with Mom's brass napkin holders. I roll them up, slip them into the holders, and place one on top of each plate.

Then I inhale.

Mom is preparing salmon en croûte, one of her specialties. My mom is a great cook, and her breads are almost as good as Ava Steel's.

I return to the kitchen, and Mom hands me a platter of assorted cheeses and crackers. "Put this on the coffee table in the front room."

"The front room?"

We almost never use the formal living room. Always the family room.

"Yes, the front room. This is company, Rory."

Right. Company.

Her daughters and their boyfriends.

In Callie's case, her fiancé.

But not just any boyfriend and fiancé. *Steels.*

One of the Ping-Pong players inside me shoots one out of bounds.

Why am I so freaked out?

I set down the tray just as the door opens. The dogs are outside, so there's no commotion.

"Hey, we're here," Callie calls.

"Hey, guys," I say.

"So . . ." Donny smiles a big Steel smile. "You and Brock? Never saw that one coming."

"Neither did I." I return his smile. "But I'm not complaining."

"Neither is he apparently. Never thought I'd see the day, at least not for another ten years or so."

"Give her a break, Donny," Callie chides. "This is new for both of them."

"All right, all right."

Mom comes bustling in, gives Callie and Donny each a hug. "Go on down to the family room. Frank will fix whatever you want to drink."

I follow them, taking Mom's cheese platter with me.

"Rory, I told you the living room."

"Dad and all the booze are downstairs. He'll be more comfortable down there, and so will Donny and Brock. I swear."

She sighs. "All right. If you're sure."

"Trust me. I'm sure. Plus it's bigger, and the furniture is more comfortable."

She lifts her hands in the air, shakes her head, and sighs.

Good. I won that round.

I set the tray on the table next to our makeshift bar. We don't have a built-in bar like Brock has in his parents' guesthouse or like I'm sure every other Steel house possesses. Our bar is a shelf of liquor, a mini fridge, and two high tables.

"What'll it be, Don?" my dad asks.

"Whatever you've got open, Frank."

"What's your mixed drink of choice?"

"Margarita, but I don't expect you to go to all that trouble."

"Nonsense. It's no trouble at all."

My father, though not a drinker himself, enjoys tending bar. He put himself through college doing exactly that.

"Diet Coke for you Callie?" Dad says.

"Hey, if you're making margaritas, I'll have one of those as well."

"Coming right up." Dad pulls the blender off the shelf.

Then the doorbell.

Brock.

My stomach tumbles. "I'll get it."

I walk out of the family room, through the foyer to the door, and open it.

Brock Steel stands there, looking as though he just stepped out of the pages of *GQ* magazine. He's wearing black slacks, black loafers, and a light-gray button-down, two buttons open. His hair is actually combed, and he's holding a bouquet of yellow roses.

My jaw drops. "For me?"

He smiles. "Actually, they're for your mother, Rory."

I can't help laughing. "Oh my God, she's going to love you."

"Were you afraid she wouldn't?"

"Are you kidding me? You're a Steel. And you have a Y chromosome. You're everything she dreamed of for her bisexual daughter."

Mom comes to the door then, wiping her hands on her apron. "Good evening, Brock."

"Hello, Mrs. Pike. These are for you." He hands her the vase of flowers.

"They're lovely," Mom gushes. "How did you know I love roses? And yellow ones too."

"Just a good guess."

Not really a guess at all. I'm not sure I've ever met a woman who *doesn't* love roses.

Mom hands them to me. "Rory, would you put these on the table? They'll make a beautiful centerpiece for dinner."

"They'll be too tall, Mom. We won't be able to see each other."

"Nonsense. They'll be lovely."

"Okay, if you say so."

"And Brock," Mom says, "let me show you to the family room. Frank will get you settled with a cocktail."

"Yes, ma'am."

Ma'am? He just called my mother ma'am?

I set the vase on the table and then join the others in the family room after checking to make sure Mom doesn't need any help.

My dad has the blender whirring with margaritas. When the sound stops, he shakes the container a bit, and then pours two margaritas for Donny and Callie.

"Good to see you, Brock," he says. "What do you want to drink?"

"A beer would be great, Mr. Pike."

"Frank, please. A beer it is. I've got Guinness and Coors extra gold."

"It's been a long time since I've had a Guinness," Brock says. "That sounds great."

"Rory?"

"I think I'll start with water, Dad." I steal a glance at my abdomen. You never know...

"Good enough."

Dad pulls a bottle of Guinness out of his mini fridge, and then he pours me a glass of water from the tap.

"Go ahead and sit down. Maureen put together some cheese and crackers to tide us over while we wait for her dinner."

Callie and Donny make themselves comfortable on the couch. That leaves a couple of chairs and the love seat.

I grab the love seat and pat the seat next to me. Brock takes the hint and joins me.

Dad of course takes his recliner. He's drinking water, same as me.

My dad just doesn't like liquor. He's not an alcoholic, and he will have a glass of champagne on special occasions. Other than that, though, except for the occasional beer, he just doesn't drink.

My mom on the other hand . . .

She comes down, her apron no longer covering her.

"Dinner will be ready in about twenty minutes." Dad begins to rise, but she stops him with a gesture.

"Don't bother, Frank. If there are any of those margaritas left, I'm going to try one."

"Yep," Dad says. "In the blender."

Mom pours herself a margarita and takes a chair that just happens to be closest to Brock.

"We are thrilled to have you here," she says to him.

Donny and Callie snicker at each other on the couch.

And the Ping-Pong player inside my stomach hits another out of bounds.

"I'm happy to be here, Mrs. Pike."

"Maureen, please."

"Of course. Maureen."

"So, Rory tells us you had a wonderful time in London."

"Yes, ma'am. I wish we could've stayed longer, but you know."

"Oh, of course, all the work to be done around here. You Steels are never idle."

"That's no lie." This from Donny from the couch.

Mom means well, but I wish she'd shut up. She has no idea what Callie and I are going through, let alone what the Steels are going through.

It's not really something I can tell her. *Oh, Mom, by the way, when I was in high school, I got drugged, and someone took photos of me in very compromising positions.*

Yeah. Not happening.

Small talk.

It's going to be twenty minutes of small talk before dinner.

Then more small talk *at* dinner.

Why did I agree to this?

Brock is a trouper though. He engages my mother, asking her questions and answering all of hers. He's so good at conversation that I don't have to say a word.

So I don't, until someone says the word—

" . . . fire."

Who said that? Who brought up the damned fire?

I glance at each person's face, and I zero in on the regretful expression in my father's eyes. It was him, but why? I've been so taken with Brock and his ease with my mother that I wasn't listening to anything else.

"You know," Donny says, "anything you need. Just ask."

"Your father and uncles have already told us that," Dad says. "We're doing just fine. But thank you so much for offering. We appreciate it."

My dad is rigid, tense. It flows off him in waves. He's pinching the bridge of his nose, his shoulders slumped downward. He's the one who mentioned the fire, so he brought this on himself. He knows that.

My father will never take a nickel from the Steels. He's too proud.

And again, I want to pummel Pat Lamone for ever calling us gold diggers.

We are *not* gold diggers. If we were, my dad would take the Steels up on their offer.

Mom stands. "I think dinner's ready. Frank, get everyone settled at the table, and I'll bring it in."

"I'll help you, Mom," I say.

"Oh no, you show Brock to the table. Callie can help me."

Callie gives me her patented *what the fuck?* look. I shrug. What can I do? Mom wants me focused on Brock. Callie already snagged her Steel.

Fine. She wants me focused on Brock? I'll be focused on Brock.

CHAPTER TWENTY-SIX

Brock

Rory takes my hand, squeezes it, and then pulls me up from my place on the love seat. She gently nudges me out of the room and toward the dining area.

"What's going on?" I ask.

"My mother wants me to show you to the dining room, so I'm showing you to the dining room."

Six places are set, complete with cloth napkins and what looks like fine China—not that I'd know for sure.

"I know Maddie's at college, but where's Jesse?" I ask.

"I don't have a freaking clue," she says. "Now, I wonder where her royal highness wants you sitting? Here. I'll put you right next to her. That'll make her happy. I'll sit on your other side."

Frank and Donny enter the dining room a moment later.

"Why don't you take the seat across from Brock, Don?" Frank says. "Then Maureen can pepper the both of you with questions."

"Works for me." Donny takes his seat.

Rory folds her green cloth napkin onto her lap, so I do the same. A full glass of red wine sits in front of my spot, along with a glass of ice water.

Maureen and Callie come bustling in, carrying platters

and bowls. Once we're all seated, Maureen begins passing the bowls around.

"I hope you like salmon, Brock."

"There's not much I don't eat, ma'am."

"Please, stop with the ma'am. You're making me feel old." Mom laughs.

"Okay. Maureen."

Rory looks a lot like her mother. It's common knowledge that Maureen Pike was once a beauty queen in local pageants. All her children favor her over Frank.

But Rory... There's something special about Rory. Her beauty is almost ethereal.

And yes, I just used the word *ethereal* in my thoughts. I've got it bad.

I fill my plate, handing dishes to Rory as we pass them. She takes very small portions.

I get it. She's nervous. This is our first dinner as a couple with her family. But Callie and Donny are here. Shouldn't that calm her nerves a bit?

And then I wonder...

Did she ever bring Raine over here for dinner? Any of the others? Or am I the first?

Probably not. She and Raine were together for a while, and she's had two other relationships. That's three more relationships than I've had. Surely she's done the family dinner thing before, so why does she seem so uneasy?

"Tell me, Brock," Maureen says. "How are things at the ranch?"

I smile. Maureen lives on a ranch herself—albeit a tiny one compared to mine—so she knows there's no easy answer to that question. Does she really want to know how things are going on the ranch? Of course not.

"Fine, ma'am. I'm sorry. Maureen."

"I'm so glad to hear that. And how are your parents?"

"They're fine. Mom is working on a new book."

"That's fascinating," Maureen says. "Your mother is such an intelligent woman."

"Yes, she is."

"My Callie is intelligent like that," Maureen says.

Rory goes rigid next to me.

"Book smart, you know," Maureen continues. "Jesse and Rory are a different kind of smart."

"I got straight As," Rory says. "In high school and college. So did Jesse. And Maddie, by the way. You have another child."

Maureen's cheeks pink. "Oh, of course, I know that. You're all brilliant. You always have been."

Ouch. I'll never accuse my parents of labeling Brad and me again. They totally don't do what I just witnessed. I don't think Maureen meant to make Rory feel bad. She just has her own pictures of who her children are. I suppose my parents did the same thing, but to a much lesser extent. My mom would never make a comment like that in front of dinner guests, for example.

Donny and Callie are eerily silent and, surprisingly, so is Frank. Perhaps he's still feeling strange about the fire talk.

I hold back a sigh. Seems it's up to me.

"In my family," I begin, "Brad was always the brain and I was the brawn, despite the fact that I always got straight As in school as well."

"Isn't it funny," Maureen says, "how we get ideas about our children?"

"Not too funny from where I'm sitting," Rory mutters under her breath.

I place my hand on her thigh and give it a slight squeeze. I can make this better. "Did Rory mention that we're planning a Christmas concert?"

Maureen's eyes widen. "No. What are you talking about?"

Rory tenses further, but I continue.

"She's going to put together a program for the city."

"And I think it's a fabulous idea," Callie says animatedly.

Much more animated than she usually is, and Rory glares at her.

"Oh yeah, me too," Donny says. "I know my family is looking forward to it."

"How am I the last to know about this?" Maureen says.

In truth, she's the first to know other than Donny and Callie. Rory and I haven't made it public at all.

"You're not," I tell her. "It's only in planning stages so far."

Rory speaks then. "I've talked to Jesse. He's going to sing with me, I hope."

That gets Frank's attention. "You know I love to hear the two of you sing together. When will this be?"

I clear my throat. "Friday, December fifteenth. About a month away."

"I'm thrilled. Jesse has such a great voice, and though I love his rock and roll, I will enjoy hearing something not quite so head banging." Frank takes a sip of his wine.

"That reminds me," Maureen says, picking up her own glass. "We should have a toast."

"To what?" Rory says.

"To our company, of course. Brock, we're so happy to have you here. And of course Donny as well." She raises her glass. "To our guests."

We all clink glasses and take a drink. I don't even like wine much, and I know Donny doesn't either. But we'll make do. These are our future in-laws.

I drop my jaw, but close my mouth quickly.

Our in-laws?

No.

Donny's future in-laws.

Rory and I aren't there yet.

Are we?

I'm twenty-four years old. *I'm* not there yet.

Only then do I notice Rory's wineglass.

It's still full. She raised her glass and clinked with the rest of us, but she must have only pretended to take a drink.

Tension flows through my body, but I try to relax. What if she *is* pregnant? Is it the worst thing in the world?

No. I love this woman.

And if I ever have children, I want her to be their mother.

God, this is crazy thinking coming from me.

But I mean it. I mean it with all my heart.

Rory seems focused on Donny and Callie at the moment, for which I'm grateful. The word *wedding* floats around. I squeeze Rory's thigh again. My touch seems to relax her.

It relaxes me as well.

★ ★ ★

After dinner, I find myself outside on the Pikes' small redwood deck, enjoying a brandy and a cigar with Donny and Frank. Rather, I'm enjoying the brandy, but I hate cigars.

"How do you like your cigar cut?" Frank asks me.

Since I don't have a clue what he's talking about, I say, "However you do yours is fine."

He snips off the end of the cigar with some kind of blade and hands it to me. I light it, take a puff, taking care that no smoke goes anywhere near my throat or I'll choke up my guts. I take a sip of my brandy.

"It's great to have you two here," Frank says. "I know Maureen is tickled."

"We're happy to be here, Frank," Donny says.

"Yeah." I clear my throat. "Of course."

"Brock, don't let Maureen scare you away. We know you and Rory are just at the beginning of your relationship. No one is expecting anything."

An odd comment, to be sure.

"Oh?" I take a shallow draw on the cigar.

"Maureen and Rory," Frank continues, "they have a... sometimes difficult relationship. In so many ways, they're very much alike, being the great beauties of the family and all. But in other ways... not so much."

Rory's bisexuality. He may as well say the words. They're clear as day.

"You mean her bisexuality?" I say.

Donny shoots darts at me with his eyes.

But why? Why should we not speak about it? It's part of who she is, and it's part of what I love about her.

"Well... a bit," Frank says. "It doesn't bother me one bit. In fact, I liked Raine Cunningham. I liked her a lot."

"And Maureen didn't?" I ask.

"Maureen liked her fine. She loved the way Raine did hair."

"I see."

"Maureen... She's traditional. She's not prejudiced in any way, but when it comes to her own children... Well, she's

180

not as open as she'd like to think she is. She tries, though. She loves all our children equally, but she sees them in little boxes sometimes."

That much was apparent from the dinner conversation.

"And you?" I ask.

"All I care is that my children are happy. If you make Rory happy, great. But if she had ended up with Raine? Or any other man or woman? That would have been great as well, as long as Rory was happy. Same for her and Jesse following their hearts with their music. But Maureen sees that and compares it to Callie and all her ambition. If you knew her mother, you'd understand. It's not fair and it's not right, and Maureen and I have had many words about it over the years. But she's a wonderful woman. A wonderful wife and mother. She cares as much as I do about all our children."

I like Frank Pike more and more, and I feel terrible for what happened to his ranch.

"That's a great attitude, Frank." From Donny.

"It's the only attitude a father can have, in my book. But like I said, Maureen is a little more traditional."

"So she's pretty glad I'm here," I say.

"Son, I'd say pretty glad is an understatement." Frank takes a puff on his cigar and smiles. "But like I said, we know this is new for both of you. Frankly, I'm surprised Rory invited you over tonight. Maureen asked her to, but she hedged at first."

"Did she?"

"Rory doesn't rush into things. She's usually with someone for a couple of months before she invites him or her over to meet us."

"I suppose it's different. You already know me."

"Brock, this is a small town. We already know all of them."

I can't help it. I chuckle. "When you're right, you're right, sir."

"Frank."

"Frank, then."

He eyes my cigar still sitting in the ashtray. "You don't really like cigars, do you?"

"Well..."

"You just need to be honest with me. It's okay if you don't like cigars like your cousin here."

"I don't want to waste it."

"Don't be silly. There's no need to smoke if you don't want to." He smiles and rises. "Now, if you gentlemen will excuse me, I need to see a man about a horse."

Once Frank is in the house, Donny turns to me. "They're good people, Brock. And they do love Rory."

"I never thought they didn't."

"Just don't judge Maureen too harshly. She accepts Rory."

"But does she?" I take a sip of brandy. "I don't like what I heard."

"I knew you wouldn't. Callie and I didn't like it much either, but Callie insists their mother loves them all equally, as Frank says. Even Rory knows it."

"Well, they don't love Rory more than I do."

"They do, just in a way different way." Donny smiles. Then he drops his jaw. "Wait... You *love* Rory?"

Really? Did I really just say that out loud?

But I can't lie to my cousin.

"I do. Surprised the hell out of me."

"That's great, dude. That's amazing."

"You think?"

"Yeah, especially if she loves you back. Does she?"

"She says she does."

"Brock Steel. Brock Steel and the most beautiful woman in Snow Creek." He smiles. "Actually, second-most beautiful."

Donny gets a dreamy look on his face. Man, is that guy in love. The thing is? Callie is beautiful. She's almost as beautiful as Rory.

"So what do you plan to do about it?" Donny says.

"Well, I'm not you."

"Meaning..."

"I'm not thirty-two. I'm twenty-four."

"True enough."

"This is new. New for both of us. And frankly, with all the other shit going on—"

"Hey," Donny says, "don't let our family bullshit stand in the way of your happiness. I'm not. Sure, Callie and I could wait. We could wait until all the Steel family crap comes to a head, but who knows when that will be? How long is it going to take us to uncover everything? I don't know, and I don't want to wait that long to be happy."

"It's not that," I say.

"It's not?"

"Well, it's kind of that. But it's also just... This isn't me, Don."

Donny chuckles. "Boy, do I know what you mean."

"But it's different," I say again. "You're so much older than I am."

"Love comes when it comes, and if you want my advice, cuz, you need to embrace it."

He's not wrong.

"I have. How else would I have even accepted it?"

"She is amazing. Almost as amazing as her sister." Donny grins.

Again, he's not wrong. Except for the *almost as amazing as her sister* part. I love Callie, but Rory?

Rory is everything.

CHAPTER TWENTY-SEVEN

Rory

Callie and I are helping in the kitchen.

While the men are outside smoking and drinking brandy.

Does Brock even smoke?

So much I still don't know about him.

But my mom is ever the traditional housewife.

Women in the kitchen, cleaning up, and men outside, doing nothing.

I roll my eyes at my sister.

She glares at me. Finally, when Mom excuses herself for a moment—

"I know. I hate it as much as you do, Ror. When we have our own household, you can bet Donny will be in here helping me."

"Are you kidding? You and Donny will have a housekeeper or cook in here doing this."

"Yeah, probably." She laughs then. "I can't even fathom that."

I absently touch my abdomen.

But Callie notices. "You'll know soon."

I look over my shoulder to make sure Mom isn't anywhere nearby. "I know, Cal, but if I am pregnant, Brock and I . . . He wants to be involved."

"Great! That's what you want, right?"

"I don't know how to tell you this, Callie, but I want . . ."

"What?"

I look around the kitchen, wave my arms around. "I want this. I want a family. A family where men and women share all duties, of course, but a family."

"That's not any different from what you've always wanted."

"No, it's not. It's just that . . . I think I found the one I want a family with. It's crazy, isn't it? Brock Steel?"

"Well, you've made Mom happy." Callie scoffs.

"God, I know. I honestly never knew whether my forever would be a man or a woman, but I always knew what Mom wanted."

"You know she loves you no matter what."

I sigh. "Yeah, I know. I get that. But she makes her desires clear."

"So what? Mom is limited in some ways. We accepted that long ago."

"Part of me feels like I'm letting her have her way."

"Letting her have her way? Rory, you can't help it that you fell in love with a man."

"I know."

"If you make Mom happy, it's a simple side effect."

"Now you make me sound awful. It's not that I don't want Mom to be happy."

"You know she'd be happy if you were happy. The fact that *she* wants one scenario over the other doesn't make her a bad person. It just means she's . . . Mom."

"Yeah, whatever."

"Don't you dare hold back with Brock just because you think it's making Mom happy. You do *you*. If Brock is the one who makes *you* happy, hold on to him. You deserve happiness and more, Ror."

"Here's the thing, Cal. I *want* Mom to be happy."

"I know you do. You just want her to be just as happy either way."

"Is there anything wrong with that?"

"There's nothing wrong with that, and you know Mom would be happy either way. Just slightly happier one way."

I sigh and hang the dish towel on the rack. "I know. And you know what I'm going to do right now? I'm going to join my boyfriend, your fiancé, and our father out on the deck. For a brandy. Or rather, for some water. Because women don't always need to be in the kitchen."

Callie laughs. "You're telling me? I'm the one who's going to be a freaking lawyer. Let's go."

We run into Dad going back out.

"You two done in the kitchen already?"

"Yeah," Callie says. "We definitely are."

Dad grins at us.

He knows Mom, and he understands.

"You all go on out. I'll finish up in the kitchen with your mother."

"How did we get such a great dad?" I kiss him on his cheek.

"Same way I got such amazing daughters. Go on out and talk with your boyfriends."

I jar at Dad's use of the term *boyfriends*. Donny is so much more than Callie's boyfriend, and Brock... What are we, exactly? Boyfriend sounds so juvenile. We're in love, but it's still so new. Is there a correct term?

Or does it matter?

Maybe all that matters is that we're happy.

That's all that matters to my father. And to ultimately my mother . . . in that warped way of hers.

The four of us laugh and chat about nothing in particular, until Donny's phone rings.

He regards it. "It's Dale."

"You should take it," Brock says.

Donny nods. "Yeah, Dale?" he says into the phone.

Pause.

"I'm not sure. Brock's with me now. We'll be right over."

"What is it?" Brock asks when Donny ends the call.

"Dale says we need to talk to my dad. Now."

"Is everything okay?" I ask.

"Yeah. I mean, no one's hurt." Donny shoves his phone in his pocket.

Brock rises. "I'm sorry, sweetheart."

"Don't be," I say. "Take care of business."

Callie nods. "I agree. Unless you want us to come with you."

"Not this time." Donny drops a kiss on Callie's lips. "We'll let you know as soon as we know anything."

I rise then, melt into Brock's arms. "Call me after?"

He drops a kiss on my forehead. "Absolutely." He holds me close and whispers in my ear, "I love you."

"I love you too."

CHAPTER TWENTY-EIGHT

Brock

My two cousins and I sit in Uncle Talon's office. In his hand, he holds the orange diamond ring that was stolen from his safe.

Donny's eyes widen. "You found it?"

Uncle Talon clears his throat. "I didn't find it. I'm the one who *took* it."

"And left a feather in its place?" Donny says. "What the fuck, Dad?"

"I didn't leave a feather in its place. The orange feather must have fallen off my new black Stetson."

"Since when do you wear your best hat around the house?" Dale asks.

"I was going out, Dale, and I was wearing it when I opened the safe and took the ring."

"Why?" Donny rubs the bridge of his nose. "You freaked me out. You should have told me."

"I don't make it a habit to inform my sons every time I open my safe," Uncle Talon says. "I never have, and I don't plan to start now. I took the ring to get it appraised."

"I already did all that, Dad," Donny says.

"You did. I wanted to have someone else look at it. Someone who might be able to determine what the LW stands for."

"I wish you'd mentioned it," Donny says. "I thought someone had broken into our house again. I was thinking all these really strange things."

"Like what?" I ask.

"I was in a bad way. I kept thinking about the phoenix."

"My horse?" Uncle Talon says.

"Well . . . yeah. How you named him after the phoenix, what the symbolism meant to you. And I kept thinking that the phoenix had fallen into ashes again, and we need to rise again. And then when I saw the orange feather . . ."

"Come on, Don," Dale says. "You didn't actually think it was a phoenix feather."

"Of course not. But guys, all this shit that's coming down? Our dad was shot, for God's sake."

"Not by a phoenix," Dale says dryly.

I stifle a chuckle.

"Of course not," Donny says. "But the ring was gone, and a feather was there. My mind went places. I figured whoever stole it was trying to tell us something."

"About a phoenix?" I ask.

Donny rolls his eyes at me. "Fuck off." Then, to Dale, "And you fuck off too."

"We're just giving you shit, cuz."

"Unfortunately," Uncle Talon says, defusing the situation, "I wasn't able to uncover anything more about the ring. If the ring did belong to my mother, I think we need to assume that she got it from her mother, Lucy Wade, whose initials were LW."

"But you said—" Dale begins.

"Yes, she didn't come from money. But maybe it was an heirloom? I don't know that there's any way to find out."

"There has to be a way," Donny says.

"Maybe. I don't know. But I've talked to the rest of the family, Don, and we want you to have the ring. We want you to give it to Callie."

"I agree," Dale says.

"So do I," I offer.

Donny shakes his head, though. "I would like Callie to have it one day. I mean, the ring was made for her, and it was left for me in a safe-deposit box in my name. Someone wanted me to have it. But until we know who left it, until we know what all of this means, I want the ring kept here in a safe place."

"All right. We'll keep it here in the safe," Uncle Talon says, "but I'm changing the combination."

Dale and Donny both widen their eyes.

"You haven't changed that combination in"—Dale pauses—"at least since I turned eighteen and you gave it to me."

"I haven't," Uncle Talon says, "and that was negligence on my part. From now on, I will be changing the combination every month. I'll leave it in a safe place. Only your mother will know where it is."

"Dad," Dale says, "that's not enough."

"I agree, so you, as my firstborn, will also know. And only the two of you"—he nods to Donny and me—"will know who has it. That's it."

I clear my throat. "You don't want to tell my dad?"

"If your dad needs it, he'll know where to find it."

"He will?" I ask.

"He will come to me."

"I think what he means is . . . What if something happens to you, Dad?" Dale says.

"First of all, nothing is going to happen to me, but if it does, anyone who needs the combination will go to your mother. Or to you, Dale, as my firstborn. And if they don't think to do that, if they go to Donny instead, or to you, Brock, you will know where to direct them."

"And no one else is going to know?" Donny says. "Not Diana or Brianna?"

"This is my decision for now. I may change my mind, but for now, only you and your mother will know where to find the combination, and only Donny and Brock will know who else has it."

Uncle Talon is being overly cautious, but I can't say that I blame him. No one broke into the safe and left a feather, thank God, but someone did get into the house and leave that safe-deposit key for Donny, not to mention Uncle Talon's shooting.

Uncle Talon rises and removes the painting of the horse named Phoenix to reveal his safe. He opens the safe, places the ring inside, and then closes it.

"Now"—Uncle Talon takes his seat behind his desk once again—"it's time for the three of you to level with me. What hasn't your father"—he nods to me—"told me?"

I gulp.

What am I allowed to say?

Can I tell Uncle Talon that my father and Uncle Bryce have deliberately kept things from him and the rest of the family over the years?

Does he even know about Pat Lamone and his alleged claim to the Steel fortune?

Surely my father told him that much.

But I have no idea. I don't feel like I know my father at all.

And I'm not sure I know my uncle either.

But these two blond men, my cousins, I know them.

And together we'll figure this out.

"Uncle Talon?"

"Yes, Brock?"

"Have Dale and Donny told you about the nurse who poisoned you?"

Uncle Talon draws in a deep breath. "They have."

"So what do you think? Who could be behind all of this?"

"The only people who I know for sure could be behind this are dead," Uncle Talon says.

"My father says the same thing, but what if they're not?"

"They are."

"But *are* they, though? My father also told me that his father—your father—faked his own death twice."

"Yes, he did."

"And the other guys—the ones who . . ."

"It's okay, Brock. You can say it."

Except I can't. I can't say those dreadful words. Something in my throat keeps them lodged. So I continue as if I said them. "Are you sure they're all dead?"

"Tom Simpson, Uncle Bryce's father, killed himself in front of your father."

"Yes. He told me."

"And Larry Wade died in prison, so either he was killed, or he killed himself."

"And what about the other one? Aunt Ruby's father?"

"Wendy Madigan killed him, and we were all witness to it."

"I know. I get it. But my father said he was witness to our grandfather's death as well. Twice."

"Brock," Donny says. "These people would be really old by now."

"I know that. But damn... Who else would have something against us?"

"It could be any number of people," Uncle Talon says. "My father had his share of enemies."

"But why?"

Uncle Talon shakes his head. "We don't know all the answers, Brock. I wish we did. I know for sure that Tom Simpson is dead. His brains were splattered all over his own kitchen. Just ask your father."

Just ask your father...

But that also means trusting that my father is telling me the truth.

And I hate to say it, but... I no longer trust *any* of these people to tell me the truth.

"Who would want you dead, Uncle Talon?"

"I don't know, Brock."

"Who would want *my* father dead?"

"Again... I don't know."

"Uncle Talon... damn it. What aren't you telling us?"

"Hey," Dale says. "Watch it."

"I get it, Dale. You're totally protective of your father, and I don't blame you, but we have all these pieces to a puzzle, and none of them fit together."

"It's okay, son," Uncle Talon says to Dale. "Brock has valid questions, and I wish I had valid answers."

"We're going to find the motherfucker who tried to kill you, Dad," Dale says. "I will take that to the grave."

"Don't you take anything to the grave, son. That would kill your mother. Besides, you have a new wife. You'll have a family soon. You will *not* give your life for any of this. Do you understand me? That goes for the two of you, as well." He nods to Donny and me, and then he rises. "You know what? I think we could all use a drink."

I rise as well. "I'm going to pass. But thank you."

"Brock, I love you. I love you like you're my own child. I feel that same way about all my nieces and nephews. We all do."

I nod. "I know that."

"Trust me when I say we only kept this information from you because we thought we could protect you."

"That's what you get for thinking, I guess." I walk out of Uncle Talon's office, down the hallway, through the foyer, and out the door.

On my way I text Rory.

Meet me at my place. Please.

CHAPTER TWENTY-NINE

Rory

It doesn't even occur to me to say no. I'm tired, and my nerves are on edge from the dinner with my parents and then Dale's phone call to Donny.

But Brock needs me.

So I go.

I'm waiting in my car when he drives up.

"Hey," he says. "I'm sorry. I figured I'd get here before you did."

"No problem."

"Easy enough. I'll get you a key, and all the security codes. That way you don't have to wait out here."

"That's not necessary, Brock."

"It is. I love you, Rory, and I don't want to keep any secrets from you. I've seen what secrets do to relationships."

"Giving me a key to your place isn't like telling me a secret," I say.

"But it is. Don't you see? I want you in every part of my life."

I warm all over. "You do?"

"Yeah, I do. And yeah, it scares the shit out of me, but it is what it is."

I smile, and he leads me into the house. Sammy rushes

around us, pimping herself out for scratches behind her ears, and we oblige. Then Brock lets her out the back door to do her business.

He touches my cheek. "Thank you for coming."

"You said please." I smile.

"I did. Is that why you came?"

I shake my head. "I would have come anyway. I love you. But you don't strike me as the kind of man who says please a lot."

"I seem to say it a lot now. With you."

"I like that. I like that you want me with you that much. That you're willing to say please."

"Oh, sweetheart . . . you have no idea how much I want you. But I honestly didn't call you over here for sex."

"It doesn't matter if you did."

"I won't turn you down"—he gives me a rakish smile—"but I just wanted to be with you. You're like my safe place, Rory."

"And you're mine."

"I never thought I'd need a safe place."

"There's no shame in needing a safe place." I trace his lips with my finger.

"I know. It's just . . . I never thought . . ."

"It's okay. Families aren't perfect." I sigh. "I should know."

"I never thought they were. But I did at least think that my family—the Steels—were upright citizens. The best of the best."

"Maybe they still are."

"I don't know, sweetheart. I just don't know."

"Let me take you to bed," I say. "You can forget about it, at least for tonight."

He kisses me then. A beautiful kiss—and though it's not

as raw and needy as most of our kisses, it's full of love. Full of safety.

Which is what he needs.

I take the lead, which I'm not sure I've ever done with Brock, but I feel he needs it right now. I don't mind taking the lead. In fact, I like it.

I entwine his fingers through mine and walk toward his bedroom.

His bed is unmade, and I can't help a smile. Doesn't matter.

I cup his cheeks, look into his dark eyes. "I love you."

He groans. "God, I love you too, Rory."

I unbutton his shirt slowly, even though I want to rip it in half and watch the buttons fly.

But I feel like slow is what he needs right now.

Slow and safe.

With each new inch of skin I expose, I trail my lips over him. Over his warm flesh, his bulging muscle. When I get to the last button, kissing his abdomen, I part the shirt and brush it over his shoulders.

I stand back for a moment, admire his beauty.

And he is beautiful. Masculine and magnificent and so beautiful.

Of all the men and women I've been with in my life, no one compares to Brock Steel in pure physical magnificence. In the pure lustful attraction that I feel.

I kneel before him, unbuckle his belt, unsnap his jeans.

I push them over his strong hips along with his underwear.

His giant cock springs forward, alert and ready.

I kiss its tip, and he lets out a moan.

"God, sweetheart."

"You're beautiful," I breathe.

"No, you are."

I wrap my lips around his cockhead and suck gently.

His hands go into my hair then, pulling it out of the ponytail and letting it flow over my shoulders.

"Rory..."

I pull back, widen my eyes.

"I need to be inside you."

"In good time." I return to my work on his cock.

He's amazing—beautiful and amazing—and giving him head is pure pleasure. I suck on him for a few moments, relishing the groans coming from his throat, and then I rise, push him to the bed, and pull off his boots, socks, jeans, and underwear. Then I kneel back between his legs and take his cock between my lips once more.

"You're wearing too many clothes, sweetheart."

"For now," I say and then return to this gorgeous cock.

I suck him slowly, languidly, the ultimate tease.

I don't want him to get too worked up, because he wants to be inside me and I want him there.

But for now? This is a safe place, and I want to do this for him.

Once he's lubed up with my saliva, I add my hand to increase the friction.

Slowly, a painful tease, I'm sure ...

Until he pushes my head away.

"Need you. Now."

I stand and remove my clothes. Then I turn. "Where are your condoms?"

"Forget the condom," he says through clenched teeth. "Get back here. *Now.*"

I obey him.

I obey him because even if I'm not pregnant, I'm at a point in my cycle where it's unlikely I could get pregnant.

I obey him because I want him now, sans barrier.

I obey him because, even though I never thought I'd obey any man, it feels right to obey Brock Steel in the bedroom.

I climb on top of him and sink down on his hard cock.

And I'm filled. Filled to the brim, and my God, he stretches me so exquisitely.

"Brock..." I breathe.

He captures my lips in a kiss. This is no sweet kiss like before. This is a patented Brock Steel kiss. Harsh and passionate, and I feel it through every part of my body, all the way down to the tops of my toes.

But mostly I feel it in my pussy that's full of his cock. I position my knees and begin moving around on him, savoring the delicious burn, the flares of fire as he tunnels into me.

He groans into my mouth, into my whole body, and I quiver as lightning strikes me.

My mouth is still fused to his, and my groans...my screams... They're muffled, but they're there.

My whole world becomes my body, my pussy, my heart joined to this man.

I move quickly, letting the orgasm flow through me because I want him to join me.

Up, down, up, down ... I fuck him hard, fast, and with each stroke, my orgasm plummets me further within the cocoon that is protecting me, enveloping me.

He breaks the kiss then and lets out a long groan. "Coming... Coming so hard..."

He presses me down on his cock, and he's buried in me

balls deep, the end of my orgasm still flowing through me as I feel his release pump into me.

We sit there, my head embedded in his shoulder, our chests clamped together with perspiration.

We stay that way.

For a long, long time.

CHAPTER THIRTY

Brock

Just what I needed.

Rory can read me like no other. She knew exactly what I needed, and she gave it to me.

I hope someday I can do the same for her.

I have no idea how long we stay joined together, her on top of me and my dick embedded inside her.

But it's a long time.

"I love you," I whisper against her neck.

"I love you too."

I maneuver us gently and pull the covers over us. I kiss her on the top of her head. "Stay. Please."

"I'm not going anywhere."

★ ★ ★

I wake before my alarm, which is unlike me. Rory has moved to the other side of the bed and is softly snoring.

Yes, the most beautiful woman in Snow Creek snores.

I won't tell her. It's too cute.

I pull her close to me, and she lets out a soft sigh without opening her eyes.

And I'm thinking . . .

I move downward, taking the covers with me.

I think I want pussy for breakfast.

I lick her softly, slowly. Sweet, sweet Rory.

Above me, she moves, making the soft noises of someone waking up relaxed.

I nibble on her clit, and her hands thread through my hair.

"Morning..." she murmurs.

"Morning," I say against her wet thigh.

"Feels good..."

"Tastes good..." I growl. And then I continue my work.

Within a few seconds, she's coming, and I crawl forward and push myself into her wet heat.

Slowly we make love as the morning sun begins to rise.

Afterward, we lie in each other's arms, until Sammy rustles me up.

"I've got to let the dog out," I say.

"Okay." Rory rolls away from me.

I rise, throw on my jeans from last night, and make my way to the kitchen to let Sammy out the back. Then I put on a pot of coffee and make Sammy's breakfast. Once she comes back in and is eating, I pour two cups of coffee and go to get Rory.

I nudge her. "Sweetheart, I have to get ready. Do you have lessons today?"

"Mmm-hmm. Not until ten, though."

"Do you want me to set your alarm for you?"

"No. I'll get up with you." She doesn't open her eyes, though.

"You're so cute," I say.

That gets her eyes open. "I'm not cute, Brock Steel."

"Did I say cute? I meant beautiful. Breathtakingly beautiful."

"That's better." This time she stretches her arms above

her head and actually pulls herself into a sitting position. "I should go home. I've been neglecting my poor dog."

"Why don't you bring your dog over here?"

That gets her wide awake. "What?"

"Move in with me."

Her jaw drops.

And I have to keep my own jaw from dropping. Did I really just ask this woman to move in with me?

"Brock..."

"I know. Crazy, right? But I really want you to."

"I..."

"What is it, sweetheart?"

"I mean, you just sprang this on me."

"I love you," I say.

"I love you too, but moving in... That's big, Brock. Really big."

Yeah, it's big. Part of me can't believe the words came out of my mouth. Me. Brock Steel. Infamous Steel playboy.

But I don't regret the words. Not at all.

"Maybe I *want* big with you, Rory."

"But we haven't talked about the future..."

"No, we haven't. Why do we need to talk about the future? We're happy today. We love each other today."

"Moving in is a big commitment."

"It doesn't have to be."

"Are you kidding me?" She stands, paces around the room in her glorious nakedness.

"I'm not kidding about anything," I say.

"Brock, we've been in love for... what, a day? Two? Moving in is a big step."

I've heard the stories about my parents and all my aunts

and uncles—the stories about how we Steels fall hard and fall fast. Then I watched it happen to Dale and Donny.

I never believed it would happen to me. Never in a million years. But it has. It has totally happened to me.

"It doesn't have to be such a big step, Rory."

"How can you not see this?" She shakes her head as she shimmies into her jeans. "Moving in together is one step below marriage."

"Then marry me," I say.

The words are as big a surprise to me as they are to her.

But I can't unsay them. I don't want to unsay them.

"For God's sake, Brock." She steps into her shoes. "I'm not marrying you or anyone."

"Ever?"

"Not today, anyway."

I rub at my jawline. Has she forgotten she may be pregnant? Why isn't she all over this? "Rory, where is this going, then? I mean . . ." I glance at her abdomen.

She sighs. "I just got out of a relationship, Brock. You know this. And I love you. I love you more than I loved Raine. I love you more than I've ever loved anyone. But it's too soon. How can you not see that?"

"How can you say it's too soon when you might be pregnant with my kid?"

Her eyes widen.

I went a step too far.

"Rory . . . I'm sorry."

"Oh, God . . ." She walks into my arms. "I'm the one who's sorry."

"You haven't done anything to be sorry for."

"The truth is, I love the idea. I just don't *want* to love the idea."

"Moving in? Getting married?"

"Both." She sighs. "I love them both."

"How long did it take Donny and Callie to fall in love?" I ask.

"Not long."

"It didn't take us long either."

She pulls back and looks at me. "I feel like it's not fair to you, to be honest."

"How can it not be fair to me? It was my idea."

"I know, but I don't want people to say I married you on the rebound."

"Who gives a fuck what people say? I don't."

"I really don't either." She shakes her head. "I gave up giving a fuck what people said years ago. You kind of have to when you're bisexual."

"Then what's the problem?"

"It's just too soon."

"Rory, look at me."

She meets my gaze, and my God, her eyes are beautiful. So loving and tortured and beautiful.

"Do you love me?" I ask.

"More than anything," she says. "You know that. I love you so much, Brock."

"And I love you. I've never been in love before, Rory. It's all new to me. But I can't imagine, for one moment, ever *not* being in love with you."

"I can't either," she says, "but Brock, this is new. It's exciting. What if it doesn't..."

"What if it doesn't work?"

She sniffles a bit. "What if it doesn't last, Brock?"

I step backward. Surely she can't be thinking...

"Oh God, that look on your face." She touches my cheek. "I don't mean it that way. I love you. I love you so damned much. I can't imagine ever not loving you either. But…with everything else that's going on, Brock. For all I know, Pat Lamone has already sold my pictures to some sleazy social media outlet."

"Then I'll kill him," I say, totally meaning it.

"You have your own issues."

"Your issues *are* my issues, Rory. Don't you see? You're mine. I'm yours. It's a package deal. All of the good with all of the bad."

"I get that, it's just…"

It dawns on me then.

What I'm going through is bigger—much bigger—than the high school drama she's going through.

"You don't want to be saddled with all my issues. Do you?"

She bites her bottom lip.

"Just say it. Rory."

"It's not that. Your problems don't scare me. It's just… I have no way of helping you, Brock. I live paycheck to paycheck teaching music to kids. My family lost almost everything in that fire. My dad is working at the hardware store to help make ends meet."

"I can help your family."

"That's not what I'm saying. I wish I could just drop everything and be there for you."

"Rory, I'm not asking you to drop everything and be here for me. I'm asking you to be a part of my life. To share everything, the good and the bad. I could help your family if you'll let me."

She shakes her head vehemently. "My family will never accept."

"Maybe they will. If not from me, maybe they'll accept it from Donny. He's marrying Callie."

"You heard my father at dinner. He's too proud."

For the love of . . . A sliver of anger wells in me. Why won't they let me help?

"There's pride," I say, "and then there's stupidity."

I clamp my mouth shut.

Rory reddens.

This time I went too far, and I instantly regret it.

CHAPTER THIRTY-ONE

Rory

No, he did not.

Brock Steel did *not* just call my father stupid.

My father, who is the proudest man on the planet. My father, who accepted me without question when I came out to him. My father, who I knew would always accept a man or a woman in my life, unlike my mother, who only gives lip service to it.

I curl my hands into fists, turn, and walk out of Brock's bedroom.

Only to be yanked back in.

"Sweetheart, I'm so sorry."

"Save it." I tear my arm away from him.

"I didn't mean that. I just . . ." He rakes his fingers through his hair. "I like your father. I respect him. I don't for a minute think he's stupid. I just want so much to help you, and helping your family helps you. I want to take care of you. Do everything for you."

"But don't you see? I can't have you do everything for me. Or for my family. We need to stand on our own feet, Brock."

"But I have—"

"Don't. Just don't. Yes, you have everything. Everything material, anyway. You never have to worry about money. You never have to worry about how the bills will get paid. Or about whether you'll eat steak or hamburger for dinner. You don't have to worry."

"I know. I have enough for five lifetimes, and I want to share it with you. With your family."

"I'm not ready."

"Rory . . ." He gazes at my abdomen, which I'm absently stroking. "What if . . ."

"What if, indeed? Let's find out. There are tests now that can determine HCG levels within five days before a woman misses her period. We could find out now, Brock."

"Fine." He finishes dressing quickly. "But we're not relying on any drugstore test. We're going into the city. You can see a real doctor."

"I have lessons. I just took time off to go gallivanting around London with you and—"

"*Gallivanting* around London? Is that what you think that was?" He shakes his head as he pulls on his boots. "Gallivanting. I can't believe you just said that."

I'm blowing this.

I'm blowing this so badly, and I don't want to. Seems we're both saying things we shouldn't.

"I didn't mean it that way," I say.

"Exactly how did you mean it, then? We went to London to get information from a man—an elderly man who is important to my family. An elderly man who lost the one love of his life when he was a young man—the love of his life who was probably killed because of *my* family."

"I know, baby. I'm so sorry."

"Just get out of here, Rory."

"But . . ."

"Please. Just go."

God. What have I done? He called my father stupid, and I lashed out. I just lashed out. I loved my time in London with him, and I loved meeting Ennis Ainsley and helping Brock deal with his family problems.

And now? I'm screwing this up. Big time.

I reach toward him, wanting to feel his soft flesh against my fingertips, but he brushes my hand away.

"I need to cool off."

"Are you ... Are we ...?"

"Over?" he says. "Is that what you want to know?"

I gulp. "Yes. That's what I want to know."

"If we are, it's your choice. Not mine."

"What's that supposed to mean?"

"It means I love you, Rory, that I was serious when I asked you to move in with me. I was even serious when I asked you to marry me. I was serious when I said we should go into the city to find out if you're pregnant. I was serious about all of that. About sharing your life. About sharing your fucking problems. And about you sharing mine."

"Brock—"

"If we're over, it's your decision, not mine. But for the moment? I need to cool off. And I need you out of my sight."

I chew on my lower lip. I want so badly to touch him.

I screwed this up. But so did he. I open my mouth to say as much, but he shakes his head.

"Please. Don't."

Please. He said please.

And I do have a weakness for him saying please.

I nod then, turn, and leave.

★ ★ ★

Once my lessons are done for the day, it's slightly after three p.m. I don't dare go buy a pregnancy test at the local pharmacy, so I get in my car and drive to Grand Junction.

I'm in line at the pharmacy, ready to buy a pregnancy test that claims it can detect pregnancy within five days of the due date of your period, when I change my mind. I take it back to the shelf and replace it.

I get back in my car and drive, not sure where I'm going, until I end up at the Western Slope Family Planning clinic.

I sit in my car. Inside is Davey. And pregnancy tests. What the hell am I doing?

But I'm here now.

They have pregnancy tests here, I'm sure. Plus... I want to talk to Davey. I leave my car and enter the clinic.

"May I help you?" the receptionist asks.

"Is Davey here today?"

"She's with someone at the moment. Did you have an appointment?"

"No. I... I saw her a while ago, and our meeting didn't end all that well."

"Did the two of you have a problem? We could assign you to another counselor."

"No, Davey was lovely. I know I should have called to make an appointment, but..."

"But what?"

"I really just need to get a pregnancy test," I say.

"Oh, of course. Were you inseminated here?"

"No..." I look over my shoulder at the few women who are sitting in the waiting room. "I'm so sorry. This was a big mistake."

"Would you like me to leave a message for Davey?"

"No, it's fine. I'm sorry to have troubled you." I turn to walk out the door.

"Rory?"

I turn back at my name.

Davey stands there, having just come out from the back. She looks as pretty as ever, wearing her white lab coat, which is in stark contrast to her dark skin. Her hair is different than the last time I saw her. It's slicked back into a tight bun, which accentuates the fine lines of her face.

"Oh, Davey," the receptionist says. "This young lady was just looking for you."

Here goes nothing. I smile...or attempt to. "Good afternoon, Davey."

"Is everything all right?"

"Yes, fine. I was just wondering if you and I could talk for a moment."

"I have about fifteen minutes before my next appointment," she says, "so you're in luck. Come on back."

I follow Davey back to her office, where I met with her previously.

"Okay," she says. "What can I help you with today?"

"Do you mind if I sit?"

"Not at all."

I take the same chair I sat in during our heated appointment. "First, I need to be honest with you. I've decided to give the other relationship a go."

"You didn't have to come all the way here to tell me that, Rory. You made yourself very clear on the phone, and there are certainly no hard feelings on my end."

"I know that. I didn't think there would be. If it weren't for this other relationship, I really would be interested in dating you."

"I understand. What brought you in, then?"

I chew on my bottom lip. "I think I might be pregnant."

Davey smiles. "Did you end up going to another sperm bank?"

"No. The relationship I'm in, as I told you, is with a man, and ... well ... We got a little overeager one time—"

"I see. So you're not on the pill, obviously, or you wouldn't have come to a sperm bank. What do you normally use?"

"A condom. But we forgot it. And that's not the worst part."

"What's the worst part?"

"I was ovulating at the time. I took one of those tests."

"I see." Davey nods. "I've been where you are."

"But you didn't end up pregnant."

"No. But why would you assume that?"

"Because the last time I was in here, you told me you were inseminated here."

"Right. I did." She smiles and shakes her head. "I don't tell that to all my clients. I felt a connection with you right away."

"I felt it too. But believe me, I'm in love with this man. And I want a baby so badly. You were right last time. I haven't thought this through. But now it might be happening."

"So you've missed your period, then?"

"Technically not yet. It's due in four or five days, give or take a little. But I've heard there are tests now that can ..."

"Yes. The newest tests can detect pregnancy hormone up to six days before a missed period, so you're well within the time frame. We have them here. I'll be happy to give you one."

"Davey? You're a lifesaver."

"You know you can get those tests at the drugstore, right?"

"Yeah, I know. I just wanted to talk to someone."

"You can talk to me anytime. Just because we're not going to date doesn't mean we can't be friends."

"Thank you for being so understanding about this. I mean, I just barged into your day."

"You're lucky that I happen to be free"—she looks at her watch—"for about five more minutes. The test doesn't take long. Wait here."

I wait, sitting on the edge of my chair, while Davey leaves and then returns about thirty seconds later with the pregnancy test.

"The bathroom's right around the corner." She shows me as she hands me the test. "You know the drill. Pee on the stick and wait sixty seconds."

"And if it's positive…?"

"Then you need to talk to your boyfriend, but I can give you a referral to the best ob-gyns here in Grand Junction."

"I'd appreciate that. And Davey?"

"Yes?"

"Thanks."

"You're very welcome."

"I'll be back," I say. "Hopefully before your appointment gets here."

I take the test, head through the door that Davey motions to, secure the lock, and sit on the toilet. Only to have stage fright.

"Really?" I say out loud. I get up, go to the sink, and turn on the faucet.

Yep, works every time.

Once the stick is sufficiently wet, I set the timer on my phone for one minute.

The longest minute ever.

Clocks seem to slow down to a crawl when you're on edge, and I'm definitely on edge.

The seconds draw out, one by one, until—

The timer buzzes.

CHAPTER THIRTY-TWO

Brock

I work outside all day.

I should be in the actual office building helping my father, helping Uncle Bryce. I love them both, and I'd take a bullet for either of them, but I don't want to see them today.

So I work outside. I do hard labor. Whenever something's bugging me, this is where I end up—interacting with the land, the livestock.

I'm superfluous out here, of course. We have enough hired men and women to take care of everything, but still... Nothing takes the edge off like good old hard work—another lesson from the man who fathered me. The man I'm avoiding.

After six hours of hauling grain and tending to animals, I'm still tense, so I take off early in the afternoon. I shower, and then I walk the pathway between my guesthouse and my parents' home. I head to the pool house, change into my trunks, and then execute a perfect dive into my father's lap pool. He's not home, of course. He's at work, conversing with Uncle Bryce about God knows what.

Probably more secrets he can keep from the rest of us.

I cut through the water like a great white, my strokes in perfect form.

I swim and I swim and I swim. I lose count of how many

laps I've done, and I keep going, keep going, keep going...

Until—

"Brock!"

My mother. My mother's voice.

I come to the edge of the pool and bring my head out of the water. "Yeah? What is it, Mom?"

"What are you doing here?" She sits down at one of the tables by the pool, wearing a fleece jacket and jeans.

It's an early November day, a little brisk at around fifty-five degrees. But my parents' pool is heated, and I feel fine.

Mom rises, walks into the pool house, and returns with a large towel. She hands it to me. "This is heated. Wrap it around yourself. Then go change and come talk to me."

My mother is a professional talker.

She's a medical doctor—a psychiatrist who specializes in childhood trauma.

I didn't have any childhood trauma.

I had an idyllic childhood, unlike my cousins Dale and Donny.

I take the towel, go back to the pool house, and change back into my clothes.

When I return, Mom has lit the gas-powered fire pit.

"Sit," she says. "Patrice is bringing some water. I want you to drink up."

That's Mom, always taking care of everyone. She knows how dehydrated I get when I go crazy swimming laps like that.

"You're a dead ringer for your father right now, Brock," she says. "So many times I'd find him out here, swimming until his muscles could no longer move. But you can't swim your troubles away, son."

"I can sure as hell try."

Mom smiles, and Patrice walks over with the waters.

"Thank you, Patrice," Mom says. Then to me, "Drink up."

I down an entire glass of water flavored with lemon, and then Mom pours me another, nodding.

"This one too."

"Making my bladder burst isn't going to help anything," I say.

"Two of these glasses is twenty-four ounces altogether, so nothing is going to burst your bladder, Brock. Trust me. I'm a doctor."

"A head doctor."

"I went to medical school, and I did all my rotations. I know basic anatomy, and I know how the bladder works. So do you, for that matter, so stop arguing with me."

She's right, of course. I'm not sure why I'm arguing. I down a second glass of water. The tartness of the lemon helps quench my thirst.

"All right," Mom says. "Spill it."

Spill what? There are so many things to spill. How much does my mother even know?

"Why has Dad kept so much from me?"

"It wasn't my idea," Mom says. "I got outvoted."

I jerk backward in my chair. "*You* got outvoted? The one who knows the most about children and their minds? Their psyches? You wanted to tell us the truth?"

"Maybe not the whole truth, but some of it."

"But they voted against you? The one person who understands children better than any of them?"

"You're repeating yourself. Yes, they did, and they had their reasons."

"Which were ...?"

"They made some good points. Dale and Donny had just come into the family, and you know what they've been through. Your father and the others wanted to make things as normal as possible for those two boys, and that meant not dredging up all the things that had just occurred in our family. Plus Brad was a newborn, and so was Diana. Aunt Ruby had just gotten pregnant with Ava. We had all these innocent souls coming into the world, and we didn't want to poison them."

"But still ... You disagreed."

"I did." She sighs. "Burying the truth is never a good idea. There's no healing that way."

"But we didn't have to heal."

"No, you didn't. But Dale and Donny did."

"Yet here I am, a grown man, and now I have to deal with all this. Why wasn't anyone watching?"

"I can't begin to describe the torment of those times," Mom says. "It's all very intertwined. Fate seemed to bring us all together. I had a connection to the Steel family through my patient Gina Cates, Aunt Ruby's cousin. And Aunt Ruby had a connection to the family via her father, Theodore Mathias, who was—"

I hold up a hand to stop her. "I know who the hell he was."

She nods. "Right. It was so much to deal with, and once everything came full circle, when your grandfather, Bradford Steel, died in prison, we all thought it best to leave it be. To raise our children in a happy environment."

"We *all*?" I say.

"Not all. Not me."

"How could they not listen to you? You're the one who's an expert."

"They did listen. They listened very intently, while I

explained that hiding the truth from anyone is rarely a good idea. But then they decided—and we each had one vote—that it was over and we would do our best to keep the past in the past."

"Did anyone vote with you?"

"Only one."

"Which one?"

"Aunt Ruby did."

"Why do you suppose she did?"

"Because Ruby understood what it was like to have something thrust upon you when you weren't prepared. She didn't know who her father was until she was about fifteen, and when he came out of the woodwork, he tried to molest her, tried to sell her into slavery."

I say nothing. If I open my mouth, I'm surely going to hurl.

"Aunt Ruby is strong. She escaped him and lived on her own for three years as a minor, and then when she turned eighteen, she supported herself waiting tables until she could enroll in the police academy at twenty-one. Anyway, she agreed with me. If she had known who her father was from day one, she would have been prepared."

"Maybe there was no way for her to know."

"That was her point. There wasn't. But there *was* a way for you kids to know the obstacles that might flare up."

"Obstacles, Mom? Really?"

"Not the best word, I know, but in the family's defense, we all thought it was over. The three men in question were dead, and so was Wendy Madigan."

"Uncle Ryan's birth mother."

"Yes. And your cousins Ava and Gina don't know that yet, so you're going to need to keep it to yourself. It's up to Uncle Ryan and Aunt Ruby to tell them or not to tell them."

"Of course. I would never..."

"Not on purpose, you wouldn't. But you have your father's hot streak, Brock, and if you got angry enough..."

"Mom, if I got angry enough, I would still think of my cousins and what's best for them."

"All right, Brock."

I'm not sure if my mother believes me or if she just thinks it best not to press this particular point. It doesn't matter in the end.

"Dad told me what they did to you."

"Dredging up those old memories wasn't pleasant," she says.

"Maybe that's what the rest of the family wanted, then. To never have to relive all this." I shake my head. "But they were wrong. It's not fair to us now."

She nods. "Things are never better left buried, Brock. If there's something there, it will always rise to the surface eventually, and it's best if we're prepared for it."

My mom isn't just brilliant, she also has common sense. Why didn't they listen to her all those years ago? Why didn't they listen to Aunt Ruby? She was a cop, for God's sake. She and Mom are best friends. They have been forever. They were each other's maids of honor.

"Your father will figure out how to handle this current situation," Mom says. "You're going to have to trust him."

"That's just it, Mom. I hate to say this, but I *don't* trust him. He has lied by omission all these years."

"We all have," she says, "and he's still your father, Brock."

"And you're still my mother. So what? I'm a grown man, and I have to take responsibility for myself. For my own actions."

She smiles then. That big broad smile that makes her so beautiful. "You were such a strong baby," she says. "You were nearly ten pounds. You are my miracle baby, Brock. I didn't think I could have another child. I was forty-two when you were born. You fought to come into this world. I shouldn't have been able to get pregnant, but you made it happen."

I've heard this all before. Yes, I was a miracle. Yes, I was huge and I almost ripped my mom a new one. It's one of those family stories we hear at Christmas every year.

But my mom isn't done speaking.

"Even then, I knew how strong you would be. I love both of you, both of my sons, but you have a gift your brother doesn't. His personality is so much like mine. He's very in touch with his feelings, he's a hard worker, and he knows how to listen to people. But you? You're like both your father *and* me. You have all my good qualities and all his, without much of the bad. You have your father's hot streak, but you're able to control it much better than he can, and believe me, that will come in handy. Nothing can stop you, Brock. Not when you've made up your mind about something."

I can't help smiling. "I was talking to Rory about this. About how Brad was always the brain and I was the brawn."

"If we made you feel that way, I'm sorry."

"You didn't. Not really. I mean, I know we were equally loved and all that."

"You're the brawn *and* the brain, Brock. Don't ever forget that. You aced your way through every class you ever took. You're strong, you have a good heart, and you have an amazing sense of justice and morality. That's why all of this is bothering you so much."

"I suppose so," I agree, "but that's not the whole of it. It's also bothering me because I don't feel like I know my family anymore."

"I promise you that your father is the same man he always was. He's a good strong man, the love of my life, and he was a good father to you."

"I never said he wasn't."

"No, you haven't said that, but he made a choice. A choice he has to live with now. Don't turn your back on him."

"I won't."

"Good. Because there may come a time, before this is all over, that you want to. And I'm telling you now, Brock. If you do that, it will kill him."

CHAPTER THIRTY-THREE

Rory

Not pregnant

These tests actually say the words. Pregnant or not pregnant.

Not pregnant

It glares at me, and though it's in blue, it seems like it's red and flashing.

Not pregnant

Not pregnant

Not pregnant

After washing my hands, I return to Davey's office and see that she's still alone.

"So . . . good news?" she says.

"Depending on who you ask." I walk in and show her the stick.

"So it's unlikely you're pregnant. Although I would definitely test again if your period does end up being late."

"I was ovulating, Davey."

"That's no guarantee. Surely you know your biology, Rory."

I plunk into the chair across from her desk. "Yes, I know."

"Is this good news or bad news?"

"I'm not sure. But I'm a little . . . sad."

"That's natural, for someone who wants a baby."

"Yeah. This relationship is still so new, though."

"You'll have plenty of other chances to be pregnant, Rory."

"What if I can't? What if this means I'm infertile?"

Davey smiles. "You're not infertile, Rory."

"You can't tell that just by looking at me."

"Okay, you're right. Chances are you're not infertile."

"Are you a doctor?"

"A midwife, actually. Certified."

I gasp and smile. "You deliver babies! That's wonderful."

"Well, I work here now. But yes, I do offer my services to our clients who choose to use a midwife instead of an ob-gyn."

Davey's phone buzzes. "Yes?"

"Your next client is here, Davey."

"Okay, thank you. I'll be right out." She clicks the phone off. "I'm sorry, Rory, but I need to take my appointment."

I rise. "I understand. Thank you so much for your time."

"Call me anytime. And if you don't get your period on time, take another test."

"But…?"

"But… chances are it will also be negative."

I nod and leave her office.

Brock will be relieved. I guess we go back to using stupid condoms.

Then I laugh out loud as I walk to my car. Was I truly hoping to be pregnant just so we didn't have to use condoms? Have I truly gone bananas?

It's all of this. It's the stupid fight I had with Brock this morning.

It's Pat Lamone and those photos.

It's Brock and his family and everything they're going through.

It's my mother and my father and Donny and Callie and Jesse and my students and the recital and my unfulfilled opera career and ... and ...

It's certainly better not to bring a baby into this mix. Not right now anyway.

I need to think of this as a blessing.

I must get through everything else, and then, if Brock and I are still together and if we still love each other and if he still wants to marry me ...

That's a lot of *ifs*.

If Brock still wants to marry me ...

Marriage to Brock—the idea fills me with elation ... and also with fear.

Why, though? Isn't this what I wanted? A baby? A family? I always wanted a partner. And I *am* in love with the man.

The love I feel for Brock is almost ... palpable. I love him so much that it hurts, but in an exquisite way.

My eyes fill with tears.

I don't see it coming, don't even feel it coming ... but within seconds, I'm sobbing, sobbing so hard that I have to pull over onto the side of the road.

I weep and I sob and I cry, and then I flail around my car, searching for a tissue. I finally find an old one on the floor in the back seat.

One blow and it's soaked.

I cry and I cry and I cry.

All of it.

It's just all of it.

CHAPTER THIRTY-FOUR

Brock

I don't reply to my mother right away.

I may want to turn my back on my father?

How much do I still not know?

I want to ask her, but I don't want to ask her with just as much intensity. So much is already going on. Do I really want to know more?

"I'd like to ask you something," Mom says.

"I can't. I can't promise anything about my feelings for Dad."

"No, I'm not asking about that. I want to talk to you about Rory Pike."

Rory? Who I kicked out of my house earlier? I've cooled off, and I feel like shit about that. I need to call her. "Sure. What do you want to know?"

"She's a lovely young woman."

"She is."

Of course we just had a doozy of a fight.

But I don't really want to get into that.

"Her family's been through a lot," Mom says. "And she just broke up with someone. So . . ."

"What's the question, Mom?"

"I guess I want to know if you and she are both in the same place."

"You want to know if she's on the rebound," I say.

"Maybe she is and maybe she isn't. But women are different from men, Brock."

"Yeah, Mom, I know. I used to play post office."

"You know very well what I mean."

I sigh. "I asked her to marry me, okay? So that should tell you where I stand, at least."

My mom drops her mouth open. "I've never known you to be serious about any woman."

"I never was. Not until Rory. And I didn't mean to be. But we got—"

"*We?* You mean she returns your feelings?"

"Yeah. She does." Warmth surges through me at the thought, and for a moment, the argument we had no longer exists.

Except that it does.

Mom rises abruptly. "Stay here."

"Where are you going?"

"To get something. I'll be right back."

I pour myself another glass of lemon water and wait. Mom returns a few minutes later, holding a red velvet box.

Oh, geez . . .

I know what it is. It's the ring from her grandmother. Her pride and joy. The pink star sapphire.

"Mom, I—"

"Don't," she says. "Don't say you're not ready, or it's too soon, or whatever. It's yours. It's always been yours."

"What about Brad?"

"He'll get the diamonds from your father's mother. This is for you."

"But you love that ring."

"I do. It was my grandmother's, as you know, but I rarely wear it. The pink clashes with my green eyes. Everything clashes with my green eyes. But on Rory Pike? This ring will be perfect."

She's not wrong. This ring will look stunning on Rory's left hand. But our fight...

Mom slides the velvet box across the table to me. "Take it."

"I can't."

"You can. If you're serious about Rory, you should have this in your possession when you need it."

"But this morning..." I shake my head. "We had a ridiculous fight. I told her I needed to be away from her."

My mom pats my hand. "Fights happen, but they rarely signify the end of a relationship. Do you want to tell me what happened?"

"No, not really. It was stupid. I need to fix it."

"Then fix it, Brock. If you love her, you have to fix it."

I grab the ring box and rise. "I will. Thanks, Mom."

She smiles at me. "Don't turn your back on love. Not ever. And for what it's worth? I think Rory Pike is wonderful."

And with my mother's words, I know exactly what I need to do.

★ ★ ★

Rory's not answering her phone.

I've called three times, left two voicemails, and I've texted.

I decide to try one more time.

I get a breathless, "Yes?"

Her voice doesn't sound right.

"Sweetheart? It's me. What's wrong?"

Sobs then. Racking sobs.

My heart drops. She's upset, really upset, and it slices into me like a butcher knife, gutting me. "Where are you, Rory? Tell me, and I'll come right away."

"On"—gasp—"my"—gasp—"way"—gasp—"back"—gasp— "from"—gasp—"Grand Junction."

"What were you doing in Grand Junction?"

"You told me"—gasp—"to see a doctor."

"Rory, I said we'd go together."

"You told me to get out. You told me—"

Then a clatter.

Damn! Where is she? God, I hope she pulled over. If she's crying like that, she shouldn't be driving.

"Where are you? I'll come get you."

Rustling. A big sniffle. Then— "I'm fine."

"You're not fine."

"Oh, but I am. And you're fine too, Brock. Because you know what? I'm not pregnant." Big gasp. "You didn't knock me up. So yeah, we're both just fine." Sniffles again. More sobs.

My Rory. My sweetheart. Sadness sweeps through me, and I know what I have to do. I have to get on the road to Grand Junction and find her. I don't want her to be alone right now.

Together we can deal with the grief.

For it is grief that I'm feeling. Sadness and anguish and pure grief.

For a baby I didn't know I wanted … until now.

★ ★ ★

I find Rory still on the side of the road. After getting her into my truck and arranging for someone to transport her car back to her parents' house, I drive her to my place.

Once inside, I take her in my arms right in the foyer. "What can I do for you?"

"Nothing."

I cup her cheeks. Her eyes and lips are swollen and red, her nose even redder. Still, she's the most beautiful woman I've ever seen.

"Please tell me," I say. "What do you need?"

"I don't know."

"When I'm upset, I swim. It helps."

"I don't want to go swimming," she says.

"I didn't think you would want to. It was just an example. It helps me when I'm upset."

She doesn't reply.

I walk her to the kitchen. "Do you want a cup of tea? My mom likes to have a cup of tea when she's ..."

When she's what? Crying? Sobbing? Just found out she isn't pregnant?

"No tea," she says.

Rory stands in the kitchen, leaning against a counter.

I take her hand and lead her to my bedroom, though I'm not sure what we're going to do when we get there.

Maybe a shower?

She walks straight into my bathroom and turns on the faucet. I watch her as she splashes water on her face and shudders. "I know I must look like a fright."

"You're beautiful, as always."

She scoffs. "Don't bother lying to me, Brock."

"I'm not lying to you. You're beautiful to me no matter what."

"You told me to get out," she says.

"I did. I needed to cool off. I was angry."

"I know, and I'm sorry. I shouldn't have been so nonchalant about a trip to London. We weren't gallivanting about London so I could be missing my work. I wanted to be there for you. I wanted to help you. I was just..."

"I understand."

But do I? I want to. Are we in the same place? I asked her to move in with me. Hell, I said I'd marry her. My great-grandmother's ring is in the pocket of my jacket.

I don't want to bring these things up now, not when she's so distraught, but eventually I'm going to need to know where she wants this to go.

She's still standing in the doorway of the bathroom. Looking past her, I see the huge, jetted tub that I've never used. I always use the shower that's detached from the tub.

A bath. Maybe a bath would relax her.

I walk past her into the bathroom and twist the tub faucets. I test the water several times until it's at a warm temperature that I think she'll like, that I think will be soothing to her.

I don't take baths myself, though I've been known to sit in a hot tub now and then.

To use a hot tub, though, I'd have to go to my parents' house, and I don't want to do that. Rory needs to be by herself.

What do women like in their bath?

Bath salts? Bath bombs?

I don't have any of that.

Bubbles? I don't have that either. I have shower gel. Would that work?

I go to the shower, grab my bottle of Evergreen shower gel, and squirt a stream of it into the tub as it fills. Sure enough, bubbles form.

Once the tub is full, I find Rory sitting on the bed. I pull her up and undress her slowly.

"Brock..."

"Quiet," I say softly. "This isn't about sex or anything else. This is about me taking care of you."

Once her clothes are off, I try not to stare at her beautiful body. Instead, I lead her into the bathroom, make sure she has towels, and help her get into the tub.

"Just relax, sweetheart."

She closes her eyes and sighs.

I move toward the door to leave—

"No," she says.

"I want to give you some privacy."

"I don't want any privacy, Brock. I want you."

"All right. I'll stay in here with you." The only place to sit is the toilet, so I close the lid.

"No," she says. "In the tub. With me."

I guess there's a first time for everything. If my first bath must be with a beautiful woman, so be it. I'm not going to deny her anything right now. She's so upset, not just because I told her to leave earlier, but because she found out she's not pregnant.

I shed my clothes and get into the tub with her. My dick is hard, of course. It's always hard when I'm around Rory. Especially around naked Rory.

I climb in behind her and nestle her against my chest.

"Sorry," I murmur in her ear, as my cock pokes her back.

"About what?"

"About...you know."

She turns around and faces me. "We can take care of that." She climbs on top of me and sinks down onto my cock.

I groan as she settles onto me, takes me into her body.

She's in control, and she goes slowly.

Part of me wants to grab her, move her up and down on my cock quick and hard, splashing water everywhere.

But I'm here for her. I will let her take it slowly if that's what she wants. Besides, I didn't even think we were going to have sex in the bathtub.

No condom.

But I find that I don't really care.

Rory's not pregnant, so Rory could become pregnant.

And I don't care.

I'm going to take life as it comes.

But she stops. She rises, gets out of the tub, and pulls a towel around her wet body.

"Sweetheart?"

"No condom," she says.

"It's okay, Rory."

"No, it's not okay, Brock. It's not okay until we discuss this. Until we—the two of us together—decide where we're going and what this thing is between us, we have to be careful."

"But you *want* a baby."

"I do want a baby. I want a baby more than I can breathe. But I don't want a baby with someone who doesn't want one."

"You know how I feel about you." I close my mouth. I want to tell her how sad her news was. How much I'm grieving a baby I didn't realize I wanted. But she's right. I'm not ready for a child, no matter how much I may want one. Still, I was ready to go without a condom. To make her happy.

"I think I do," she says. "But this is new for both of us. We don't want to bite off more than we can chew."

I can think of a few things I'd like to bite right now, and

they're all on Rory's body. My cock is still hard as a rock, and I don't want to be in this tub.

So I get out, splashing water everywhere. Yeah, I'm making a mess, but I don't care. I'm not angry exactly, except maybe I am. Rory started this. She's the one who turned around and climbed on top of me.

Now she's sitting, still wrapped in a towel, on the edge of my bed.

God, I'm trying. I'm trying to do what she needs here. I've got a rock-hard cock and a woman who spent the afternoon crying in her car on the side of the road.

I wrap a towel around my waist and join her on the bed. "I'm not a mind reader. You're going to have to talk to me, Rory."

"I don't know how to say what I need to say," she says.

"This is me. The man who loves you. Say whatever you want to say."

"I ... I really wanted to be pregnant."

"I know you did."

"Part of me wants to try again now. To get pregnant right away. But ..."

"But what? You're the one who got off me because I wasn't wearing a condom."

"I know. Because as much as I want a baby, I don't want to force you into anything."

"You're not forcing me into anything. And you're right, I don't want a baby. Not now. But I do want one in the future. I want one with *you*, Rory."

CHAPTER THIRTY-FIVE

Rory

A surge of warmth spears through me. He *does* want a baby with me. He just doesn't want it now.

I stroke my abdomen through the towel.

I guess I really thought you were in there. A part of me really thought I'd meet you in nine months.

"Rory," Brock says, "I love you so fucking much. But you've got to help me out here. Where am I going wrong?"

"I love you too," I say, "and where you're going wrong is nothing that either one of us can control. I'm twenty-eight, and I want a baby. You're twenty-four, and you want to wait."

"Rory, sweetheart, this is not an insurmountable problem. We both want the same things. It's only our timing that's a little off."

"Timing is everything, Brock."

"That's ridiculous, sweetheart. What about compromise?"

I don't reply, partly because he called me ridiculous, and partly because I want my way, which I know is childish and— dare I say it?—ridiculous, just as he said.

"Rory, you understand compromise. I know you do."

He's not wrong. I understand compromise better than the average person. When you have your dreams torn out from under you and the best you can do is teach music to the students in your town, you know compromise.

You also know settling because that's what compromise is a euphemism for.

Why should I settle now? I had to settle on my career. I had no choice. New York didn't want me. They didn't care that I was the most beautiful woman in Snow Creek. They didn't care that I was the most talented woman in Snow Creek. I was never more than Colorado good.

I don't want to settle anymore.

I don't have to wait to have a baby.

I can have one now.

I just can't have one with Brock.

Damn.

Damn it all to hell. I had to go and fall in love with Brock Steel, who doesn't want a baby.

Correction—he doesn't want a baby *now*.

But he does want a baby in the future, and he wants that baby with me.

Compromise.

Maybe it's not like settling.

Maybe it's like . . .

"Are you going to say anything?" Brock asks.

"Yeah, I am. Give me just a minute."

My mind races. He doesn't want a baby now. But he did ask me to marry him. I'm not ready to marry a man I've been with for less than a month. But my God, I'm ready for a baby. For the pitter-patter of little feet.

But moving in . . . That's something I could do. It's still too soon for marriage, but we could test the waters. See if we're compatible. Get our dogs together and explore our parenting techniques.

Damn. I just compared Sammy and Zach to a baby.

I've gone completely bonkers.

"Let's do it," I say. "Let's live together."

A smile splits his face. "You mean it?"

"I do if you do."

"I do, sweetheart. Sometimes I can't even believe how much I do."

"But there's one thing I want..."

"Anything. You name it."

"We need to *talk* about a baby, Brock. If this is forever love, I don't want to wait. I don't want to be having babies in my late thirties."

He kisses my cheek. "We can talk about babies all you want." He kisses my lips. "And we can practice a lot too."

"You mean like with the dogs?"

He lets out a guffaw. "I mean practice what it takes to make one."

I can't help it. I punch his upper arm. "I'm serious. You probably don't want a kid until you're forty. That's not going to cut it with me. I'm willing to compromise, Brock, but I need you to compromise too."

"Rory, don't you know by now that I'd do anything for you?"

"Anything?" I tease.

"All you have to do is ask."

"Then give me a baby. Now."

He rolls his eyes. "You're incorrigible."

"A little," I admit.

"Tell you what," he says. "Let's practice."

I nod and reach for the drawer on his nightstand.

He grabs my hand. "No."

"We're using a condom, Brock. I won't be that woman."

"I know a little about women's physiology. I grew up on a ranch."

"I'm not sure how to tell you this, but human women are different from cows."

"Ha. You're funny, Rory. What I mean is that you're close to getting your period, so it's unlikely you'll become pregnant if we have unprotected sex."

"True, but it's no guarantee."

"Then let's take a walk on the wild side," he says, his eyes sparkling. "I want to make love to you. Just you and me with no latex separating us. I want to feel all of you, Rory, and I want you to feel all of me."

Then his mouth is on mine, and he's wrangling the towel off my body.

My face is still a swollen and red mess, but he wants me. I feel it in his kiss, in his movements. He wants me, and he wants me without the barrier of a condom.

I won't get pregnant—most likely anyway.

And part of me isn't ready to stop being sad yet.

But part of me ...

Part of me is horny as hell and wants Brock's hard dick inside me now. Make that yesterday.

I grab his cock through his towel, grasp it, and squeeze.

"God..." he groans into my mouth.

My nipples are hard and taut, and they want his lips, teeth, tongue ... But I won't be the one to break this kiss—this kiss that's like a narcotic.

A narcotic, and I'm addicted. So addicted.

And my pussy...

God, my pussy...

It wants his lips, teeth, and tongue ...

It wants his cock. His hard cock, thrusting, thrusting, thrusting ...

But I *won't* break this kiss.

I won't break—

I jerk at the sound of my phone ringing.

Brock leaves my mouth, nibbles over to my ear. "Ignore it," he whispers.

Good advice. I'll ignore it.

The ringing eventually stops.

But then it starts again.

I pull away.

"Sweetheart ..."

"I'm sorry. If it wasn't anything urgent, they wouldn't have called back right away."

I fumble for my purse, find my phone. It's Callie.

"Callie? What is it?"

"Thank God you answered. It's Dad. He's had a heart attack."

CHAPTER THIRTY-SIX

Brock

Donny and I sit in the waiting area of the hospital. Rory, Callie, and Maddie have gone into the back with Maureen to talk to the doctors. Jesse hasn't arrived yet.

"Steel!"

Donny and I both look up.

Jesse's running into the waiting room. "Where's my mother?"

"In the back with your sisters," I say. "They're talking to the doctor."

Jesse plunks down in a chair across from us. "Damn."

"Go in there," Donny says. "They need you."

"Shut the fuck up, Steel."

Donny shakes his head. "Really? You want to play the high school card? When your father is lying in the ER?"

He rises. "No. I'm not playing any card. I just need a damned minute."

I raise an eyebrow at Donny, hoping he gets the idea. Now is not the time to bring up their stupid high school football rivalry. They're eight years older than I am, and *I* feel like the mature one here.

Jesse rubs his forehead and temples, and then he stands. "Where?"

I point to the door. "They're back there somewhere."

He nods, heads to the reception area, talks to someone in scrubs, and then goes through the door.

"Unreal," Donny says. "We were just having dinner with Frank."

"I know. He's in good shape. How does something like this happen?"

"Hell if I know. He'd better not die, damn it. If he can't walk Callie down the aisle for our wedding, it will crush her. She loves her old man."

"So does Rory. He understands her in a way Maureen doesn't."

"I know. Callie's always talking about how close they are. With everything else she and Callie are going through . . . This can't happen."

I scan the room. The ER isn't crowded today, but the few people in the waiting area all look haggard and frightened. They're all waiting for news of their loved ones. I let my gaze drift to the door of the ER. A man and a woman walk in, speak to reception, and then sit down.

Another man walks in, and—

"Fuck," I say.

"What?" Donny asks.

"Is that . . . ? Seriously . . . ?"

Donny follows my gaze and then rises and walks toward reception. "Lamone, what the hell are you doing here?"

Pat Lamone is indeed here, in the freaking ER.

"I'm having cramps," Lamone says.

"You fucking son of a bitch." Donny lunges at him.

"Sir!" the receptionist yells. "What are you doing? Security!"

I pull my cousin off Lamone. "Calm down, for God's sake. You want to get arrested?"

Donny brushes off his shirt and jeans. "What are you doing here?" he says through gritted teeth.

Two security guards approach us. "What's going on?" one of them asks.

"Nothing," I say. "We're good."

"You sure about that?" The other eyes us, and he doesn't look happy.

"Yeah, fine," Pat says.

They don't look convinced, but they head over to reception and talk to the woman there.

"What are you doing here?" Donny asks again.

"None of your business."

He's right. It's not our business. But isn't it interesting that he's here while the entire Pike family is in the ER, waiting for news on their father?

"Tell me," Donny says, "or I swear to God you'll walk out of here limping."

"I think security might have something to say about that," Lamone says.

"Go sit down and cool off," I tell Donny.

"Fuck you," he says.

"For God's sake." I grab Pat's arm and lead him toward the door of the ER. "Now. Tell me. Why are you here?"

"I told you before. It's none of your business."

"How did you know?" I demand.

"How did I know what?"

"That we'd be here?"

"It may interest you to know, Steel, that my entire life doesn't revolve around the two of you. I'm here to visit someone."

HELEN HARDT

"In the ER?"

"No. In the hospital. I usually come through the ER because the parking's better."

"So you're not—"

I stop. I won't volunteer any information. Perhaps this is truly a coincidence.

"Not what?"

"Never mind." Out of the corner of my eye, I notice Rory and Callie heading back toward Donny. Shit.

"Go, then," I say to Lamone. "Get the hell out of here."

"Not that I need your permission, but I've got someone waiting for me." He walks away through the hallway and out of the ER. He doesn't seem to notice Callie and Rory.

Thank God.

I walk briskly back to the corner where Donny, Callie, and Rory are.

Rory falls into my arms.

"Hey, it's okay," I tell her.

She pulls back. "It's not okay."

I swallow. "God, please don't tell me—"

"No, no," she says. "He's not dead. But he's got some blockage. We're waiting for them to take him to the OR for a triple bypass."

Callie is crying into Donny's shoulder.

"Where are Maddie and Jesse?"

"They're still in the back with Mom. Cal and I wanted to come back out and let you and Donny know."

"What can I do for you?" I ask. "Anything."

"I don't know. It's all so surreal. I want to feel something, but I'm numb. This is my dad. My rock. The one who takes care of all of us."

245

"Did the doctor tell you about his prognosis?"

She nods. "It's pretty good. It's not an uncommon procedure. But it's open-heart surgery, Brock."

I kiss her forehead. "I know. I'm sorry, sweetheart."

"We'll be here for a while. You don't have to stay."

"Of course I'll stay. I wouldn't be anywhere else."

She leans into me. "It's okay. You've already seen me at my worst today. I don't want to put you through any more."

I pull back slightly and meet her gaze. "Hey. This is where I want to be. Exactly where I want to be."

"Are you sure? Really sure?"

"Come with me." I take her hand and lead her away from Callie and Donny so we have a bit of privacy. "What do you think it means when I say I love you? It means I'm here for you. For whatever you need, Rory. I *want* to be here."

She leans her head on my shoulder. "There's nothing you can do here."

"I can be with you."

"I know. I love you for it. But—"

"Tell you what. I'll get you a room at the Carlton. Not just for you but for Callie, your mom, everyone. You can stay here in the city, close to the hospital. I'll go to your house and pack you a bag if you want. I'll take care of your dog. I'll do whatever you need."

She cries then. Softly into my shoulder. "I didn't think I had any tears left today."

I kiss the top of her head. "It's okay."

"It's not okay, Brock. I cried buckets today over a baby that never existed. And now... Now, my father. *This* is real. *This* exists. And I wish it didn't."

"He's a strong man. There's no reason to believe he won't come out of this."

"That's just it. He's strong. In great physical shape. He eats right, and he gets lots of exercise. He hardly ever drinks. How did this even happen?"

"I don't know, sweetheart. Life just doesn't make sense sometimes."

"Oh, Brock... I'm sorry."

"For what?"

"For... I don't know. You're going through so much right now."

"Hey. My father is healthy. He's not in the hospital. It's okay to think about your own problems, Rory. It's okay."

"I don't want to be selfish. I feel like I've already been so selfish."

"You're not being selfish. Cry if you need to. Yell if you need to. I'll take you outside, and you can yell at the universe if you want to. Whatever you need, Rory. I mean it."

She sighs, choking back a sob. "I just need you, Brock. I just need you."

CHAPTER THIRTY-SEVEN

Rory

My tears dry out quickly, and I feel terrible. Terrible that I cried over a nonexistent child and now I don't have any tears left for my father.

My father, who gets me in a way my mother doesn't. My father, who truly doesn't care whether my life mate is a man or a woman.

My father, who taught me how to be strong.

My father, who taught me it's okay to change directions when things aren't going as planned.

My father … My rock …

He'll be okay. He has to be.

I have to concentrate. Pray. Send healing vibes. Stay positive.

Which means I can't think about the fact that I saw Pat Lamone with Brock when Callie and I came back out here.

I don't want to ask about it. I want to shove it into a compartment and forget about it until my father is out of the woods.

But I can't.

"Brock?" I choke out.

"Yeah, sweetheart?"

"What was Pat Lamone doing here?"

"Shit. I was hoping you hadn't seen him."

"I was hoping I hadn't either, but you just confirmed it."

"He says he's here to see someone in the hospital, and he parks at the ER because it's easier."

"So he doesn't know about Dad?"

"If he does, he didn't indicate it. He could be lying, of course."

"Yeah. He probably is."

"But Rory, why would he be here if your father's in the ER?"

"I don't know. Kick us while we're down?" I scoff.

He kisses my lips. "I don't think so. He was here to see someone."

"Who?" I ask.

"It doesn't matter who," Brock says. "You concentrate on your dad. Forget about Pat Lamone. He doesn't matter."

CHAPTER THIRTY-EIGHT

Brock

Rory opens her mouth to answer and then widens her eyes.

I follow her gaze. Jesse has come back into the waiting area, and he's talking to Donny and Callie.

"Come on." I lead Rory over to where the others are standing.

"Good, there you are," Jesse says. "They've taken Dad up to the OR. There's another place in the hospital where we can wait, and it's more comfortable."

"All right," I say. "Let's go."

"Thing is . . . It's family only," Jesse says.

"Donny's family," Callie says.

"So is Brock," Rory says.

Oh God.

"I'm sorry," Jesse says. "There's already five of us up there, and Mom thinks . . ."

"You mean *you* think," Callie says.

Rory touches Callie's arm. "Callie, it's okay. Let's just go. We can let Donny and Brock know what's going on."

"That's not—"

"Callie," Rory says, in a voice that sounds like she's talking to a child. "It'll be okay. Donny and Brock have a lot on their minds as well."

"Rory—" I begin.

"No, Brock. It's okay. Callie and I will be okay. Jesse, Maddie, and our mom are there. We'll keep you informed."

My Rory. She will be a great mother. In her way, she already is one.

I kiss Rory on her lips. "If you're sure."

"Yeah." Then she comes to my ear and whispers. "You've already seen me break down once today. I don't want you to see it again."

"Oh, sweetheart..."

"Please," she whispers.

"All right. I've got you if you need me."

"I know."

Donny gives Callie a kiss, and then the three head back.

"Now what?" I say.

"Now we wait. I guess."

"Or...we could figure out why the hell Pat Lamone is here and who he's visiting."

"Brock, you do know that hospital records are confidential."

"Yeah, I know that. I also know I've got a couple of Benjamin Franklins in my pocket."

Donny laughs. "God... Are we truly becoming our fathers?"

"No. Well, maybe. But apparently our grandfather..."

"What?"

"I've been talking to my dad, Don. Evidently our grandfather wasn't above holding a gun to a person's head to get what he wanted."

Donny's jaw drops. But almost as quickly, he recovers and says, "Now why doesn't that surprise me?"

"Yeah, why doesn't it? It surprised the hell out of me."

"Listen, Brock. I've been racking my brain for the past couple of weeks, trying to figure out how the hell all of this fits together."

"Any conclusions?"

"Only one."

"Care to share it?"

"Sure. What we have are a bunch of puzzle pieces, and none of them fit together, but they must all be related somehow, right?"

"Maybe. Hell if I know."

"Anyway, whether they're related or not, there's one thing that doesn't fit. How a fucking rancher in Colorado turned his business into a billion-dollar enterprise."

"Investments," I say. "Start-ups probably. I mean, tech was just beginning back then. He probably invested in Apple and Microsoft. Intel and HP."

"Yeah. We could easily find out by talking to Uncle Bryce. If he'll talk to us."

I nod. "Yeah. If."

"Then you see what I'm saying."

"Yeah, I see what you're saying. There's also our great-grandfather—the one who spawned this half great-uncle from whom Pat Lamone is allegedly descended."

"Honestly? I think maybe that's where we start. Great-Grandpa Steel, and then Grandpa Steel. If we can find out where they went wrong, maybe we can figure out the rest from there."

"But this was years and years ago," I say. "If there was any dirty money involved, it's been laundered and then laundered again. It's squeaky clean by now."

"True." Donny rubs his forehead. "All right. We're here now, so let's do what you said. Let's figure out why Lamone is here and who he's visiting."

"If he's even visiting anyone," I say. "He could've been lying."

"Absolutely. He absolutely could've been lying. Let's go on the assumption, for just a minute, that he's not. Maybe there is someone here."

"And if there is someone here..." My mind races. "He told me he always parks here, at the ER, because it's easier. Which means...he comes here a lot. Or he's been coming here for a while."

"And that means... If there is someone that he's visiting, assuming he's telling the truth, then it's a long-term patient."

I nod. "Which means palliative care or mental health care."

"So Lamone has someone—a relative possibly—who's either dying or mentally ill."

"Right." I gaze around the ER waiting area. "Let's go. He went this way."

CHAPTER THIRTY-NINE

Rory

I'm cold, and then hot, and then cold again—all while feeling numb. It makes no sense, but that's what I'm feeling.

Callie and I are sitting together on a small love seat across from Jesse, Maddie, and my mother.

"He'll be okay," Callie says to me.

"God willing," I reply.

"I know how close you are to him. We all are, but you and he..."

Good. She stops talking. I really can't go there right now, or I'm going to explode into tears again. I've done that enough for one day. I'm not sure I have any water left in me. In fact... I rise.

"I need something to drink. Do any of you want something?"

Mom shakes her head. "No."

"Nothing for me," Jesse says.

"Maybe a Diet Coke." From Maddie.

"All right. One Diet Coke and a water for me. Callie, come with me." I pull her out of the chair.

We walk together out of the waiting area.

"I guess we find a vending machine," Callie says.

"No, we need the cafeteria," I tell her. "You and I need to talk."

"Really, Rory? Now?"

"There's nothing we can do for Dad," I say. "I wish there were, but we won't know anything until we know."

"Well, true."

"So you and I should talk. Pat Lamone is here."

Callie stops walking and turns to face me. "What?"

"Yeah, he came in and told Brock something about visiting someone. He and Donny are probably looking into it."

"I should text Donny."

"You can if you want. Why don't you just try to relax a little in the cafeteria for a while?"

"What about Maddie's Diet Coke?"

"We'll bring it when we come back. In the meantime, if she gets too thirsty, she'll get up and find a vending machine."

"Rory, you're not acting like yourself."

"I'm not myself anymore. My father's lying on some OR table with his chest cut open and his life in the hands of a bunch of doctors who don't know him and don't care about him. And I found out today . . ."

"What?"

"I'm not pregnant, Callie."

"Is that good news or bad news?"

I sigh. "Honestly? Both. Brock wasn't ready for a baby, even if I was. But there was never a baby to begin with, so why did we worry?"

"It's okay to feel a loss," Callie says.

"What loss, though? I was never pregnant. It's not like I had a miscarriage."

We find the cafeteria and enter. The food service area is closed, but self-service is open. I grab a bottle of water from the refrigerator unit and then a bottle of Diet Coke for Maddie.

"Do you feel like eating anything?" Callie asks.

"Not even slightly."

"Neither do I, but we should. It will help the sick feeling."

"Will it though?" I ask.

"One way to find out." Callie walks up to one of the self-service shelves and grabs a couple of granola bars. "What do you want?"

"That's a loaded question, Cal."

"All right, let me bring it into context. What do you want from the shelf?"

I walk over next to her, grab a package of cupcakes. "This, I guess."

"Sugar high. Good call."

Callie grabs a Diet Coke for herself as well, and we pay for the items and find a quiet table. I open my package of cupcakes—the chocolate kind with squiggly white icing on top—and take a bite. Chocolate sawdust. Yum.

"Who do you think Lamone is here to see?" Callie asks.

"Hell if I know. At this point, Cal, I don't give a shit about him anymore. Let him try to publish my pictures. I don't give a flying fuck."

"Rory, you don't mean that."

"Don't I? With Dad up in the OR with his heart in some stranger's hands, do naked photos of me really even matter?"

"Change of trajectory," Callie says, "because we need to stay positive. Tell me something good. Tell me something that makes you happy. Anything."

"Brock. Brock makes me happy. Brock loves me and I love him."

Callie smiles. "Donny told me."

"You're not surprised?"

"A little, to be sure, but mostly just happy for you. Very happy for you."

"Thanks, Cal. I know there's not much to laugh about, but you know what's funny?"

"What?"

"You and I, the Pike sisters. We caught two of the Rake-a-teers."

Callie giggles. "That is something, isn't it?"

"Men who we didn't think would ever settle down."

"Wait... Are you saying...?"

"We're going to move in together. Brock and I."

"Oh my God! This is amazing, Rory."

"It is kind of cool."

I smile at my sister. She smiles back. And they're good smiles, radiant smiles, but they're only masks. Underneath the smiles, though we're both happy to be in love, we're both worried about Dad.

And everything else.

"Compartmentalizing," Callie says.

"What?"

"I'm compartmentalizing. Just Dad right now, Rory. Let's just focus on Dad right now. Trying to deal with everything else... It's just too much."

I nod, take another bite of my dry cupcake. Then I twist open the cap on my water and take a drink, washing down the chocolate sawdust.

Compartmentalizing.

Callie's good. She has an analytical mind, and she can file things away in mental folders and leave them for another time.

Good. Good for her.

The only problem is that I can't do it.

I have an emotional mind, and an emotional mind doesn't file things away. An emotional mind feels. All the feels. All at once.

"Okay?" Callie says.

I nod again. "Okay," I lie.

CHAPTER FORTY

Brock

"What do you think?" Donny says, as we gaze at the reception desk. "You think they like blond hair or dark hair?"

"How the heck should I know? At least it's not a dude."

"Yeah, that would complicate things."

Two women sit at reception. Older women, probably in their forties or fifties. One has some graying at her light-brown temples, and the other has her hair pulled back in a dirty-blond bun.

"I'm not sure either of us are going to have sway," I say.

"We've got to try."

"Let's go together. We'll turn on as much charm as we can and hope that one of them bites."

Donny and I advance to the reception station, both turning on our most dazzling smiles.

Gray Temples looks up, returns my smile—or Donny's smile. I can't tell which one. "May I help you gentlemen?"

"Yes, you can," Donny says. "A friend of ours is here visiting someone, and we'd like to pay our respects as well."

"Of course. What is the name of the patient?"

"Lamone," Donny says.

Gray Temples taps on her computer. "I don't see a Lamone . . . Crap. My computer froze up. Genevieve, can you check?"

"Sure. What was the name again?" Blond Bun—Genevieve, apparently—lifts her eyebrows at me.

I smile, giving her a look at my pearly whites and jawline.

No reaction.

Great.

"Lamone," I say, making my voice as low and sexy as I can muster.

In fact, I sound kind of creepy.

"Sure. Let me take a look." Genevieve taps.

"What's your name?" Donny asks Gray Temples.

"Mercy. What's yours?"

I freeze. Should we tell them who we are?

"Steel," Donny says. "Donovan Steel."

I guess we can tell them who we are.

"Donny Steel? Of *the* Steels?" Mercy gushes.

"Yes, that's me. This is my cousin Brock Steel."

I switch my attention from Genevieve to Mercy. "It's lovely to meet you, Mercy."

"The pleasure is mine. Genevieve, did you find the patient?"

"I'm sorry, but there's no patient with the last name of Lamone at the hospital."

"Oh my," Donny says. "We just assumed that was the last name. It's the last name of our friend. Pat Lamone. He told us he was going to be here today to visit his sick relative, and we wanted to be here to show him support."

"How nice of you," Mercy says. "Genevieve, isn't that nice?"

"Yeah. Nice." Genevieve doesn't crack a smile.

So . . . Mercy it is.

"Now what are we going to do?" I say. "We promised him we'd be here."

Genevieve meets my gaze with cold eyes. "Why don't you text him? He'll tell you what room it is."

"Now why didn't I think of that?" I dazzle her again, again with no results. I pull out my phone. "Damn, my phone is dead."

"I left mine in the car," Donny says.

"Isn't that convenient," Genevieve says dryly.

"Well, we can help you," Mercy says. "The Steel Foundation gives us a large grant every year."

"And we're happy to do it," I say.

"Yes, my father was treated at this hospital not long ago," Donny adds.

Mercy taps on her computer. "It looks like Mr. Lamone is visiting the patient in room 3520." She frowns. "That's our mental health wing."

"I know," I say, feigning no surprise at all. "He's beside himself about this."

"That's why we're here to support him," Donny agrees. "He's been running himself ragged."

"The two of you are good friends." Mercy smiles.

"That's confidential information," Genevieve says.

"Genevieve, this is the Steel family. They fund this hospital."

Genevieve rolls her eyes. "Whatever. I'm not going down with you."

"No one is going down," I say. "We promise. We'll tell Pat how great you've been. And our family. All of our family."

"How nice of you," Mercy says. "Get on up there and be with your friend."

"Thank you." Donny dazzles once more.

"Yes, we won't forget this." My turn to dazzle.

Then we turn and head for the elevators. Once we get to

the elevators, Donny starts laughing.

"Yeah, it's kind of funny, except that we just made that poor woman breach her ethics."

"I know. And damn, I hate breaching ethics. But our name. Our fucking name. I've seen it time and again. This name can work miracles. And it makes me wonder, again and again. Why? How the hell did we get here? We sure as hell did *not* get here raising beef."

"Well ... There are apples and peaches. Wine."

"Yes, I know. And you're right, our esteemed grandfather probably got into tech when it was new and innovative. Still ... there's something we're not seeing." He punches the elevator button.

"I know." I sigh. "What the hell could it be?"

"We're going to have to find out," Donny says, "and I have the sinking feeling that once we do? We're going to wish we never started looking."

A feeling of impending doom washes over me.

"This is wrong," I say. "So wrong."

"It's all kinds of wrong, dude."

"You're engaged. You're settling down with the woman of your dreams. Everything should be going great for you. You're the city attorney of Snow Creek. And me? Damn. I'm in love. For the first time in my life, I'm in love with the most beautiful woman in the freaking town. She loves me back, Don. She fucking loves me back. It's amazing, the feeling. The overwhelming elation of being in love, but it's tainted. Tainted by this whole fucking mess."

The elevator dings, and the door opens.

Donny meets my gaze. "I suppose we don't have to do this."

I walk into the elevator, turn, and regard him. "We have to do this, cuz. We absolutely have to."

He follows me into the elevator, and the doors close. Donny hits the button for the third floor.

"You're right. We have to do this. We have to fucking do this."

The elevator jolts but then ascends slowly.

"Man, we need better elevators here. What if someone has to get to the OR quickly?"

"These aren't the OR elevators," Donny says.

"Yeah. Of course not."

My mind is awash with crap. I'm not sure what I'm even thinking at this moment.

Finally, we make it to the third floor.

"What do we do when we get there?" I ask as we step off the elevator.

"We don't have to do anything. All we need to do is get the name of the person he's visiting. We can figure out why later."

"Right."

"What was the room number again?" Donny asks.

"3520." I check the sign on the wall. "We go this way," I say, heading right.

Donnie and I walk down the hallway, smile at the nurses sitting at the station.

One of them smiles back, and the others don't look up from what they're doing.

"Security here is great," I say with sarcasm.

"That's in our favor for now. We can make sure they increase security later. When we no longer need this."

"Yeah, right."

3504, 3506, 3508 . . .

FLARE

We walk, slowly, past all the rooms.

3512, 3514, 3516 …

One more room to go, and then we'll hit 3520, near the end of the hallway.

I stop.

Donny turns, meets my gaze. "You okay?"

"Yeah. I'm fine. It's just…"

"I know. We're about to find out one more fact. One more thing that won't make any sense. Believe me, I get it."

"What if it does make sense? What if there's some family member—one of our family members—in there, completely neurotic or psychotic or another kind of mess?"

"Then we'll deal with it. We already know we have mental illness in the family."

"Except…" Dare I say what I'm thinking?

"I know." Donny nods. "Dale and I aren't related to the rest of you by blood. But we also have a father who sold us out for five grand. Maybe he wasn't technically insane, but he wasn't a good man."

"I hate thinking of it in those terms. You're my cousin, man. Blood doesn't matter to me."

"Doesn't matter to me either, but I get what you're saying. Whatever bad genes the Steel family carries, Dale and I don't have them."

"Neither does Henry," I say.

"Yeah, but Henry comes straight from Uncle Bryce, and we know all about *his* father. If that wasn't a psychopath, then what is?"

He's right, of course.

No discrimination here. We are all equally fucked.

"Here we are," I say. "Room 3520."

The door is closed, and although there is a window looking from the hallway into the room, the blinds are closed as well.

"He's in there," Donny says.

"He is."

The name on the door says "Smith."

"So the relative's name is Smith," I say.

"Yeah," Donny says, "and I've got some swampland in Florida I'd like to sell you."

"What do we do now?"

A nurse walks briskly by then. "Can I help you gentlemen?"

"We're just waiting for our friend. Visiting Mr. Smith."

"You mean Mrs. Smith."

"Right, of course." I flash my smile.

"Would you like to go in? I can check with him for you."

"Oh no, we'll just wait for him at the end of the hall. We don't want to interrupt his visit."

I follow Donny to the end of the hallway, where there's a small sitting area. We each take a seat in uncomfortable olive-green chairs.

"Now what?" I ask.

"We wait for him to come out of the room. Or we wait to get a text from Rory or Callie. Whichever comes first."

"But it's getting late. It's almost seven p.m. Aren't visiting hours over?"

"Hell if I know," he says.

"Okay, then," I say. "I guess we wait."

CHAPTER FORTY-ONE

Rory

Callie and I head back up to the waiting area, and I hand Maddie her Diet Coke.

"Took you long enough," Maddie says.

"Sorry," I say, "Callie and I needed to ... I don't know."

"It's all right, Rory," Mom says. "We all deal in our own way."

Callie and I sit down with Mom, Jesse, and Maddie.

"Any news?" Callie asks.

"Nothing in a while," Mom says. "But—" She jerks as a woman in scrubs comes out and heads straight toward us.

I swallow, but it doesn't dislodge the lump in my throat.

"Mrs. Pike," the woman says.

"Yes?" Mom doesn't stand.

But Jesse does. "I'm Jesse Pike, and you are?"

"I'm Dr. Alonso, the resident on your father's case. The attending cardio thoracic surgeon sent me out with an update. Your father has been moved onto the heart-lung machine now."

"And what does that mean exactly?" Jesse asks.

"It's actually called a cardiopulmonary bypass machine," Dr. Alonso says. "It works to provide blood and oxygen to the body when the heart is stopped for a surgical procedure."

"In English please," Jesse says again.

"I'm sorry, let me try to explain better. I know you're all upset and worried. Your father has significant blockage in his coronary arteries, so the surgeon needs to redirect the blood to the heart—in other words, bypass."

"We understand," Callie says.

"In order to do the procedure, the heart has to stop while the surgeon is making those bypasses."

My mother goes white. "His heart is *stopped*?"

"Yes, but it's no cause for concern, ma'am. The heart-lung machine is directing blood and oxygen to his body while his heart is stopped."

"Oh, God," Mom says. "I just can't deal with this."

"Ma'am, your husband is doing very well."

"You just said his heart is stopped."

"Yes, so we can make the repairs. So we can redirect the blood flow."

I stand then. "Doctor, you're talking to a scared wife and scared children. Is our father okay?"

"Well, your father is on the operating table, and he's on the cardiopulmonary bypass machine. But the surgery is going well."

I sigh. "I understand. That's all we're going to get out of you."

"She can't say anything else," Callie says. "No doctor can guarantee a successful outcome. That would be a malpractice nightmare."

"This is not bad news," Dr. Alonso says.

I nod. "Thank you, Doctor." I sit back down.

"I need to get back to the OR. I'll update you again as soon as I can." Dr. Alonso leaves.

"She was just a breath of fresh air, wasn't she?" Jesse says dryly.

"She needs a few lessons in bedside manner," I agree.

"She's a resident," Callie says. "Probably first or second year. She doesn't know any better."

"Well, she should," I say. "Especially when a person's husband and a person's father has his chest open on a table."

"Rory…"

"I mean it, Callie. Maybe you can compartmentalize, but I can't. I'm worried about this and about so many other things. The least that woman could've done is come out here and smile."

"I agree," Jesse says. "She was awful."

"I agree too." From Maddie. "I don't want her touching our father."

"You guys," Callie says, "she's probably very qualified. I mean, come on. Do you want the most qualified doctor? Or do you want the doctor who's the nicest?"

Classic Callie.

"Fine," Jesse says. "She'd better be damned good."

I say nothing.

I sit in my chair, watch my sister drink her lukewarm Diet Coke, and try not to let my mind wander.

Which is a surefire recipe for it to do just that.

It wanders first, of course, to my father—who I love, who understands me more than anyone—lying on a table with his chest wide open and his heart stopped.

It wanders to Brock, who I also love, and who's probably still out in the ER waiting area. Or maybe he and Donny left, or maybe—

My mind wanders then to Pat Lamone, who's somewhere in this hospital. Brock and Donny are probably investigating, and—

My mind wanders to the trouble they could be getting into. I don't trust Pat Lamone, and the hospital has security.

Next my mind wanders to everything else going on with my family and with Brock's family. It's all too much.

And then it wanders to where I was only hours ago, on the side of the road, sobbing my heart out over a baby that never even existed.

That seems so ridiculous now when my father's life is at stake.

It was always ridiculous, with everything else that's going on.

I close my eyes, try to concentrate. My family's not religious, but I feel like I should be praying or asking the universe to protect my father.

I need him so much. Someone in the room who understands me.

Thank you. Thank you for Brock. Thank you for everything you've given me in this life.

But you've taken a lot from us too, so please . . . Please don't take away my father.

CHAPTER FORTY-TWO

Brock

Half an hour elapses.

I quickly text Rory to see how her dad is doing. She texts back that he's on the heart-lung machine, and the doctor says everything is going well.

Good.

Another half hour elapses. I text Rory again. No additional news.

She doesn't ask where I am, and I don't tell her. She needs to concentrate on her father right now.

One more half hour, and just as I'm about to text Rory to check in—

Pat Lamone walks out of the room. He doesn't look toward this end of the hallway where Brock and I are sitting. He walks the other way, toward the elevators.

He stops at the nurses' station, stands there for a bit.

"Who is in that room?" Donny whispers to me.

"I don't know. But we're going to find out."

Donny and I keep our heads down, only looking up when necessary, to see if Pat is still at the nurses' station. Finally, we look up and he's gone.

"It's now or never," Donny says.

"This is the mental health wing," I say. "We can't just walk into that room. Whoever is in there might freak out."

"You got a better idea?"

I sigh. "No, I don't."

"We'll go in really quick, see who it is, and leave."

I nod. "Okay."

We both rise, head toward room 3520.

The nurses are busy. I reach my hand out to the door and twist the knob. Donny and I enter swiftly and quietly, shutting the door behind us.

The person in the bed appears to be asleep, thank God. I place a finger over my lips, indicating to Donny to be quiet, and I slowly approach the bed.

A woman. Her face is aged, her hair silver.

If I had to guess, I'd say she's in her late seventies, possibly early eighties. But who knows? Mental illness can affect people strangely.

Donny looks around while I pull out my phone and snap a picture of the person on the bed.

"We have to get out of here," I say to Donny.

"Yes. We do."

We walk toward the door, open it, and—

"What the hell do you think you're doing in there?" A uniformed security guard stands next to the door.

"Honest mistake," I say.

"Yes," Donny says. He holds out his hand. "I'm Donovan Steel."

"Do I look like I care who you are?" the guard says.

"I'm Brock Steel." I hold out my hand as well. "From the Steel family. Our family funds this hospital."

"And you think that gives you the right to go skulking around in people's rooms?"

"As my cousin said"—I move my hand back down to my side, since he clearly has no intention of shaking it—"it was an honest mistake. My mother, Dr. Melanie Carmichael Steel, is a retired psychiatrist. She used to have privileges here. Our foundation is thinking about offering to expand the mental health wing of this hospital, so my cousin and I were here looking around."

"At this hour?"

"A friend of ours is in surgery having a triple bypass," Donny says. "My future father-in-law, actually. Since Brock and I were here, we figured why not have a look?"

Finally, the guard seems to soften. "I'm sorry to hear about your future father-in-law. Is his prognosis good?"

"For now," Donny says.

"What exactly were you doing in a patient's room, though?" the guard asks.

"Like I said, honest mistake," Donny says. "We thought we heard screaming, but it must've been coming from somewhere else."

"You thought you heard screaming coming from this room?"

"Yes," I back Donny up. "But the patient in that room is asleep, so we were mistaken."

"We'll be going," Donny says.

I smile. "Yes. We didn't mean to cause any trouble. We just thought that because we were here, we could have a look around. Maybe give some information to my mother and the rest of the foundation."

The security guard doesn't look convinced, but he finally nods. "All right. Looks like you weren't up to anything nefarious. Sorry to bother you, but the next time you decide to look around the hospital, let the nurses' station know."

"Absolutely," Donny says. "We're really sorry for neglecting to take that step. It's just... We're very worried about my future father-in-law. We weren't thinking clearly."

"I understand," the guard says and turns, but then he turns back toward us. "Your future father-in-law's name is?"

"Frank Pike," Donny says.

"Thank you so much," I say, holding my hand out again.

This time the guard takes it. "No harm done."

Donny shakes his hand as well, and then we head to the elevator.

Once on the elevator, I heave out a sigh. "That was freaking close."

"Yeah. Too close for comfort. I can't believe you took a picture."

I absently slide my hand over my pocket where my phone is. "Yeah, that did take some balls. But you know me. Balls of steel."

"Ha," Donny says, not even close to laughing.

"I'm not sure it'll do us any good, but we know this much at least. Whoever this person is, I'd bet her name is not Mrs. Smith."

"Probably not."

"If Lamone is a relative of mine, this woman might be a relative as well. And maybe that's why he's coming after the Steel money."

"You think? He's trying to save his granny? Or his mother? Whoever the hell it is?"

"Maybe. Though why is he messing with Rory and Callie? They don't have any money."

"Except they do. Our money. I'm pretty sure Lamone got

wind of the fact that Callie and I are together. And now you and Rory."

I nod. "Right. But it can't be all for the woman in that room. Pat Lamone is a lot of things, but altruistic is not one of them. I just don't believe it."

"Neither do I, cuz," Donny says. "Neither do I."

My phone buzzes, and I pull it out of my pocket.

"It's a text from Rory. Frank is off the bypass machine. Doing well."

Donny regards his own phone. "Just got the same from Callie. I guess I should turn my ringer back on."

"Yeah, I don't know what I was thinking. I should've turned it off while we were up there."

"No harm done now. We're going to have to be more careful. We weren't really thinking."

"No," I agree. "We weren't."

"We need to be thinking about Rory and Callie right now. We can take them to a late dinner. Maybe get their minds off Frank for a bit."

"I agree."

I text Rory.

> *Donny and I want to take you two to dinner.*

> *Not until he's out of surgery. But it shouldn't be long.*

> *I understand.*

We end up back in the ER waiting room where we began.

"I'm going to book a suite at the Carlton," Donny says.

"Good idea. There's five of them, so maybe two suites?"

"Yeah. Two. Jesse and his mom can stay together, and the three girls."

"Sounds good. I'll see if I can help Rory with canceling her students or whatever."

"Good idea. I'll let Callie know she doesn't need to come into the office until she feels she can."

"And what after that?"

"I guess we wait."

CHAPTER FORTY-THREE

Rory

An hour later, Dad is out of surgery. He's in the ICU, and only one person can be in there with him, so of course it's Mom.

Callie and I go back to the ER waiting room to let Donny and Brock know what's going on.

I melt into Brock's arms. I have no more tears left in me.

"It's okay, sweetheart," he whispers.

I shake my head into his chest. "It's so not okay. But he's alive, and his prognosis is good."

"Do you feel like dinner?"

"Do you mind if we invite Jesse and Maddie along?" I ask.

"If it's okay with Donny, it's okay with me."

★ ★ ★

After a rather awkward dinner—Donny and Jesse together is a recipe for awkward—Brock and Donny take us to the Carlton, where they've reserved suites.

Jesse is rigid. It's clear he doesn't want to be beholden to the Steels.

I leave that to Callie and Donny to deal with.

In the meantime, Brock takes Maddie and me to the suite he's reserved for us. As much as I want Brock to stay, I know he has to get back to the ranch.

"What else do you ladies need?" he asks Maddie and me. "I'll have it delivered to you."

"You've done plenty," I say.

"Yeah," Maddie says. "We can get a toothbrush and toothpaste from housekeeping. And we'll just sleep in our underwear."

"Listen," Brock says. "We're going to be family when Callie and Donny get married. We want to do whatever we can to make this easier on all of you. So here's what I'm going to do. I'm going to open up an account"—he fiddles with his phone—"on Instacart for you, and I want you to order whatever you need. Got it?"

"All right." I nod. "Thank you, Brock."

He cups my cheek then, presses his lips over mine. "Anything you need. And I mean anything."

Maddie goes into the other room to give us some privacy, and I wrap my arms around Brock's neck and kiss him. A deep, loving kiss.

"I wish you could stay," I say.

"Me too, but you need your family right now, and your family needs you."

I nod and kiss his lips once more. "I love you."

"I love you too, sweetheart. I'll text you when I'm home. Okay?"

"Okay."

"You text or call if you need anything. You hear me? Anything. Let me know how your dad is doing."

"Thank you."

And then Brock leaves.

Maddie returns. "Daddy's going to be okay, right?"

"Yes, we're going to think positive. Dad is going to be okay."

Maddie sighs. "You and Callie are so lucky."

"Why do you say that?"

"You each have a Steel."

"I suppose so."

"I wish I had a Steel."

"You're twenty-one years old, Mads. You're way too young to be thinking about settling down."

"I know. I've been crushing on Dragon for so long."

"Dragon? Please. He's Jesse's age, for one. That's like what—eleven years older than you are?"

"Yeah, I'm kind of getting over him. A week ago at Murphy's, Dave Simpson was paying a lot of attention to me, and he's about the prettiest Steel there is."

"So now you're into pretty boys? After Dragon, the dark prince?"

"I don't know." She sighs. "I just want to think of something other than how worried I am about Daddy."

"I hear that."

"So tell me. Tell me about you and Brock. I heard you tell him you love him."

"It's still new, Mads."

"You can still tell me. I'm twenty-one. Legal and everything. You and Callie have always been so close, only two years apart, and you tell each other everything. I've always kind of felt left out."

"We don't mean to leave you out."

"I know, but I can't help the way I feel. It's like I don't belong. And then, at school, with the awesome foursome, I'm always the odd man out. Like I don't belong again."

I regard my youngest sister. Maddie is beautiful. In truth, she resembles me more than Callie does. People always say I look the most like Mom, but in truth, Maddie does, with hair a shade lighter than mine and eyes a shade darker. I was seven when she came along, and she was my baby. Maddie's birth is what made me want to be a mother myself. I've wanted it for so long, and I've wanted it because of my littlest sister. I had no idea she felt so left out with her sisters and her friends.

"They're your best friends," I tell her, "and we're your sisters. We all love you."

Maddie sighs. "I know. I love you too, and I love my friends. But they're the Steels. And I'm the lowly Pike."

Her words piss me off. "Hey, first, get rid of the word *lowly*. That is no way to be thinking of yourself."

"It's not what I think of myself. Not really. But I hang out with the awesome foursome, who have all the money they could ever want. In the meantime, I'm wearing Callie's hand-me-downs."

I laugh. "You haven't worn hand-me-downs since you were in middle school. We've all been the same size since then."

"I know. It's a metaphor."

"I get what you mean, Mads, but think about everything we *do* have."

"Like what? Our dad's in the ICU after a heart attack. A fire destroyed our livelihood. I'm lucky I can stay in freaking school. Callie had to give up law school."

"Except she's not giving up law school."

"Well, not now. That's only because she snagged a Steel as a fiancé."

"Still, things worked out for her. And for you. You didn't have to leave college in your last year. Everything's going to be fine, Maddie."

Maybe if I say it to Maddie, I'll begin to believe it myself.

Maddie, of course, doesn't know what the Steels are dealing with right now. She also doesn't know what Callie and I are dealing with right now. I can't tell her, and even if I could, I wouldn't. I don't want to further shatter her world when she already thinks it's shattered the way it is.

So I do the only thing I can do—try to take her mind off it.

"So tell me," I say, "about you and Dave Simpson."

Maddie blushes a little, though her cheeks are already red from crying about Dad. "He just showed me a few pointers for pool. He's easily one of the best-looking Steels, though."

She's not wrong. Dave Simpson is gorgeous. He looks a lot like his mother, Marjorie Steel Simpson, but he has the blue eyes of his father, Bryce Simpson. Mixed with Marjorie's dark hair and tan skin, it's an intoxicating combination. Plus his features are fine and sculpted. Definite cover boy material.

But I've never been one for a pretty boy. If I'm attracted to pretty, it's in a woman, not a man.

In men? I like the rugged masculine type.

I like Brock Steel.

"Dave is twenty-four, I think," I say. "I'm pretty sure he and Brock are the exact same age."

"Right. They're a year younger than Diana," Maddie says. "Anyway, he's dreamy, and . . . I like him a lot, but oh, Rory . . . How can I even think about liking a guy when my father . . . ?"

Okay, so talking about Dave Simpson isn't going to help.

"Do you want to talk about Dad?" I ask.

"No, not really."

"We don't have to talk at all, Maddie. I noticed you didn't eat hardly any of your dinner."

"How could I?"

I simply nod. Callie and I didn't eat much for dinner

either, and I feel pretty guilty over the fact that Donny and Brock sprang for an expensive dinner for us, and we picked at it.

Jesse, being a guy, of course, scarfed his down. Men can always eat.

"I think I just want to try to go to bed," Maddie says.

"Okay. Go ahead and take the single bedroom. Callie and I can share the other."

"Are you sure?"

"Of course. Callie and I have been sharing a room most of our lives. Joined by a bathroom, I mean."

"Thanks, Rory. I think I'll take a shower."

"Okay. I'll put in an order on that Instacart Brock set up for us, and hopefully it'll be here soon. Underwear, toiletries. Anything special you want?"

"No thanks," Maddie says. "Your boyfriend's the best."

And I nod. Yes, my boyfriend is the best.

The very best.

CHAPTER FORTY-FOUR

Brock

I wake at five a.m., and after taking care of Sammy, downing two cups of coffee and a piece of day-old bread from Ava's bakery, I head over to the Pike house.

I got the combination to their front door from Rory. She asked me to take care of Zach and Dusty. I key in the code and enter.

The dogs bark at first, but they settle down when I call them by name. "It's okay, guys. It's okay." I let them out the back way to do their business, and then I look through the kitchen to find the dog food.

Their water bowl is bone dry. Poor pups.

I find the bag of kibble in the pantry and fill the bowls. Then I refill their water.

"Come on in, guys," I yell through the door.

Once in, they both lap up water for what seems like five minutes but is only a few seconds, and then they eat their breakfast. I'm on dog-sitting duty until the Pikes get home, and who knows when that will be?

Frank will probably be in the hospital for five days at least, but once he's out of the ICU, I imagine Rory and Callie will come home. Only Maureen will stay at that point.

Once the dogs are done with their food, I let them out again.

Rory asked me to stay awhile, to keep them company, so I make myself comfortable in the kitchen. I need more coffee, so I brew a pot, and then I look in the refrigerator. There are a couple of eggs and some bacon, so I make myself a second breakfast.

The day-old bread was good, but I need some protein.

I'll restock their refrigerator. In fact... I have a wonderful idea.

I'm going to have their house completely cleaned and all their cupboards restocked.

For Rory.

I want to do this for Rory and her family.

A smile splits my face. Just making Rory happy has that effect on me.

Once the coffee is done and I finish my breakfast, I sit on their deck and watch the dogs play. I pull my phone out to see if anyone has checked in about Frank, and when I see that they haven't, I pull up the picture that I took last night.

The elderly woman in the mental health wing at the hospital.

The woman Pat Lamone was there to see.

Who is she?

One person might know.

I call my father and hope he's in the office and not out on the ranch.

"Brock," he says.

"Good morning, Dad. I'm going to be late getting in today. I'm over at the Pikes'."

"Oh?"

"Yeah. Have you heard? Frank had a heart attack last night."

"Oh God. Is he...?"

"He's okay. He had a triple bypass, and he's in the ICU. All four of the kids are in the city at the Carlton, so I'm taking care of their dogs."

"Of course. Whatever they need," Dad says.

"Yeah, I'm working on that. In the meantime, though, Donny and I saw Pat Lamone at the hospital last night."

"What was he doing there?"

"That's what I'm trying to figure out. Apparently, there's an elderly woman in the mental health wing. He was visiting her."

"Who is she?"

"The name plate says Smith, but I'm pretty sure that's an alias."

"Most likely. His mother maybe? A grandmother?"

"I don't know. I was hoping you might have some ideas."

"I have the names of his mother and father," Dad says. "And they're not Smith."

"Yeah, I figured. I took a photo of the woman. I'm going to forward it to you now."

"You took a photo of a mentally ill woman in the hospital?"

"Yeah, not my best look. I get it. Don't tell Mom."

"I hate keeping things from your mother, but you're right. She won't understand that."

"I know. It's unlikely the photo will do us any good anyway, but if you have even a slight recognition..." I hit send. "Should be coming through soon."

"Got it." Pause. "Doesn't ring a bell. What do you think, late sixties? Early seventies?"

"I was thinking eighties. It's hard to tell. People age so differently. I mean, Mom is sixty-five and she looks amazing."

"Yeah, but your mom is not strapped down to a bed in a mental health facility."

I widen my eyes. "She's strapped down?"

"Yeah, didn't you notice?"

I pull the photo back up. Sure enough, her wrists are secured with white bindings. I didn't notice because the white is the same color as her gown and the sheet, and I wasn't looking at her wrists. I was concentrating on her face.

"I didn't notice. Donny and I were just trying to get out of there as quickly as we could."

"I can't believe you were able to get in."

"Yeah, we had some issues with the security guard. But we got out of it, dropped the name."

"Yeah, that's usually all it takes."

"So can you look into this? See if you can figure out who the hell she is?"

"Yeah, I will. But honestly, Brock? Pat Lamone and his claim to the Steel fortune is the least of our problems right now."

"I know that, Dad."

"It's more important that we find out who's been hijacking our property and moving... cargo."

"Cargo, Dad? Really?"

"It's just an easier word to say, son."

"I suppose. But we can't let ourselves get easy with this, Dad. It's a harsh reality. I don't want to get comfortable with it."

"This has nothing to do with getting comfortable, Brock. You know that."

"Yeah, I know that."

"All I can tell you is this. I understand that Pat Lamone

means more to you because of what's going on with you and Rory. I get that, and I understand. But we really need to find out who left that information for Donny. Someone wanted us to find out what's going on on our property. Whoever it is, we have to consider them a friend at this point."

"Do we?" I ask. "That's pushing it, in my opinion."

"In mine, as well. But whoever has hijacked our land for these horrific purposes is the enemy for sure. Someone wants us to know, and you know what that means. The enemy of my enemy is my friend."

"Maybe, Dad. But if they're a true friend, why didn't they just come to us? Why sneak around and leave shit in Donny's bathroom? Who the hell does that?"

"Someone who doesn't want to—or can't—reveal themselves to us. Which means—"

"They're probably working with the enemy," I finish for him.

"Exactly."

My mind races. "There's got to be a connection, Dad. That ring. That ring that belonged to your mother. With the initials LW on it. That's got to be some kind of clue, right?"

"Yes, but I haven't been able to figure out what. We have to look deeper, Brock. Whoever wanted us to have that information, those GPS coordinates, also left the ring. But why? I've been racking my brain to try to figure this out, and I haven't yet. But I will, and you're going to help me."

"I will. Donny and Dale will too. But do we keep it among the four of us for now?"

"I'm going to bring Talon in. After all, he was shot, and at this point I think we have to assume that his shooting is related to the rest of this."

"Is that a reasonable assumption?" I ask.

"Reasonable? Hell, I don't even know what reasonable is anymore. But my brother gets shot, in a place where he almost never goes? And the next thing you know, all this other shit comes to light? The puzzle pieces have to fit together somehow, Brock."

"But there's more, Dad. The stuff Brendan Murphy uncovered under his floorboards."

"I'm not completely convinced that is related," Dad says. "But it is something else we need to figure out."

"Hell, yeah, we need to figure it out. Because whatever else was left under those floorboards is no longer there after Murphy's place got trashed."

"I know, son. I know."

"We need to go back, Dad. Tonight. Rory's going to be involved with her father for a few days. That gives me the chance to deal with some of this stuff. We'll check out Doc Sheraton's land. Talk to him about the guard dogs. We have to figure out who's behind this. We *have to*."

"I agree with you. And we will."

"Except..."

Zach and Dusty waggle up to the deck to have their ears scratched. I oblige, stroking their soft heads.

"I have to take care of the Pikes' dogs."

"We can get someone else to take care the Pikes' dogs. What about your brother? Or Dave or Henry?"

"Yeah, I suppose Brad could do it. Someone just needs to come over here in the morning, feed them, and let them out, and then do the same thing in the evening."

"Perfect. Call your brother and get that all arranged. If he can't do it, get Henry or Dave. I'm going to talk to Bryce about taking a few days off. Let's get started as soon as we can."

"I'm in. All in. At least while Rory's occupied with her father." I sigh. "I just wish . . ."

"So do I," Dad says. "I get it, Brock. It's a tough thing. But at this point, it's ride or die, son. We figure this out, or we go down."

"I understand."

I end the call.

Ride or die.

I breathe in and hold it, drawing strength for what I must do. What I must do for my family. For Rory. For the future of the children she and I will have someday.

They deserve everything I have to offer, everything my name has to offer.

The Steel family will *not* go down on my watch.

CONTINUE THE STEEL BROTHERS SAGA
WITH BOOK TWENTY-FOUR

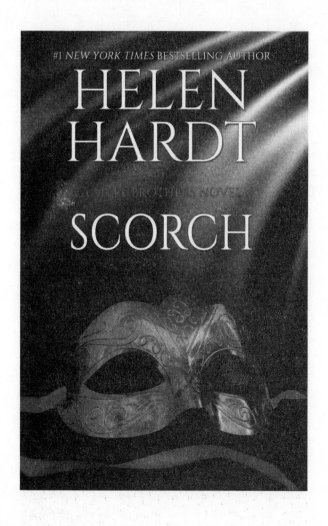

MESSAGE FROM HELEN HARDT

Dear Reader,

Thank you for reading *Flare*. If you want to find out about my current backlist and future releases, please like my Facebook page and join my mailing list. I often do giveaways. If you're a fan and would like to join my street team to help spread the word about my books, please see the web addresses below. I regularly do awesome giveaways for my street team members.

If you enjoyed the story, please take the time to leave a review on a site like Amazon or Goodreads. I welcome all feedback. I wish you all the best!

Helen

Facebook
Facebook.com/HelenHardt

Newsletter
HelenHardt.com/SignUp

Street Team
Facebook.com/Groups/HardtAndSoul

ALSO BY HELEN HARDT

The Steel Brothers Saga:
Craving
Obsession
Possession
Melt
Burn
Surrender
Shattered
Twisted
Unraveled
Breathless
Ravenous
Insatiable
Fate
Legacy
Descent
Awakened
Cherished
Freed
Spark
Flame
Blaze
Smolder
Flare
Scorch

Blood Bond Saga:
Unchained
Unhinged
Undaunted
Unmasked
Undefeated

ACKNOWLEDGMENTS

We're getting closer to answers...but of course there are always more questions! This is the Steel Brothers Saga, after all. Brock is becoming a new favorite of mine, which is no surprise, since of the three original Steel Brothers, my favorite is his father, Jonah. It's been great fun revisiting him and Melanie.

Huge thanks to the always brilliant team at Waterhouse Press: Jennifer Becker, Audrey Bobak, Haley Boudreaux, Yvonne Ellis, Jesse Kench, Jon Mac, Amber Maxwell, Dave McInerney, Michele Hamner Moore, Chrissie Saunders, Scott Saunders, Kurt Vachon, and Meredith Wild.

Thanks also to the women and men of Hardt and Soul. Your endless and unwavering support keeps me going.

To my family and friends, thank you for your encouragement. Special shout out to Dean—aka Mr. Hardt—and to our amazing sons, Eric and Grant.

Thank you most of all to my readers. Without you, none of this would be possible. I am grateful every day that I'm able to do what I love—write stories for you!

Rory and Brock return in *Scorch,* which has a surprise in store for you. Be prepared to say hello to some old friends!

ABOUT THE AUTHOR

#1 *New York Times*, #1 *USA Today*, and #1 *Wall Street Journal* bestselling author Helen Hardt's passion for the written word began with the books her mother read to her at bedtime. She wrote her first story at age six and hasn't stopped since. In addition to being an award-winning author of romantic fiction, she's a mother, an attorney, a black belt in Taekwondo, a grammar geek, an appreciator of fine red wine, and a lover of Ben & Jerry's ice cream. She writes from her home in Colorado, where she lives with her family. Helen loves to hear from readers.

Visit her at HelenHardt.com